emma janson

DISCOVERING
SANITY

a novel

For more information, to inquire about rights to this or other works or to purchase copies for special educational, business or sales promotional uses, please write to:

Incorgnito Publishing Press
A division of Market Management Group, LLC
300 E. Bellevue Drive, Suite 208 Pasadena, CA 91101

First EDITION
Printed in the United States of America

ISBN:978-1-944589-65-3

10 9 8 7 6 5 4 3 2 1

DEDICATION

To the people who give "free fish".

Contents

MOVING UPSTATE

Ignacio Cheyez picked up a brochure from the passenger seat of his uncle's borrowed car. He wanted to double-check his destination's address since the roads were simply empty highways lined with trees. Upstate New York in 2016 was definitely "The North Country" like everyone had told him, since the land stretching between farmhouses seemed to last forever. As he drove past signs descending in miles toward Canada, though, he really began to question whether he was on the correct path to better health.

When his favorite Latin radio station fell to complete static, Ignacio changed the channel to Canadian pop hits in protest. Some of the commercials were spoken in French.

And the road kept going. Ignacio had been on the road for so long that he'd even forgotten about the beanie on his head and how much it irritated his scalp, despite his shoulder-length hair. He stretched his neck the best he could while thinking of his mother and the reason he was driving upstate at all, and the car began to veer off to the right of the slow lane. This jolted him upright for better focus on the road, but he couldn't help being somewhat distracted. His mother had long been his obsession since her own mental diagnosis had institutionalized her by the time she'd turned seventeen. Unlike Ignacio, she was a threat to society, but this didn't hinder his thirst for answers. His youth was plagued by an overwhelming sense of longing to know her.

By the time he'd turned seven, in fact, his disrupted mind and unanswered questions about his mother had begun to melt together into truths and lies. The trauma of witnessing her homicidal attempt on a dusty VHS tape had itself catapulted a deep curiosity that had formed into his current obsession. At twenty, now, and driving to a specialized behavioral health facility, he didn't even know what the beginning had been or where his story began. Oh well – he'd have to figure it out. The announcer on the radio posed a question in French and Ignacio answered in the style of a rap.

"I don't know what I'm doing, yo. Driving upstate for me. Faking insanity. Be the intake for me. Fuck all humanity. Burning mistake, you see. It's a calamity. I do know what I'm doing, though." His beat, boxing between phrases and fragments, put him in a better mood, but 8 hours of gas station food was irritating his stomach. He hoped that his navigational system was correct, as it displayed only a few hours left until his arrival at the vineyard-based mental health facility he was headed toward.

After another pit stop to fill his gas tank, Ignacio scurried back to his uncle's car. There was something about the air in upstate New York that made it feel colder than the city. Had the elevation changed? Was it the realization that he was so far away from home? Were the wind currents really that different when it came to the space between buildings or along land without obstructions? Regardless, he was cold; he turned the heater up to calm the chill that permeated his bones, and then he put his crumpled beanie next to the Northern Lights brochure he'd received in the mail.

This time when he picked it up, he opened the brochure to read more than just the address. Ignacio read back over the information about the early years of the institution – it was reassurance that this was the place for him to get out his maternal angst. According to their brochure, Northern Lights was a premier licensed residential mental health facility in a remodeled mansion surrounded by vineyards, and not a mental institution. Opening its doors in 2005, the owners, Mr. and Mrs. Reed, had revamped and re-designed the luxurious establishment as an alternative to a traditional clinical setting. The care they provided was designed to treat people suffering from psychiatric disorders and emotional disabilities. Flexible with admissions, their deluxe facilities welcomed walk-ins once a week, but their focus remained on patients in need of extended stays. Some of their treatments included: Art Therapy, Yoga, Adventure/Exposure Groups, Specialized Nutrition, and Pottery Classes. Additionally, there was a fitness center and an indoor pool on the premises. The Reeds had thought of everything necessary to making a mental health visit as comfortable as possible for their patients.

He smiled while thinking of this stay as a two-month vacation from being poor, because not everyone could afford such a posh mental health facility as Northern Lights. Ignacio Cheyez was certainly in the category of people who, prior to this, had sought treatment through free state programs. Northern Lights had only entered his world through the trauma of his mother's homicidal urges, his own inability to let it go, and researchers looking to validate links between mental disorders and genetic predisposition; in other words, he'd kind of gotten lucky, in some weird way. Globally, researchers had actually fought to sponsor him, but in the end it had been a group out of Germany that was subsidizing his September stay and looking to study his condition. He'd been chosen due to his "unique circumstances" – a repeated phrasing that appeared throughout his file.

Ignacio didn't directly blame his grandmother for their living conditions, but the truth was that Northern Lights was a luxury resort compared to her hoarded New York City house on Elliot Street. And without his backstory, he'd have been trapped with her rather than driving from the chaos of the city to a mansion.

His grandmother, Maria, was a short matriarchal woman who'd never thought his mother Juana would get pregnant at such a young age. She'd felt Juana would become a cop or a Marine because she was so consistently fearless of all things that frightened other children. Her attempt to kill the boogie man formed only one of the stories that had solidified this way of thinking. At six years old, Ignacio's mother had hidden in the closet with a knife, an extremely elaborate booby trap winding throughout her room. According to Maria, *el cucuy* wouldn't have stood a chance – if there'd been such a thing as a boogie man. To Maria's disappointment, though, the path that her daughter could have excelled on didn't come to fruition. Rather, Juana's rebellion began shortly thereafter, and lasted eight years…until the birth of her only son, just before her fifteenth birthday.

The family had assumed her pregnancy was a youthful mistake, Ignacio knew, but it had really been planned, and viewed as something else altogether in the eyes of a girl suffering from an undiagnosed mental illness. Juana's son, whom she would name Ignacio, had for her represented the highest point reached in the heavens by her celestial body – a zenith. He became the capstone to strange ideologies. Essentially, Ignacio had been born from a child with a tormented mind, this event serving as Part One of the unique circumstances that were leading a dimple-cheeked twenty-year-old to Northern Lights.

When Juana had been institutionalized, Maria had become the guardian of baby Ignacio. She'd raised him like her own, loving him as if she'd borne him with her own body. When he became inquisitive about Juana's disappearance, Maria explained with mixed emotions that it had occurred on the day her daughter had "died" and her new son, Ignacio, had been born. Each elusive answer had a tidy, uplifting bow. Maria and other relatives were equally vague about the incident that had changed Cheyez family history, but what was made clear to Ignacio was that Juana had been a rebel, mentally unstable, and needed to be locked up forever. The details in between were a blur of shame, denial, and secrets that he was not allowed to discover because he was just too young. However, Ignacio was always searching for the truth.

At seven years old, he thought he was a big boy – big enough to know what had happened to his mother. What was the Cheyez incident that his grandmother spoke of in whispers on the phone? Why did she cry sometimes for no reason, and collect newspapers and books on psychology that she didn't understand? His mind was lost, and he only wanted to know the simple truth…where was Juana? Who was she? Since he was big enough to discover the truth about Santa Claus, why not so for the facts about his mother?

Merely a child that Christmas, he followed his questions until his mother's reality presented itself in a shockingly raw manner. While searching for presents, as every seven-year-old does, he found a shoe box buried deep under Grandma's bed. It was surrounded by psychology books and newspapers. Nearby lay neatly wrapped gifts labeled for Ignacio. The shoe box didn't have wrapping paper, though; instead, it had been hastily taped shut and was covered with dust. With his body tucked halfway under the bed, Ignacio scanned the brightly colored images of snowmen and his favorite cartoon characters in elf hats, but they didn't hold his attention.

At seven years old, he *should* have grabbed any brightly colored package, but he didn't. Between his curiosity and some overheard conversations from months before Christmas, he chose to push the snowmen aside in order to get at the dirty shoe box. His decision to choose truth was a compulsion developed from his family's hushed words. He'd learned that his mother had been jumped into a female Latina gang just before her tenth birthday. She'd been violently beaten by all members as part of the initiation. At the time, Grandma hadn't believed her daughter's gang affiliations were true, as she was convinced that her strong-willed child was better than the rumors. She was adamant about Juana's strength... until the second jumping resulted in two broken ribs and an embedded false fingernail in her daughter's cheek. No one denied the meaning of the crescent shaped indentations – not even Juana's mother, Maria.

Juana catapulted herself through the ranks via her high pain tolerance, her thirst for mischief, and eventually her own demands for respect. Once she'd been inducted into the gang, there was nothing Maria could say or do to pull her daughter away from the life. By Juana's fourteenth birthday, she was a rank away from being the leader of the sisterhood, and in celebration of her right-hand position being obtained at such an unheard of age, she was given a boyfriend of her choosing from another local gang. Since she couldn't decide between the five top choices of young boys, she then lost her 'virginity' several times. No one ever agreed upon the true identity of Ignacio's donor – not that it ever mattered.

When Maria came out of the bedroom after that fateful conversation which Ignacio overheard, her makeup was freshly done over swollen eyes, and Ignacio never held another false fantasy regarding his conception. He was seven when he discovered there was no Santa Claus, and seven when he discovered that he was the result of a planned pregnancy of a crazy girl with moons on her face.

THE CHEYEZ INCIDENT

Given the curious nature of little boys, Ignacio was eventually bound to discover the secrets in the box under his grandmother's bed, but he wasn't ready when he did. No seven-year-old boy would ever have been ready. Inside the mysterious box was a plastic evidence bag marked "Exhibit A" which held a VHS tape.

He was ashamed to discover it.

He should have believed in Santa another year. He should have returned the box and its evidence bag to beneath the bed and chosen instead to peek at the year's Christmas presents. But he didn't. All of those brightly colored gifts hid strange books and a curiously dusty box. He knew it was a clue to his mother's story that no one would tell him, unless such knowledge came through an adult conversation he was never meant to hear…but this box was a shortcut to all of that knowledge he'd been dying to retrieve.

He gingerly walked the box and its VHS tape to the television at the other side of Grandma's room. Clutter overwhelmed the home, but Ignacio was used to it, and he knew where to step so that nothing was disturbed. He carried the tape past books on conscious theory, circa 1926 - 1997, and right by stacks of unopened bundled newspapers. He placed the tape into the VCR's slot and watched it descend, and then he removed the remote from the stack of new magazines on top of Grandma's dresser. He could hear his grandmother banging pots and pans around in the kitchen for another meal's preparation, so he exhaled and placed his finger on a button.

Play.

White noise on the television flashed and faded. Darkness lightened into images he didn't recognize. The remaining contents of the tape split his world apart then, essentially exposing him to the beginning of his current mental status.

In Latino cultures, the Quinceñera of a girl marks the transition from childhood to womanhood, much like the celebration of an American girl's growth on her sweet sixteenth birthday. The tradition comes from either presenting the girl to her future husband or presenting the girl as available for marriage, back in the time when it was acceptable to do so. That purpose has since passed, but the formalities of today are just as rich as they once were. Most of them are as prescribed, if not more so, than those for a wedding. The ceremony varies from culture to culture, but generally three things are consistent: a formal gathering with elaborate dresses, lots of formal dances, and toast.

When the video played, the beginning showed Juana waving to the camera in her beautiful Quinceñera dress. Dimples appeared when she smiled, as did crescent shaped scars on her left cheek. Young Ignacio glanced over to his grandmother's mirror and smiled. Their faces were the same. For what seemed like a lifetime then, Ignacio stared at the image of his fifteen-year-old mother in the mirror and then on the television, back and forth. His fingertips touched the screen where little moons were sunken into her cheek.

Ignacio could see that his mother's birthday venue had been beautifully decorated by family members who'd traveled from upstate New York, Pennsylvania, and New Jersey. He smiled at seeing his two-month-old self in the arms of his great aunt, the surrounding family cooing over his precious dimples.

The family had made an impressive effort to pull together a memorable setting filled with twinkling lights, draped fabric, and delicate flower arrangements so that Juana would always remember her special day. A custom archway had been built, stained, and assembled by uncles and nephews for her grand entrance into womanhood. The food which filled the ballroom and tantalized the noses of those excited to feast on this occasion had been prepared by Maria's sister. She and three elder family members had made sure favorite tradition-al dishes were prepared to perfection. In the video made to commemorate the birthday, family members were recorded waving the air into their noses and taking deep breaths. The sister proudly displayed a dish for the camera and presented it as if it was a pot of gold. When the operator of the camera, Uncle Carlos, reached his hand out to sneak a taste, the wom-an smacked his hand away. They both laughed. These dishes had been coordinated to be finished and set at the tables just after the candle ceremony; in their family, the candle cere-mony was considered to be the most important aspect of the whole celebration.

In this ceremony, traditionally, the birthday girl distrib-utes candles to the people whom she considers to have been most influential in her development. The gesture is accom-panied by a speech dedicated to each of the people she gifts. Each candle symbolizes the years the girl has left behind and a special memory with any person who is invited to join the ritual.

As Ignacio watched the event unfold on the video, he felt warm and loved. Everyone was happy, festive, and fondly reminiscent of the past celebrations they'd all shared together. It was light and fun, yet proper and traditional. Juan III escorted Juana through the archway in place of her father, who'd lost his battle with cancer the year before. It was an emotional moment for everyone to view, Ignacio could tell, and also emotional for Maria, who kept dabbing a tissue under her eyes and assuring everyone that she was okay.

Juana was beautiful, walking through the arch on his arm. When it was time for the speech, everyone gathered around to give Juana the floor as the lights dimmed in anticipation. Select family members and girlfriends stood to her right. Male friends stood to her left among designated men in the Cheyez family. All of them were very respectful and dressed appropriately – despite fidgeting more than anyone should in their formal attire. Everyone else was an observer to the proceedings, spread out in a horseshoe formation as close to the main, highlighted event as possible. Mothers cradled and hushed their young, fussy children. Fathers lovingly nudged their daughters as they reminisced and smiled over the speeches they themselves had been a part of so many years before. Elders were respectfully given seats as others constantly asked if they were comfortable.

Uncle Carlos, at nineteen years old, had been given the camera; he zoomed in on Ignacio's baby face and then pulled dramatically away as Juana began her speech. He slowly scanned around the room to the family's faces while they listened intently, their loving smiles clear.

Ignacio rested his elbows on the dresser and waited for his mother's speech like everyone in the video. He giggled when Carlos tried to help quiet the room and accidently cursed in Spanish. This was followed by a slap to his arm by a family member, which made the camera jerk.

Yet, Juana's speech wasn't what her family had been waiting for. Not one of her thankful stories involved family members, as everyone had anticipated. Instead, Juana described cherished memories and lessons learned from the girls who surrounded her. Worry began to take over expressions of Cheyez descendants as she gifted the candles, one after another, to her friends – her gang friends. Carlos panned and zoomed to people getting angry, uncomfortable, and deeply concerned. Elbows nudged and whispers escalated to mumbles coming from scattered sections of the horseshoe.

Ignacio's eyes stretched with intensity as he backed away from the television, unable to understand the images and words of his mother. Nervous, he glanced to the bedroom door, ensuring it was locked. His heart began to sadden for the younger-looking Grandma in the video, who was gritting her teeth and rubbing her elbow.

The camera panned back to Juana, lighting another candle and telling yet another gang member how they'd influenced her life, a bright and meaningful expression on her face. Her sincerity was the most astounding part of the whole awful experience. Maria stood next to her with pooling tears that teetered on the edge of spilling to the floor. A distant relative shot her a look from the edge of the camera frame, with his hands politely crossed over his crotch, unsure whether or not he should step in out of respect. By the eleventh candle, he was fidgeting in sweat as he mouthed for Maria to do something with wide eyes. She was too frozen with disappointment. Had her husband been alive, he would have stopped the blasphemy, but she could not.

The final four candles were handed to the leaders of the sisterhood, seeming to suggest that Juana had saved the best for last. At the end of her speech, she was in tears as all of her candle-lit friends gathered around her for a group hug which was surrounded by a bunch of offended family members who were ready to lose their composure on an epic level.

Among the crowd was an uncle, recently released after twelve years in the penitentiary. He was seething on the edge of destruction as the teenage girls huddled, almost taunting him. Carlos zoomed out to a wide shot, trying to capture the horde as he giggled unintentionally. When the girls broke from the group hug and spread themselves throughout the family members in the horseshoe, Juana addressed everyone again. Her voice was recognizable, but her attitude was another stake in the hearts of the family that had raised her.

Ignacio leaned in to the dresser, shifted a psychology magazine under his elbows, and turned the volume up.

"My transition to womanhood has begun; I leave behind my childhood." She pulled out barrettes from her delicately set, cascading hairdo and stretched her hair as tight as she could manage into a ponytail on the top of her head. Doing this exposed fresh tattoos that had been hidden until now, and they ran up and down the sides of the portion of her face and neck that had previously been covered by beautifully flowing curls. Family members inhaled in unison and grabbed at their chests in shock. Maria covered her open mouth as she battled extreme embarrassment and a swelling of explosive anger. Nobody wanted to overstep boundaries with the matriarch of the family by attempting to end the drama without her permission, though, so they all stood on edge, wound tight like soldiers ready for battle. They patiently waited for her to give them a sign.

Ignacio also watched her on the screen and waited for some sign, but it didn't come.

Carlos giggled and quietly said into the microphone, "Valiendo, Madre! It's about to get real up in this bitch, yo." He was blissfully unaware of the truth. He believed the worst that would happen was juvenile detention or time in a group home somewhere, and so he continued to record the drama so that he could laugh about it with his friends…but what he captured wasn't attitude; it was evidence of a young girl's deep insanity. It was evidence of a rebellion that was officially transitioning into a malicious act, based from a twisted mind. The act, and this video, would become Exhibit A.

Juana grabbed glasses of alcohol from a preset table and threw them at the archway, causing everyone in the room to instinctively flinch and step away just before she lit the arch on fire. She then rushed to the draperies hanging from the beautiful woodwork along the room's windows and lit them on fire while screaming, "Long live, mis carnalas!"

The girls around Juana shouted out her sentiment along with her while Carlos yelled curse words too close to the microphone and took cover behind a metal serving cart. He was screaming at his sister, *"What the fuck are you doing, Juana?"* The video was wild and uncontrolled as he continued to record the action, huddled into his protective position. The audio picked up frantic running behind more cursing as he finally focused in on the fire that was overwhelming the arch, slowly at first, and yet growing rapidly larger as it burned through the fresh paint and alcohol.

Juana's friends began lighting tablecloths on fire, as well as the dresses of family members, curtains, dried floral arrangements, and anything else that was flammable. As the smell of burning items became stronger and things were engulfed into flames, family members screamed out the need to protect the children while others tried to put out the smaller fires. The men who could have easily subdued some of the teenagers were more concerned with moving children and elders out of the building. The teens tried to block the exits, but were pushed aside or punched into submission as panic grew among the Cheyez descendants. Carlos captured his great aunt hobbling for safety while embracing two-month-old Ignacio against her frail chest, but the video showed that baby Ignacio never cried as the images became swirls of darkness and faces lost among screams. As people pushed their way out of the building, Carlos could hardly catch his breath. The smoke was thickening, too, as the next minute of tape was nothing but screaming and fire alarms.

Suddenly, a light appeared in the video and silhouettes ran toward it. Carlos did not stop coughing even as he ran to a place where the air by the road was clean, the camera jostling along at his side. When he oriented himself again, he turned the camera back to the building and vomited in response to his sister's attempt at killing their entire family tree.

Meanwhile, Ignacio kept watching the VHS tape, unsure of how to feel.

After regrouping, Carlos began counting everyone from behind the lens as he tried to breathe in fresh air. He was nearly finished counting when the teens poured out of each exit with charred skin, and scorched hair and dresses. Each one of them looked like a *chola* version of the possessed main character in the horror movie *Carrie* as she'd appeared after killing everyone at her prom. They were coughing at first, but regained composure as they walked toward the family with balled fists and demonic eyes. Some of the girls carried broken table legs with sharp, uneven tips and knives from the ballroom kitchen. Carlos zoomed in on the assemblage of teenagers as the smoke poured from the building behind them and faint sounds of firetruck alarms pierced the chaos. Juana stopped with her mob, about 15 feet from the huddled family members, most of whom were sobbing. When the Cheyez men regrouped, they stepped forward to provide a masculine barricade.

Enraged, Juana screamed at the top of her lungs, pink spit flying out of her mouth as she shook her head violently, as if possessed. "Give us our son or we will take him!"

The statement threw some of the gang members off, as they looked a little scared and surprised by what they'd heard. It appeared that the teens hadn't been acting as a collective, and that Juana was somehow masterminding their intentions. However, some were on board just because of who Juana was to them, and they began edging forward to protect their leader.

Unsuccessfully, seven-year-old Ignacio searched the television screen for the great aunt with a bundle in her arms.

"*Pendeja*, I'll go back to prison for you!" The uncle lunged to begin a charge, but the thing that stopped him at his first step was Maria's shout for him to wait, given from her crouched position in the crowd. Neither the teens nor the family members said a word as children cried and sirens blew louder in response to an emergency 911 call. But Maria heroically walked through two layers of family, stepped in front of the uncle, and addressed her daughter.

"*Hija del diablo!* Devil daughter! Ignacio shall never know your face! I turn my back on you. We all turn our backs on you!" Her fists shook in front of her tensed eyes for emphasis before she turned her back to her daughter who she'd now disowned.

Seven-year-old Ignacio couldn't believe his ears, let alone his eyes. This was not the grandmother he knew who sang silly songs of dogs with clubbed feet to make him laugh. His grandmother worried about feeding him too much and making sure he was warm. She poked at his dimples and told him that's how angels got into his face to make him smile. Yet, here she was screaming so hard that he thought the veins in her neck would burst.

When she turned around, away from Juana, the shimmering lights of the oncoming emergency crews twinkled in her tears, and yet she held her head high. Several family members slowly turned, to signify their denial of young Juana's existence as they followed the matriarch's lead. Eventually, everyone shunned her; even the hardened criminal, her uncle, turned his muscle-bound back in proof that he had become a better man. Carlos focused the camera on Juana, who watched them all turn one by one as her last remaining sensible side – that which had sought a return of her own son – was shunned for the atrocities she'd tried to bestow. The gang members looked to one another, waiting for Juana's next command, which she never gave. When the fire crews and trucks stopped up the street to connect to the water main, though, a young and unexpected hero emerged from the back of the Cheyez family's formation.

Ernesto was 14 years old, with Downs Syndrome, and the youngest sibling of Maria's deceased husband. Not only had he been born challenged, but Ernesto was morbidly obese and insanely strong. No one wanted to see what he was capable of in terms of strength, but this incident had pushed everyone to their limits…and he was no different. He was unable to compute the events surrounding him, and it only made an uncontrollable rage well inside of him. He turned opposite the statuesque group of family members to the teens, and then ran at full speed, charging through everyone. Some moved out of his way in surprise and some were knocked out of his way like bowling pins as three hundred pounds of angry Ernesto screamed out an obsessed focus on Juana.

Juana watched him charge her as he approached faster than anyone would have thought possible. Ernesto's arms were outstretched, his fingers spread like he had seen fingers displayed so many times on crucifixes nailed to his momma's living room walls. His scream was worse than any scream heard in the past, as there was screeching that permeated the sound, his voice cracking from his impending puberty.

Carlos spun the camera away from the motion of the firetrucks to capture Ernesto's break away and zoomed into the action as the girls stood frozen, waiting for the train wreck to hit. In broken English, he screeched, "Don't. You. Make. Her. Cry!" Ernesto's arms and hands clothes-lined two of the gang members on either side of Juana before he wrapped her in a bear hug, plummeting all of them to the ground. He landed on top of Juana's tiny frame and seared dress. Her feet kicked as she tried to scream for help, but she was unable to catch her first breath. Half of the gang immediately attempted to push and pry him off, the others analyzing their moral compasses as they considered shanking a fat handicapped child.

In the video, things between the main actors in the scene seemed to pause with everyone in a standstill as emergency crews began to show up to deal with the fire, working in the background of the video to address what looked like the most pressing concerns.

Luckily, the fire was extinguished quickly, but it took

some convincing before Ernesto walked away from Juana. Family members scattered everywhere, crying and holding hands, all of them incredibly lost. When most girls would have been beginning their self-discovery at her age, Juana was handcuffed to a stretcher in the back of an emergency vehicle. She then watched as her great aunt relinquished her bundled zenith to emergency crews.

As squad cars escorted the emergency vehicles out of the area, one of the field officers made a radio call to ask how to process a fifteen-year-old for arson and attempted mass murder. With this, Carlos faded the video to black in an attempt to put a dramatic closing on the already intense evening. This creative ending was what finally pacified the sounds of firetrucks, police sirens, and family members who were crying next to Ignacio. And the recording stopped.

FALLING APART

The severity of the Cheyez incident caused unified deflections every time Ignacio brought up the subject of his mother with his family. They couldn't be tricked into giving him information on Juana. Once, he asked Ernesto for his version of the story, but Ernesto just hunkered down and insisted that she was dead, refusing to look him in the eye for weeks afterward. Ignacio apologized several times, and felt wicked for asking. He never gave up wondering, though; rather, he pretended that his curiosity faded with age. Secretly, he kept notes in a diary and then, in eighth grade, escalated to collecting undisclosed audio clips of his family members talking. In high school, he spent countless hours in the library – looking through news articles and psychology books.

After graduating high school, his research into his mother's story became more intense. He managed to open sealed documents by using lots of manipulation. The patrolmen and women who'd been on the scene nearly eighteen years prior to his search had been promoted through the system. Most of them were higher ranking officers, if not retired. The remaining personnel refused to give information to him, though, for fear that it would ruin their future careers within the system.

One such detective with a thick accent tried offering his opinion without offering information. *"Son, your motha tried to torch your whole frikkin' family! What do you care where she's at and what she's doin'? If I were you, kid, I would neva' look back. She's probably locked up – where she should be."* To emphasize his insensitive suggestions, he circled his index finger around his temple. And although his answer was less than professional, he was the politest out of all the people Ignacio questioned. Others referred to her as "the Firestarter" and did their best to quickly get him off the phone or shoo him out of their offices.

But lack of closure makes trauma a looped horror that attacks a person in different ways. Years of open-ended questions and images from the VHS tape manifested into an uncontrollable force of destruction during Ignacio's freshman year of college. Between classes and football games, the things that occupied his mind were not always his studies or his girlfriends. At first, it was only nagging questions that bothered him, but then these questions progressed into lapses in time. Eventually, he experienced grand feelings such as those his mother might have had during her youth – like those that had resulted in an evidence tape. There were many nights when he felt Juana's pain as she pulled fake fingernails from her cheek. Countless nightmares included burning, crescent moons. Ignacio tried to self-medicate with marijuana, but there was a painful heat in his ribcage when he smoked, and he didn't know if it was from smoke inhalation or from his great aunt's overprotective arms as she'd run for safety with his infant body in her grip.

His obsession with his mother's story began skewing his perception of reality at the moment when an image of her tattoos seemed to appear on his neck. Sometimes he believed that his dimples hid the scarring of moons and that he was, in fact, the zenith. However, the so-called tattoos he saw were random scratches from his digging at his skin while he slept. His dimples were just dimples, and other than his unique circumstances, he was your average eighteen-year-old Hispanic male.

He tried ignoring his strange thoughts with the intensity of his family, who dismissed his questions, but the effort still left him within his mind to develop conspiracy theories. He felt as if his family had never really loved him – otherwise, he imagined they would have just told him where his mother was institutionalized. Ignacio's grades fell because constant thoughts of his mother's unknowns plagued him. Every morning, he wrote *"Where is she?"* in the steam of his bathroom mirror. He saw her fifteen-year-old face in every Hispanic girl on campus, and sometimes thought the buildings he was in would burst into flames. Finally, his theories and research took over his world; it was as if he was trapping himself within it.

Ignacio was unaware of his own decline, of course. He felt it was a simple curiosity that needed to be wrangled by a well thought out plan. On scratch paper in his film studies class, he repeatedly scribbled the word *plan*. He felt this was what he needed to get answers and to relieve his mind of his maternal obsession. Even as the professor yelled at him to pay attention, he flipped the sheet of paper over in embarrassment, but when he looked down again he saw his backward writing through the thin sheet.

Ignacio realized that he could not devise a plan for answers while thinking outside of the box, as he'd previously assumed was the only choice. He had to be inside of the box, somehow.

This was where the line of sanity twisted. Eleven years after watching the tape labeled 'Exhibit A', it was clear that Ignacio Cheyez needed professional help. Ironically, he thought he was controlling his obsession by immersing himself within it, thus setting in motion his calculated efforts to get inside of the mental health care system. Not for the sake of his own rabbit hole, but to discover his mother's. He wanted to be crazy so that he could see and understand her crazy – and he thought of his new efforts as Operation NALP. It made sense to him.

Getting "fake" treatment began with countless self-admissions for mental health care, and the resulting interviews with his college counselors. He discussed his VHS discovery and how it had ruined his world thereafter. *Nightmares. Smoke. Blackouts. Burning moons.* He expressed his one-word question that needed to be answered, no matter the cost, and he did it over and over again.

Why?

The true encounter of the documented "Quinceñera Fifteen Fire Starters" aided in his convincing tales of self-destruction, so it wasn't that farfetched for those he encountered to believe he was suffering from a traumatic stress disorder.

He walked around campus in melancholy until someone spoke to him who carried influence – like a teacher – and then he would snap in such a manner that they feared for their own safety and the safety of other students. The first few times, he laughed at the teachers for jumping the way they did. There was a certain amount of joy to be found in being fake-crazy. It was undeniably liberating to ignore social norms.

Ignacio found that, in order to perpetuate his lie, he had to admit himself to the mental ward of the local hospital about once every two weeks, setting up a visible pattern of instability. In turn, the hospital doctors referred him to several social workers and psychologists, and in two counties, who all agreed that his mental wellbeing was in flux. They were completely unaware of its depth. He left college and dorm life to move back into his grandmother's home. Regardless of these circumstances, though, she never spoke of Juana's horror story to Ignacio, and he never asked her to. Eventually, after dealing with thick packets of many signed forms, he was given a government check every month in return for his new label – mentally disabled.

Getting paid for the rest of his life without being a productive member of society took him two years of consistent lying to establish. It also took an emotional toll on his otherwise genuinely happy self – or so he thought.

Playing his part in Operation NALP became daily fruitless work when he couldn't get more funding from the state and it was made clear to him that Juana was no closer to him than when he'd started. He simply hadn't grasped how difficult it would be to maintain a lie of this magnitude…until he tried to "fake" his way through it. In truth, though, Ignacio was so disturbed that he believed he was completely sane while pretending to have serious mental health problems. He saw it as a game. It was calculated, contained mayhem, and it kept him occupied.

At twenty years old, after 30 months of pretending to be crazy, Ignacio was contacted by a researcher who'd been recommended by one of his doctors. The group the researcher represented came with binders of paperwork for him to sign, and he obliged without carefully reading any of it because he was sticking to the plan – he had to learn more about his mother, and that meant sticking to the operation he'd concocted, so far as he was concerned.

When he received the Northern Lights brochure at his grandmother's home, he lied about his plan. Additionally, there was no polite way to tell her that her hoarding up stacks of meaningless trash was cramping his style. Her packrat home had begun as fixable clutter back when Grandpa had died, but then Juana had dumped an infant on her after trying to kill the family in a fire – it was no surprise that the clutter had just gotten out of hand. She couldn't afford luxu-

13

ries and was forced into bare essential, low-income housing which manifested in her having issues with letting objects go. Granted, walkable, clear pathways through the chaos existed, though by this time the clutter was stacked to the ceiling, but it was no place to heal a broken mind. And in addition to the special conditions she lived in, her neighborhood on Elliot Street was the kind of place where random toddlers in sagging diapers stood in the middle of the road after midnight. The tearless children only added to the disturbing type of neighborhood such a good woman had ended up occupying. It wasn't her fault; it was circumstances beyond her control, but it wasn't something Ignacio could deal with – not while looking for answers and faking craziness.

Getting away from the conditions of the home was only a bonus to his plan. Lying about the plan was the worst part of the whole charade. Ignacio told her the treatment he needed worked best when it was focused and concentrated. It was the most appropriate lie. That being said, she packed him a wonderful lunch for the road trip and wished him the best without further complaint.

After a lengthy goodbye and with a simple packed bag, Ignacio began driving to the Northern Lights Behavioral Rehabilitation Center in upstate New York. He wanted the relaxing, carefree environment of the nut house to set him free from this life that he'd purposely spun out of control. He couldn't wait to be in a clean room and experience whatever it was they called art therapy.

He was sticking to the plan.

THE ACQUISITION OF THE MANSION

Hours from his destination, the blurring time faded into minutes. He finally looked around to take in the beauty of the area. So close to the mental health facility, and yet so far away, the evening sky fell upon the horizon of landscape that was ready to surrender to winter snow. The colors were the most beautiful pallet Ignacio had ever seen in his life. Here was a relief from the images he'd happened to consume at seven years old. He shook his head in an attempt to clear his mind from the tragedy that had haunted his entire life and focus on the present moment.

Though Ignacio considered his story to be pretty strange, he would have been shocked to discover the history behind his destination.

The owners, Mr. and Mrs. Reed had founded Northern Lights in 2005 under their own unique circumstances. They'd shared many dreams before then, but the facility had never been one of them.

In 1980, during Jack Reed's college days, he was a thin,

black-haired kid who was enthralled with earth sciences. He dabbled in sports on occasion mostly to keep his dad off his back. His unnecessary anxieties over controllable asthma prevented anyone from seeing his exceptional skills on the court. A little more research on the realities of being asthmatic could have put him in the games with Larry Bird if he'd worried less about inhalers he didn't need, but he had no way of knowing it.

Jill, a fair-skinned redhead, had dreams of becoming a CEO just like her power-dressing mother. She maintained an exceptional grade point average although she held her own reservations about how she would manage a career with her ideal six children, after marriage. The balance of being a successful working woman and homemaker excited her, though.

Jack and Jill's different worlds collided at a 'Save the Earth One Business at a Time' rally, in the midst of tambourine-banging hippies and young entrepreneurs who would one day design computer operating systems for Apple. They quite literally bumped into each other as Jill scanned her calendar and Jack followed a red-winged bird in the sky that was regionally out of place. They were two different kinds of dreamers who would one day share the same hopes, and their courting was fast and furious, yet innocent and loving. Their inseparable chemistry was the envy of their friends, and their given names, Jack and Jill, added to the perception that they were a perfect couple. They were so happy together that they made others around them happy, so it was no surprise to anyone when Jack eventually asked Jill's father for his daughter's hand in marriage. After graduation as a married couple, they settled down near Syracuse, New York.

As life happened, living happily instead became their priority. Three beautiful red-headed children were the focus of their joy, and so their dreams never died; they just transformed. When Jack and Jill were in their early forties, the oldest child was running her own confections business. The middle child joined the Army and married, and when the youngest left for medical school - a new dream was set in motion. It was early 2004 when they sold everything, obtained business loans, and moved into a foreclosed mansion in upstate New York. The new idea was to maintain a vacationers' luxury bed and breakfast which was surrounded by a beautiful vineyard.

The grounds had been owned by the Kirschenbaum lineage of Germany. The estate had been an active winery for 78 years, until the last widower had become senile and was found, on more than one occasion, re-enacting his time in

WWII under the fearful reign of Adolf Hitler. When the war-torn veteran bombed the staff with tomato grenades one too many times, they left one by one, and even without their last paychecks.

Thus, Mr. Kirschenbaum eventually lost the family estate to foreclosure. The Reeds' idea was to turn the 22-bedroom mansion into a bed and breakfast while maintaining the winery for profit and as a secondary, unique tourist attraction. The collective idea worked, too...until it did not. With limited funds and staff, they finally concluded that they might have bitten off more than they could chew in their first year of ownership. Something had to give, and it eventually did – if not in the way that the Reeds would have hoped.

German twins were the eventual reason for the transition from bed and breakfast to a behavioral health facility, but of course this wasn't mentioned in the brochure sitting by Ignacio's side as he drove down the highway. The brochure's text simply explained the early start-up of the facility as if it had come from a calculated business plan, though this wasn't necessarily the truth. Within the first year of the bed and breakfast operation, some unique guests arrived which changed everything – the aforementioned German twins: seventy-two-year-old identical sisters who had planned to spend their two week vacation at Northern Lights.

The pudgy sisters loved every detail of the antique décor and the novel idea of running a vineyard in addition to the bed and breakfast. They giggled at every joke Jack told within his classes on the vinification process, and found a wonderful delight in following Jill to the kitchen to help her serve dinner. Hilda and Ute Schmidt – pronounced Oo-tuh, as they frequently corrected others – were like Terriers; always alert and ready for anything. Together, they were up before sunrise to help change linens, procure breakfast, clear tables, wake the staff for early grape-picking, and welcome newcomers as they entered the grand foyer. At night, the other patrons could hear the hearty laughs of the twins echoing down hallways as they sipped their hidden liquor from German-crafted pewter flasks, as if they were teenagers. Sometimes others joined the ladies in the formal library to share stories and hear the grand adventures the twins claimed they'd been a part of in their younger days.

They were a delight to have around, and an exceptionally pleasant pair to have grace the downtrodden atmosphere of the struggling business. That was, until the sixth day of their visit, when their excitement and helpfulness was still as fresh and vibrant as it had been the moment they'd arrived.

Their tenacious appetite for joy was much more than the average person could possibly handle. Entertaining the pair was absolutely draining. It was as if two children, already excited about a trip to Disneyland, consistently feasted on meals filled with sugar. Any parent would harbor fantasies of the perfect wrestling sleeper-hold to knock each one unconscious for the duration of the trip without killing the poor darlings.

Jack was the first to become frustrated when Ute, with extraordinary enthusiasm, demanded that he teach her how to use the mechanical harvesters as she stepped up and into the driver's seat without permission. Jack insisted – with great patience – that she get down, but Ute scolded him through giggles, proclaiming that he could and would teach an old dog new tricks. Then she slapped at her overly abundant chest while roaring in laughter and wiping tears of exuberance from her beady eyes. Angered and terribly confused, Jack walked to the back of the mansion, toward a greenhouse that held the keys. He thought deeply about how he should handle the situation, should Ute wait for him in the mechanical harvester. And yes, the thought did cross his mind to physically pull and toss her old ass to the earth in between rows of vine. The fleeting image of yanking her chunky arm down as he watched her, finally in a state of shock rather than fixed in a budding smile, was temporarily relieving, but alas, Jack wasn't that kind of a man, and he concluded that calling the police was a better option for everyone.

On his walk to the greenhouse, though, Jack unexpectedly found Hilda neatly aligning eight bushels of hand-picked grapes in tidy rows. His compounding anger wasn't with her effort necessarily, but with the fact that it was too soon to get premium juice from the ill-ripened vines that she'd picked. Livid, and unable to control himself, he escorted Hilda to her sister with a gentle hand on the small of her beefy back. When they approached Ute, still giggling on the harvester, Jack firmly insisted that they retire to the house and instructed each of the twins to refrain from hindering his work again.

The twins just whispered and laughed at the idea of getting in trouble at their age. Ute, who seemed more dominant, spoke first. "Vhat vill you do? Put fraulines in prison for helping?"

Hilda agreed, "Ja, prison? However, they serve breakfast, lunch, and dinner in American prisons for free! Vouldn't be so bad." After putting this positive spin on the unfortunate life of an inmate, she hooked her thick right arm around her twin's thick left arm, and together they dismissed Jack altogether. They chatted as if he wasn't walking behind them toward the side entrance of the mansion.

"Rationed portions vould do you goot! Your middle is like 'Das ist all, folks!'" Hilda giggled as she touched her sister's stomach, which wobbled like Jell-O in her hand.

"Oh, das p-p-p-pig? Goot one! Vas ist pig's name?"

From behind the two farm-fed women with butts bigger than any video vixens, Jack shook his head and mumbled in defeat, "Porky. Porky the pig." His hand rolled over his forehead and rubbed at his temples in obvious frustration. And Hilda just squealed while Ute attempted to reenact the famous Porky the Pig's unique yet annoying laugh. After barely closing the door behind them and locking it, Jack saw the women throw themselves to the floor in hysterics that came complete with crying and labored attempts to catch their breath. Jack just walked straight to the security camera room and locked the door behind him to review tapes and get a few hours away from the chaos before he lost his mind.

Alone in the security room, Jack opened overdue bills while he reviewed footage of the facility. A hand-written letter from the Kirschenbaum estate was at the bottom of the mail pile. Within the envelope was neatly typed correspondence on official letterhead from a German government agency. It seemed strange that a letter of such professionalism would be sent with scripted addresses, Jack thought. He sank into his chair while reading the black and white text.

When he finished reading through it, he glared at the stack of bills on the edge of the desk. Captured in the monitors were the twins, busily cleaning and re-organizing the lobby. A red-headed man appeared in the corner of the screen, and his face led Jack to believe he was asking the women what they were doing. They laughed so hard that Ute couldn't stop clutching at her jiggling stomach, and Jack just watched blankly as the man attempted to escort the twins to their room with a face of deep concern. Jack shook his head, shut off the monitors, and walked to the master suite.

From his room, he and Jill could hear the twins joyously cackling in some far corner of the mansion. The echo transformed it into something menacing by the time it trickled into their bedtime conversation. Jill, who was comfortably seated under their goose-down comforter, was braiding her faded hair, now strawberry blonde with random silver streaks throughout. The braiding seemed to get a little tighter and more haphazard as the sounds taunted and agitated her relaxed mood. Jack paced at the end of the bed while retelling the story of the twins infiltrating his business outside of the guided tours. She listened to him rant as she finished her hair, then hunkered down to a position for nighttime reading.

She tried consoling him while adjusting the comforter through sighs of frustration, but it was a doomed effort. "Had I not experienced the horror of finding all of the antiques pulled from the walls and polished to a high shine, I would have thought they were just trying to help and you were overreacting." Thinking of the episode, she began to swell with anger. "However, the value is depreciated! I mean, you should have seen the sparkling objects, organized by date! By date, Jack. I was going to sell the pieces at an auction, but… well, they destroyed plan B. We are 41, but I don't even have that kind of energy! I don't think I can handle another week of this."

Jack scratched at the stubble on his face, and then finally folded his side of the comforter down to slip into bed. "I've been thinking about it all day long, and I believe those old biddies are legitimately straight from the coo-coo's nest."

"Ya think?" Jill squirted a bit of lotion into her hands and set the bottle back onto her nightstand so that she could rub it in.

Jack fussed around to get comfortable. "I feel like, as much as they pissed me off this past week, if we directed their energy better, we could use them to help get this place back on track." He wiggled his eyebrows up and down in thought.

"What are you not telling me, Jack Reed? I can feel you've got something up your sleeve. That's the weirdest thing you have said in months." Her hands rotated around each other while a few knuckles unintentionally cracked through the sound of moist aloe.

Jack's cold toes tickled at her calf. "I opened a letter today from Germany. Not *for* the Schmidt twins, but about them. Basically, a German private facility wants to pay us to let the twins stay here so that they can research their disorder. They are bat-shit crazy, with something called Hypermania, which is why they're trapped being happy. They've had their lives recorded since they were teenagers! And here's the grand finale, Jill: these researchers want to pay us whatever it takes to let them live here!" He wiggled his toes again in excitement.

Jill slapped at his shoulder with her newly hydrated hands. "You're kidding! What kind of dough are we talking here? They want to watch these women because they're happy?"

"Hypermania, Jill. Have you ever, ever seen them drop a smile or stop giggling in six days? They would pay us enough to keep this place going and hire a few more people to help with the vineyard." He snuggled up to Jill, smashing his flaccid penis against her leg, and then wiggled again. "We'll hire help with the house, too."

"Get your mush off my leg, old man." She giggled. "No one can stand being around those twins for more than an hour. The only guest who finds them remotely interesting is the crazy kid in room 19 who eats his own hair! If we let them live here, it would turn into a nuthouse! A German, government-sponsored nuthouse!" She dismissed the idea and turned to pick up her book from the top of the nightstand, opening it to the page she'd bookmarked the night before.

Jack, piney-eyed, sent her thoughts as he blinked and shouted from within his own head. Jill couldn't plug her ears from the noiseless message, either. They had been on the same wavelength for years; always in tune with the other, knowing the other's thoughts...tonight was no different. Jill huffed and puffed with pretending to read, but slid her eyes over the same sentence at least a dozen times before bashing the two sides of the book together and tossing it at the end of the bed.

"Jack, a nuthouse? You want to run a nuthouse?"

"A resort for people with mental instabilities," he corrected her as he blinked rapidly. "Behavioral health rehab –

outpatient and inpatient, whatever. We won't deal too much with the patients, honey; we just maintain the building and focus on the vineyard. The people with the PhDs will deal with the whacky-jacks."

"Is that what Germany called them? Whacky-jacks? ...We could make them pick grapes and call it therapy." She giggled at her joke and then pulled a notepad from her night-stand along with a monogrammed pen.

Jack sat up to prop a pillow behind his back because he knew a new business arrangement was about to be developed. This process was old habit since their days of dreaming and preparing for their floral shop, planning each one of their children's births and then the bed and breakfast proposal. Together now, they toiled over the details of the mother-of-all of their ideas, combining their efforts to submit a proposal to the bank and offer a separate offer to the private German organization. When the hour neared three in the morning and Jill's hand began to cramp, they smoked a celebratory joint that she'd found while cleaning one of the rooms.

By early 2016, they were established entrepreneurs of a medical facility in the first building of its kind. Their new age treatments, backed by private funding and research grants, were labeled breakthrough procedures via reviews from psychiatrists who, ironically, sported traditional German names. Doctors who heard of the facility through medical channels were more than happy to work there. They were hired by a neutral third party to ensure that patient files remained detailed and unbiased to cater to researchers. The overall appeal of Northern Lights was the controlled environment without the traditional clinical setting. The beauty of the minimal security mansion enabled its long-term patients to live as normally as possible during treatment and observation.

***

Hilda and Ute Schmidt did not share the same memories as Mr. and Mrs. Reed when it came to Northern Lights' origins. In 2004, during their extended bed and breakfast stay, a representative from their assisted living home, four distant relatives, and a lawyer had come to sign paperwork with the Reeds. The twins had seen the oncoming chain of events that followed as an unfortunate but repetitious occurrence, as this was not the first time they'd been pulled strangely from one place to another by some unknown power.

Each had felt an indefinable sadness based in their lifetimes of automatic hilarity, but vineyard staff had only seen two pudgy women dying of laughter. The situation had spun out of control when the laughter caused involuntary muscle spasms in their larynxes and diaphragms. By the time emergency crews had arrived, they'd literally been choking to death on emotion they were unable to express.

In the beginning of their eleven-year stay at Northern Lights, drugs helped to subdue the hysteria, but the sisters would never be free from their cycle of elation. Their energy was and would be far beyond their physical capabilities; however, even they were not immune to the process of aging. Inevitably, getting old takes a toll on everyone. By the time the twins shared their eightieth birthdays at the facility, they no longer helped with the wine making process and, by eighty-two, the twins stopped helping altogether with facility maintenance and polishing antiques. Still, they were quite mobile and feisty, but they just couldn't move bushels of grapes anymore. The downfall to losing strength was the question of what they were to do with such active minds when their bodies couldn't follow through? The sisters began to wreak havoc through gossip and endless schemes to bust out of the house – or, the 'bonker-haus' as they referred to it. No one ever knew if they were just bored or if they truly hated it there because their disorder veiled all their raw emotions.

As far as Jack and Jill were concerned, though, the women had indirectly helped them run the business for eleven years. They were interwoven into the fabric of Northern Lights, so the couple had taken them in fully and treated them like awkward yet loving stray dogs who you couldn't just take out to the field to put down – especially since their disorder paid the bills.

Whether they had privileges or just thought they did, the twins felt a certain respect was owed them by all of the patients and clients who entered the facility – though they tried several times to escape the vineyard mansion, as mentioned, as if it were truly a terrible place. Each attempt would have worked, too, if there'd ever been a way for them to control the giggling and laughter that always gave them away.

In fact, they were planning another scheme near the front reception area, next to a large bay window, when an olive-skinned stranger of average height walked through the doors wearing a black beanie. Their welcoming methods were overwhelming and a little insane, but Ignacio Cheyez smiled because he knew his dimples and shoulder-length hair always pleased everyone.

The Schmidt twins were, of course, unaware that the Mexican's arrival story was as twisted as their own history or the censored brochure this new patient believed in.

***

Eight hours of driving to upstate New York had taken a toll on Ignacio's patience and neck, but his relief had come in a lovely wooden sign with burned lettering that said *Northern Lights – a mile away*. This had rejuvenated him and shaken his mind away from the thoughts in his head and the burning in his neck. The magnitude of the vineyard that surrounded the mansion was unjustly captured by brochure photos. The perfectly aligned rows of grape vines around the property seemed endless in their symmetrical spacing. He rolled down his window to see if it smelled different in the North Country than it did in the city, and when he inhaled, the burst of early September air chilled his warm nose. It was crisp, this being the only word he knew to describe such a snap of freshness. As he slowly drove onward, he took note of the empty two-lane, rural road while approaching another wooden board with professionally engraved lettering. Ignacio gently stopped so that he could see the detail in such a beautifully crafted sign, and wondered if the facility would be reflective of the effort someone had placed into even this detail.

His next moment of peaceful reflection, while looking at the beautiful Northern Lights building, was disrupted by the stench of gas station junk food flatulence. He tried to fan out the distraction, which felt like a horrible reminder of the things he'd left behind. When it dissipated, he refocused on the charming location set on the top of a rolling hill with a warm, still presence.

The mansion was indeed grand from where he sat, about a half mile from the main door. His timing was accidental, but seeing the vineyard and beautiful building in the foreground of a colorful sunset made it more approachable, warmer, and intensely inviting…as if it was, in fact, home.

Without traffic to worry about, Ignacio was compelled to step out onto the grounds where he would rest for the next month, just to assess life for a moment. He immediately became emotional. The beauty of the scenery did it to him. Then questions ran across his mind, the longer he stood there looking at the vineyard. His gut told him that the answers to all his questions were coming.

As the colors of the sunset behind the building became richer, the smell of grapes gently filled his nose and lungs. His memory of the grape scent came from the fine powder drink mixes supplied by food banks. As a child, it had seemed like ghetto aroma therapy with a stinging chemical overtone. It had burned to breathe it in and the concoction always left a bitter aftertaste. The vineyard smell was soft and pleasant to inhale, though…almost smooth. This new sensation gave him pause until the cool air made him shiver. He grabbed at his arms, noticing just how steep the temperature drop had been from what he'd gotten used to in the car. Although he didn't see his breath when exhaling, Ignacio suddenly questioned his decision to pack one sweater for North Country September weather which was clearly much colder than the rest of New York's early Fall. Adding to the cold were winds from the dreaded Tug Hill region, that pushed all the bad weather down from Canada through focalized air currents. Ignacio had heard that locals called it 'Canada's piss pot' for a reason, but now he felt the truth in the statement. He shivered again and wondered why the owners of the facility hadn't picked a warmer climate.

Ignacio ran his cold fingers through his thick black hair, then tucked them under his armpits. He was underdressed in a t-shirt because, as young men were known to do, he'd neglected to think about the weather. His hands felt like ice cubes as he nestled them into the dips of his pits, but survivalists were right – it worked, and his hands felt warmer already. As for his armpits, well, the sensation was shocking to say the least. He looked down to shake off the chill that accompanied the cold blast to his upper body and, when he did, he second-guessed the shirt he was wearing. It was classic white with a hand-sized Mexican flag screen printed on the front. Over the graphic was text that read: 'Are you a Mexi-Can or a Mexi-Can't?' He read the upside-down words and giggled to himself. *Way to represent one's heritage.*

His body shivered uncontrollably before he rushed to return to the driver's seat of his car, and then he cranked the heat as high as it would go. He just wanted the strange freezing sensation that had somehow permeated his bones in less than a minute to go away. *So much for Mexican pride,* he thought as he thanked God that his gas had dissipated into a passive stink that didn't make him gag. He stretched his black beanie over his head again before placing the car in drive and heading toward the main entrance of the Northern Lights residential mental health facility. Nestled where it was in a mansion on vineyards, it was a vacation resort as far as he was concerned.

There were no gates, no intercom systems, and no fences to pass as he slowly drove to a small parking area that held only one other car. The front of the building was landscaped perfectly to showcase huge wooden doors and a new cement sidewalk running parallel to an older, pebbled pathway – clearly enough, the new sidewalk was built specially for handicapped accessibility. Huge windows lined the right side of the building. Seated close to one window were two older women watching him walk to the door. They appeared to giggle as he stepped closer. A hidden sensor within the bulkhead of a renovated archway alerted the security system to unlock the doors. No sounds of technology gave the security system away, though. It was as if Ignacio entered the building freely. Even when the door shut behind him, he assumed he could leave.

The lobby, once a grand foyer, was filled with beautiful seating arrangements. Some were tables and chairs, some were rocking chairs near antique lamps, and others were leather couches or chairs upholstered in fine fabrics. The area appeared to have all levels of comfort to choose from for the delicate derriere. The bookshelves were full, and a gas fireplace comforted a frail woman as she flipped through pages of her bible. To the left was a guard who stood for a moment watching Ignacio walk in. He quietly and discretely said something into the walkie talkie mounted on his uniform, then disappeared down the hall. The center of the lobby held a hand-rafted receptionist's desk in a curved C-shape with an enclosed back side running level with the front. Behind the desk, Ignacio could see a long hallway that appeared to be just as beautiful as the rest of what was in sight. The far-right corner of the lobby held modern glass doors and beyond them was another room, an obvious addition that caught Ignacio's curiosity.

Lydia, the receptionist, was filing paperwork and didn't notice him standing there – but nevertheless, he was greeted by the German sisters just like everyone else who came to Northern Lights.

Ute, now eighty-three, watched Ignacio as he walked uncertainly to the desk for admission. She rushed away from her window to Lydia, who was still seated behind the reception desk. Ute's breasts bounced and slapped together even in the supportive brazier she supposedly had on.

Ignacio said, "I just want to admit myself. Dr. Klein made arrangements for me."

Lydia seemed distracted, but she pulled out a packet of papers and began her monologue of instructions, which Ute interrupted almost immediately. "Velcome to the Northern Lights bonker-haus!"

Lydia shot her a disapproving look as Ignacio jumped at the shear tone and volume of her voice when it shattered through the hushed atmosphere. He offered Ute his hand, but she gently swept it aside to hug him – without regard to spatial comfort – before she stepped away to giggle at his shirt. "Vich one are you? Mexi-can or a Mexi-can't?" She reached up to pinch his cheeks, once again without permission. The receptionist smiled at the new client and politely asked Ute to have a seat, which was a request the older woman ignored all together.

Lydia immediately picked up the phone, and had begun to call security when Hilda bombarded Ignacio like an excited second puppy. "Oh, the most adorable thing we have seen around this place! I hope your visit ist long. Come sit, und velcome to Northern Lights! I'm Hilda und das ist mine twin, Ute. Most Americans say it like the state."

Ute interrupted her sister as she attempted to guide Ignacio to a formal chair for conversation. "You don't have to say, 'like the state' every time we meet a new person!"

Ignacio just tried to be polite. "Ladies, I would love to chat, but I should check in first." He winked at Lydia, who shook her head in understanding and then told the person on the other end of the phone to hurry.

Ute leaned into Ignacio as if to whisper, but it her voice was just as loud as when she'd been speaking before. "She thinks she's spry." Ute circled her index finger near her temple and looked over to Hilda, smiling at her mirror image.

Hilda laughed in perfect timing with her sister while they both used Ignacio's shoulder to keep themselves upright as a fit of hysteria began to boil inside of them. The women escorted him to a nearby couch. He didn't resist the happy elderly twins; in fact, Ignacio thought they were cute. As he removed his bookbag to lighten his load, he said, "They say that laughter is the best medicine. I suppose check-in can wait a moment."

To which the women roared and grabbed at their pudgy stomachs while their faces turned nine shades of red. Ignacio sat with an uncomfortable smile, five feet away. Hilda tried to catch her breath, but barely got through her next statement before her failed attempt to hold in the pending squeal proved to be too difficult. "Best medicine is Opium und Heroin!" Her beady eyes scrunched up so tightly that a vein popped bright blue under the thin skin at her lower eyelid.

Ute practically lifted herself from the couch as she shouted with even more force, "Morphine!" The two released themselves from holding any emotion at all in and began their jovial fit – so intensely that they slapped at each other and cried as if the devil himself were tickling them from the inside.

Ignacio had initially wondered why these women were

in a mental health facility, and thought perhaps they were visiting. They'd seemed happy enough and definitely in good spirits. Their comments had since made his eyebrows shoot to the top of his hairline, though. They were obviously patients based on the hilarity and on the receptionist's negative reactions, but the insanity of their hysteria was still infectious. He couldn't help but laugh. For a moment, he forgot about being crazy, faking crazy, his mother, and why he was actually sitting on a leather couch at Northern Lights at all. He was comfortable and happy. He did not care about the brochure, the things it said or didn't say. He didn't care how these women had ended up in the beautiful mansion, either, but he was willing to listen and learn for the next few weeks of his perceived vacation.

LYDIA & BUCK LYNN

For Lydia, it was just another hectic day at Northern Lights when the Mexican arrived – except for a mistake she'd made for the first time in six months. She'd forgotten to alert Buck to a prescription scheduled for the twins. She glanced at the clock on her desk to confirm that it was nearly an hour later than when she should have called him, and knew that she was probably the reason the sisters were reverting to full-blown Hypermania symptoms. Her stomach twisted in knots from the error, but the handsome Mexican had also added a secondary unsettling to her body.

The man had said, "I just want to admit myself." He'd partially smiled, but his eyes really sparkled as Lydia grabbed a half-inch thick folder from a preset pile; they'd been ex-pecting him.

Lydia shook her eyes away from his to place the packet on the desk between them. She was clearly nervous about something. "Welcome to Northern Lights. This is the self-ad-mission packet. Northern Lights cannot admit you until you have filled out all of the forms and…"

That's when Hilda interrupted. She ran over so fast she practically hit her face with her own unrestrained breasts.

Yep, Lydia thought, *I'm so late.*

She had indeed neglected to alert the head nurse of their scheduled medication just before the Mexican had walked in and the twins had taken over the lobby. Usually, patient medications were handled elsewhere in behavioral health facilities, but this was Northern Lights – and nothing about it was usual. Since the situation had escalated, she had to call the head nurse, Buck, who doubled as security because the paid guys secured a different wing of the mansion and came to this side only when urgent. She was nervous about watching the sisters with any new client, but this time she was watching Ignacio simply because of her familiarity with him — and he was handsome. Sure, she might be fired within the next hour for her mistake, but she couldn't take her eyes off this man's dimples and his hair that sort of made him look like a renegade. When they made eye contact, she removed her hands from her face long enough to wave him toward the desk again – before returning two of her nails to between her teeth.

During Lydia's wait for the head nurse to arrive, she watched Hilda and Ute Schmidt in their episode of Hypermania even as she kept an eye on the new guy. From behind the desk, she bit hard on her manicured tips while hearing Ute shout something about morphine from the lounge couch. They heckled like witches and slapped at each other with jovial tears, and from experience, she knew not to interfere. The last time she had, Hilda, in a fit of laughter, had punched her in the shoulder and knocked her onto the hearth of the fireplace. Lydia didn't care to experience Hilda's profound strength for a second time.

The Mexican turned to look at her with flushed cheeks. She was embarrassed, but waved him over again in an attempt to rescue him from the twins' never-ending throes of hysteria. The man walked without hesitation, recognizing his opportunity for relief. His bookbag dangled from his right shoulder. Closing the gap between them, she saw that his gorgeous eyes were a rich chocolate brown that sparkled with each step he took. She would have been impressed and intentionally flirtatious...had he not worn that awful Mexican pride shirt asking if he was a Mexi-can or a Mexi-can't. Not to mention the fact that she wasn't a receptionist at a fancy hotel; this was Northern Lights. Her current job was to welcome patients, and yet keep her distance for safety. Everyone had their reasons for being in this place, though; God knew she had hers.

***

She was there by circumstance. It had been a Wednesday afternoon, six months before this, when her beautiful face had lit up after reading local job placement ads on a website: *Receptionist/Intake Clerk needed; must be patient and willing to work in a unique medical environment.*

At least this job opportunity sounded interesting and didn't involve stripping. She was tired of that life, although it paid the bills while military survivor benefits from her dad's death were being held under investigation. This job posting was quite possibly the best stroke of luck in her two-month search to find legit work. She didn't have to think twice about calling because it was two in the afternoon and she was jobless. After clearing her throat, she smiled several times as hard as she could. Her mother had told her years ago that it loosened facial muscles and helped relax her energy. Admittedly, it seemed to warm something in her cheeks and make her feel better.

After shaking her head at herself, she dialed the number listed at the bottom of the laptop screen. Per her mother's previous insistence, she resumed her smile when she spoke on the phone to sound alert and more attentive to the person on the other end. She had no reason to dismiss this potentially valuable advice, after all – especially since it had worked when she'd hustled her exotic mixed ethnicity to a customer who preferred blondes at the strip club. The phone rang a few times before a voice boomed from the other end like a sweeter version of Darth Vader, "This is Northern Lights. How can we help you today?"

Lydia paused for a moment to analyze the familiar and yet unfamiliar speech she'd heard, and then she resumed her smile before speaking. "Um, yes, sir, I was calling about the ad for a receptionist; I'd like to know more."

The man spoke almost too loudly, and Lydia flinched before pulling the cell phone away from her do-rag. He was clearly using one of the headsets they issued at call centers, with the microphone at his lips. "Yes, ma'am, I'll direct your call to Mrs. Reed. She oversees hiring for this position and will handle all of your questions." His deep baritone permeated the air around her, and she guessed it was coming from a huge chest to have harbored such a sound, but the twang in his speech was a surprise that almost tickled her ear.

Lydia took a chance when she heard the identifiable southern accent rumbling out of his voice, thinking suddenly that she recognized his deep tone. "Buck? Is that you?"

"Ma'am? Yes, this is Buck. How can I help you?" He

was clueless about this person who knew his name, and waited while pushing the headset ear piece closer to his ear.

"It's me, Lydia!" With strained excitement, she held her breath after saying her name, and then exhaled and grabbed her mouth to hold in her emotion, as she knew he wouldn't exactly share her enthusiasm. Her nerves traveled throughout her body with an electric burst.

"Well, bless your heart; Daddy's favorite child." With a bitterness that only southern people managed through backhanded compliments, Buck continued, "I can't give you money, Lydia honey. Daddy didn't leave me and my momma anything, remember? We discussed this. Are you stalking me? I moved to New York for a fresh start and you are like a wart on my black butt that keeps coming back."

A gulp could be heard at both ends of the phone.

Lydia answered, "I'm calling for a job, Buck. Receptionist position, remember? It's just a crazy thing that you answered...my mom and I didn't get anything, either, and I'm looking for work. You know it's still with the military court system or criminal investigation people or sitting on somebody's desk. I don't know. Listen, we didn't even know about you until after Daddy's funeral. Come on, Buck, this isn't our fault and you know it." She dropped her fake smile to scratch at her scalp. Executing this conversation would be delicate but she was trying to maintain character.

Buck pushed the microphone closer to his mouth and tried to whisper to Lydia, who had to pull her cell phone away from her ear again. "First of all, we didn't know about *ya'll.* Lydia, I know you are a nice girl, but don't give me the 'Papa Was a Rolling Stone' speech. He was a good dad until he up and left us in North Carolina when I was nine. You hear me? Nine years old and my daddy leaves to fu...sleep with a white woman. Now, I am sorry that he passed on while he was overseas, but Momma and I just want a piece of our lives back. It's the fair and right thing to do." Buck scratched his eyebrow and checked his teeth in a small compact mirror that he'd pulled from his orderly uniform, and then he pulled a small jar of Carmex from the same pocket and smeared it over his thick lips. He was trying to maintain his composure; otherwise, he would have waved his hands in the air and rolled his neck for emphasis. "Now, I am at work and I cannot afford to get fired over this unauthorized personal conversation!"

She quickly interjected, "You are my brother. I told you that before. I don't want to suddenly be your sister after eleven years, but I just think it would be cool if we got to know each other. I'm sorry about all of this." She wondered if he could hear the sensitivity she was desperately trying to convey.

Buck held back the sudden tears and the lump in his throat. He paused for a moment, scanning the room for anyone in earshot. "Honey, I know. It is painful for all of us. I am sure ya'll understand. But listen, I have got to go. You need to speak to Mrs. Reed if you say you want this job. It's a decent place to work."

Lydia had never known their father to be a gigolo or anything other than a hardworking man, a respectable soldier, and an outstanding dad. The twenty-one gun salute he'd been given at Arlington Cemetery had been as honorable as it could get, too, but it had all seemed like a lie after Buck's mother had made the shocking call that shattered everything they thought they knew about him. The discovery of another 'first' family had ripped her apart like a second death. The two families had eventually spoken several times over the phone, and met twice in court, but these encounters had been failed attempts to come to a resolution on how to manage the remaining assets. The paperwork portion of determining beneficiaries was holding everything up – right along with the military, civilian, and veterans group fraud investigators.

Marriage certificates, paternity tests, and gathering proof that everyone involved shared a legal right to the death money wasn't paying anyone's bills, though, and had only created strain on everyone...emotionally, financially, and otherwise. All four parties involved had finally ceased and desisted to allow the slow-moving government legal system time to do its job, as the fighting had only been adding fuel to the already burning fire. Despite his heroic and honorable death, her daddy really had been a rolling stone.

In her head, Lydia ran through the years of tears her mother had shed, the legal paperwork, and the few conversations they'd shared with Buck and his mother.

Buck covered his mouth over the microphone to protect his whisper. "Listen, I cannot have this conversation at work. We are understaffed and I'm pulling two duties because the last clerk slapped a client, which is exactly what I would like to do to our daddy this blessed day." He pulled his hand away from the microphone and his mouth to take a breath, and then with a false energy, he shouted, "But if you would like me to patch you through to Mrs. Reed, I can surly do that for you, ma'am!"

Her voice quivered. "I want you to know that I hope we can be friends if I get the job." She held her breath as concerning emotions scrunched her beautiful caramel features together, and then she closed her sweeping, almond-shaped eyes – the same inherited eyes that graced Buck's face in a different shade of black.

He felt she was genuine from the sound of her voice.

Buck paused, his eyes gently rolling around the lobby, to the fireplace where a woman was swallowing paperclips. His eyes traveled again and stopped on a man who was getting loud and angry next to laughing twins. Again, he knew Lydia just wanted to know her half-sibling; there was no harm in that. He sighed. "You should look this place up first. Can you multi-task well; specifically, with human distraction? I know that is one question she may ask during your interview. It will make sense when you research this facility. Lord, I really need to go…" His deep, sweet voice trailed off for a second then, and in the background Lydia heard uncontrolled belly laughing and another man saying 'nigga' repeatedly.

"Oh my God, did that man just call you a nigger?"

Buck laughed, "No, he just called two German white ladies a nigger. Research this place and call back if you think you want to work here. Every day is an adventure."

A month later, Lydia drove herself to the North Country – an hour and a half from Syracuse, twenty minutes from Canada – to work in a looney bin. The routines were difficult at first, but she was adaptable and a quick learner. Six and a half months after developing a bond between herself and her sibling, she'd blended into the dysfunctional family that was the Northern Lights community and become exceptionally proud of her hardworking sibling. Although this job was hectic, it is where they'd found family in each other and the other staff. When the Mexican arrived, she called Buck first because of this familial connection – however, she also knew the hired security guards from the clinical wing would take too long.

WELCOME TO NORTHERN LIGHTS

Relieved that the beautiful receptionist had waved him over, Ignacio broke free from the sisters to stand at the front of the desk. He glanced down to see if she had a name tag on her chest, but then he was distracted by movement from a hallway behind her. The oncoming man barreled through the space with long, intentional strides. There was a unique sway in his hips as he dangled the keys hanging from the tip of his extended finger. His strength, and the quick pace with which he rushed the lobby, prepared Ignacio to get out of his way, should he need to pass for any reason. Any reason at all. Behind Buck was an old security guard who could barely keep up with the pace let alone catch his breath. Through bursts of groveling and panting, the muscle-bound nurse bent down to enter a key code in a safe tucked under the front desk. He twisted one of his many keys in the safe's second security device and it clicked open with full access granted. He removed a tin that he could practically hide within his huge hands, and then he stood upright to direct a comment at Lydia.

"We can't be late on treatments, Ms. Lydia," he said.

His deep Barry White voice blended uncomfortably with a southern gay accent and stunned the newcomer, whose only reaction was a nonchalant shift of the bookbag hanging from his shoulder.

The receptionist tried not to be argumentative in front of Ignacio. "I know. I forgot to call you." She smiled his way through embarrassment and Ignacio smiled back.

Buck looked at the stranger and double-locked the safe with the key and a pin code before walking to the laughing sisters on the couch. Hilda caught a glimpse of the tin and squealed like a child on Christmas morning. "Cannabis! Das ist the best medicine!"

The ladies laughed as they helped each other up and led the way to a back-room custom-designed for smoking medical marijuana. This, too, had a special key that only Buck possessed, which activated a German-designed filtration system. The old guard strolled past Ignacio with a strange side-eye stare then continued to walk to the smoking room where Buck was handling everything.

Lydia composed herself by tapping at her hair and adjusting her top before she refocused and pulled paperwork out for the man in front of her to read through. Once again, she tried to give her short block of instruction. "This is a welcome packet, but you need to specifically review the materials your sponsor has provided. Your stay is paid for; you just need to sign. Northern Lights cannot admit you officially until you have filled out all the forms and been seen by one of our intake counselors who's on call. Once that's completed, we will place you in a room. Do you have any questions, Mr. ...um?" She didn't get a chance to ask his name or look at his file as a reminder before the twins swooped in to steal his lovely face away, just like cackling vultures.

Ute ran back to Ignacio and relentlessly pulled his arm toward the smoking room. The old guard didn't even attempt to move her. In fact, he stepped out of her path. Buck tried to back her away and gently remove her fat fingers from Ignacio's skin as the guard finally began to shout at Ute to let go.

The little woman was stronger than Ignacio had thought possible as she pulled him with her and the imposing nurse toward the smoking room. This is the moment Ignacio understood why the guard was reluctant to touch her in any way. Ignacio shouted over his shoulder, "Cheyez! But you can call me Ignacio. Nice to meet you, Lydia!" He'd said it louder than he'd intended. Lydia blushed through her caramel complexion and pretended to fiddle around with other paperwork on her desk as if it was important.

When Ignacio turned away, Lydia stopped shuffling paperwork to watch the eighty-something-year-old twins escort him from the receptionist desk while the head nurse tried to pry their fingers from his skin. She couldn't say much to ease the incredibly awkward moment.

"Welcome to Northern Lights!" she nervously shouted as she stared at his Mexi-can ass. Every day was an adventure at Northern Lights, she thought – especially around these vineyard nuts.

MR. JENKINS' STORY

Buck was the head nurse at Northern Lights. He was also the only one authorized to open the safe boxes at reception which held clients' emergency medicines and treatments, should they need them. And he doubled as security due to his size, although Mr. and Mrs. Reed had never officially hired him for this particular position. And on top of all this, before Lydia had arrived, he'd sometimes run the reception desk, tracked and maintained nutritional schedules when the doctors were out, and pulled lots of orderly duties when the orderlies couldn't be paged. Essentially, he played a major role in keeping things together on a daily basis. Mr. Reed always reminded him that he didn't need to go beyond his stated duties, but Buck's heart was in the facility – and so letting things go wasn't an option. However, he did let it overwhelm him, and sometimes he lost track of what was happening...like any person would. Since Lydia had been hired, he'd relied on her to send him reminders. The arrangement had worked well, too, until she made her first mistake.

It happened, sure, but Buck was nearly an hour late administering a prescription because Lydia didn't give him the courtesy reminder, and he was distracted with trying to calm an aggressive patient – the alternate personality of Mr. Jenkins.

In fact, Buck was in the craft room breaking up indecent acts when the twins were bombarding Northern Lights' newest patient. The client he'd confronted was Samuel – an alternate personality of Mr. Jenkins, who suffered from Dissociative Identity Disorder. Had the hostile personality of Samuel not appeared, Mr. Jenkins would probably have been in Bible study with another patient.

Buck knew the background story of every patient in Northern Lights, but there was something about Mr. Jenkins' splitting into such a difficult personality that tugged at his heartstrings. He was not a fan of the alternate personality, of course, but he never judged or disrespected the situation. He just did his job with his whole heart.

He knew that Mr. Jenkins had once been the pianist of a church, playing uplifting solos when the Holy Spirit took over his hands. Buck believed that, somewhere along the lines, he'd simply cracked and split apart, adding a bold and limitless personality to protect the delicate nature of the first. All Buck knew was that his own goal was to keep the peace between the opposite personalities so that they wouldn't kill each other. Suicide watch for Mr. Jenkins was a constant concern for the staff.

The man's life hadn't always been this way. Before his ten-year residency at Northern Lights had begun, he'd been a mild-mannered gentleman.

He was respected throughout his little town in Ohio, having the kind of respect that resonated through all the residents, young and old. You could ask anyone about him and their response would turn into a conversation on positive personal quips. Most of the folks in town knew him from church, where he could play a mean piano to the hymns Pastor Martin chose. Some knew him from his volunteer work at the local Share N' Care where homeless folks could get a box full of clothing for a quarter. The young children knew him as "Mr. Sam" from his time directing the choir at their summer camp and his piano lessons during the school year. He even played old ragtime songs for those who were still able to dance or wiggle in their wheelchairs in his aunt's assisted living community. Mr. Jenkins was all about making people happy and uplifting spirits. His positivity and genuine nature was his projection to the world, and that's how folks around town knew him.

Tellingly, his daughter's favorite memory with her dad was from the summer of 1998, based in the time they'd spent fishing with Pastor Martin and his own daughter in the Sandusky River. Her dad was genuinely happy as they reeled and cast their lines between sips of Coke. Gloria, in her teens, had become bored after the first ten minutes, so the girls had sat off to the side and chatted quietly until everything was set up. When the sun cooled, and night was beginning to blanket the river, they packed up their gear and left with buckets of fish. The bounty was so plentiful that her dad spent the rest of the night and into the next morning scaling and smoking them while he sang hymnals, including his favorite, "Amazing Grace." The next afternoon, after a couple hours of sleep, he sat on the porch relaxing with contentment and iced tea while offering the fish for free to anyone passing by.

When Gloria asked her dad why he didn't sell the fish instead, he confidently explained himself in a short and to-the-point monologue. (He always felt that life lessons were opportunities to learn, and this was no different, but the simplicity of what he said wasn't appreciated by the teen.) Not until she was much older did she understand the valuable message he'd been trying to convey.

"See that there?" He pointed to a thirty-something Hispanic woman who got back into her car and drove off with two smoked fish. "She lost faith in humanity when her son drowned in her backyard pool last summer. Folk feel bad around here, but don't know what to say, for fear that they upset the poor woman. So, nobody talks to her anymore...but she talks to me. We talk about fish! Had a good laugh over stinking up the porch with them guts, you see. Smoked fish get people talking, Gloria. Sometimes people just need free fish."

***

The first time his alternate and completely opposite personality appeared was in 2005, when he stood before the church proclaiming God was a 'motherfucker' and then fell asleep in the center aisle. He was out cold and had to be slapped awake by old Sister O'Dell with her moles as big as dimes on her left cheek. Months of this behavior passed before his beloved congregation felt that exorcising the devil was the answer to his unexpected possessions. For them, there was no other explanation for Mr. Jenkin's uncontrollable and sudden outbursts of anger. After extensive physical testing, he'd been cleared by the local medical community and told that he was 'fit as a fiddle', and yet he continued to black out. When he came to, a colorful myriad of retold stories about the events he couldn't remember appalled him.

Buck heard this history over and over again in the time he worked at Northern Lights. He knew that Mr. Jenkins was a good man and never judged him for becoming a different person, but instead believed that his split had begun months earlier, in the summer of 2004 when he'd saved a girl known as little Tiffany from a local house fire. This act wasn't a surprise, considering the kind of man he was...however, it was big news in his small town. He received much praise and several interviews in local newspapers, as well as a two-minute run on the local news channel. He was humble enough to say that anyone in his situation would have done the same thing, but the truth was that no one in their right mind would have risked their life the way he had.

Mr. Jenkins was fifty-four years old when he happened by little Tiffany's home while on an early morning search for an address nearby, where the home owners had advertised the sale of their used lawnmower. His plan was to fix it up and donate it to the church. As he drove slowly and triple-checked the numbers on the homes against the scrap piece of paper in his hand, he heard the little girl scream from her second-story bedroom.

The fire, later determined to be a result of faulty wiring,

originating in the kitchen from a coffee pot programmed to brew at 8 AM. The wild current and fire burned through the walls of the first floor, where the child's parents had fallen asleep on the couch the night before – presumably after recreational drug use, though nobody knows that for sure except the coroner. Tiffany, a very tall two-year-old, was then alarmed by heat under her mattress and the smoke seeping into her room from the space at the bottom of her bedroom door. When her normal crying wasn't soothed by a parent's arms, her panic changed into full-blown screams that could be heard by anyone who happened to be driving by.

Once Mr. Jenkins heard the desperate screams, he parked his car in the middle of the street and began running as best he could with his bowed legs. He tried to go through the front door, but the heat singed his arm hairs from three feet away. A stubborn welling inside of him pushed at his initial reaction, which was to go back to his car and wait for the fire department. With no time to spare, he instead tried to rush through the heat, using his body like a battering ram, but the door burned the arm he led with. The paper would later quote him as saying that "God must have directed my eyes to the neighbor's house," where he found an extended ladder resting against the neighboring house that was surrounded by scaffolding and painting equipment. In a burst of adrenaline-fueled strength, he grabbed the bottom of the heavy wooden ladder and ran 30 feet or more back to the fire with it, the tool fully extended 24 feet in the air. He believed God gave him the strength for that, too.

Eye witnesses who were on the phone with 911 would say Mr. Jenkins heaved the ladder forward so the top of it would fall to the burning home near the little girl. Their accounts went on to describe how, unbelievably, he seemed to be climbing the bottom steps even before the top made contact with the siding near the window. Like a predator, he fearlessly scaled the ladder. At the top, he began punching and scratching at the screen to break through to the little girl. One of his punches bent the flimsy frame enough for him to push his finger into a dent, so that he was then ripping it out of the jamb before tossing it to the ground. Hovering 24 feet above the earth, he was enraged and wildly determined to save the girl and, although his efforts were enough to clear the window, they were also enough to throw him off balance, causing the ladder to wobble and fall backward with the weight of him at the top.

Neighbors said he violently thrashed and grabbed for the window frame. By the Grace of God, he caught the ledge and latched onto it with a claw-like grip before throwing his burnt arm inside the room. The ladder fell on the children's toys below as Mr. Jenkins hung from the window. He was rejuvenated by the screams of Tiffany, now close to his ears. He swung his body, then heaved himself up and into the room as his orthopedic shoes frantically tried to grip the siding. Recorded 911 calls replayed a scream on the ten o'clock news: *My God, I think he's going to make it!*

By the time Mr. Jenkins pulled himself into the burning home, three men from the neighborhood were already in the yard and trying to push the ladder back into place, but the three of them stumbled through it as he stood in the window, trying to catch his breath while holding the crying child. He coughed a few times, then disappeared into the smoke-filled room with the baby. The men at the bottom pushed the ladder against the house, but when they finally reached it into the smoke billowing from the window to rescue them, the screams had stopped.

The sound of the fire and rescue truck sirens grew louder in the neighborhood, the closer they got, but witnesses said they heard glass breaking through the whir of noises in the area and, moments later, Mr. Jenkins stumbled toward the crowd with little Tiffany wrapped in a wet towel. A woman from the crowd grabbed the child and ran her across the street to safety; Mr. Jenkins followed and finally collapsed with broken glass imbedded in his arms and legs.

The reporter on the ten o'clock news explained that the hero had soaked the towel the best he could in the bathroom in order to prevent burns to the child. He also reported that the man had run into a nearby bedroom, which happened to be the master room with a bay window overlooking the backyard. Having no knowledge of bay windows, he searched for a way to open it. When the heat on the floor began to melt his orthopedic shoes, he gave up on that idea and looked for anything to break the glass.

What he grabbed was a painted rock that had been on the nightstand. It had been found and painted by the little girl a mere two weeks prior to the fire. It was about the size of a softball, painted blue and gray with 'Tiff' written in her mother's hot pink, puff-paint handwriting on the front. Little Tiffany had finished the masterpiece by decorating it with glitter glue and stickers.

An unsuspecting, dispensable memento suddenly became the most valuable item in the world as it transformed into the object that would save two lives and be the last remaining reminder of a mother's love.

The ten o'clock news reduced the significance of the rock to an item the hero had used to get the girl out of the house, but it was so much more than this alone, and Mr. Jenkins couldn't stop thinking about it afterward. His mind was plagued with its potential significance. He rubbed at his ear as the image of it flashed in his mind, going beyond visual explanations to short blackouts he never told anyone about. Obsessed over the rock, he returned to the burnt remains of the home. It was taped off with posted warning signs, but the treasured rock that had saved their lives had to be found – for Tiffany. At first, he timidly and delicately sifted over the area. Then his actions became angry shoveling with his bare hands before a sudden massive headache dropped him to his knees in a pool of sooty water. He wanted to give up. He wanted to be in his favorite chair at home – a home he still had the luxury of going back to. He shook his head as he rubbed his hands over his eyes to stop the floating colored lights. Mr. Jenkins knew he needed to rest, but he couldn't. He never said the words out loud, but an inner strength screamed for him to get the fuck up as a terrible pain surged through his inner ear.

Determined, he pushed through his pain and found the rock. With his thumb, he wiped away the black water from the painted memories. Now he could see his purpose as blood oozed from the dip in his ear.

Mr. Jenkins salvaged the rock and anything else he could. By noon, his cargo pockets were full of charred trinkets and his polo shirt was drenched in sweat. He returned to his home to clean – everything, including the red stains he had not noticed on the shoulder of his shirt.

You could ask anyone, young and old, about Mr. Jenkins, the piano player at El Bethel Church. They would agree that the fire changed the man. He became angry, and an altogether different person.

It was Christmas, five months after his act of heroism, when his alter, Samuel, appeared for the first time in church. Mr. Jenkins, who had to hear about it from Sister O'Dell, was mortified with what he had done...but he held no memory of it. All the respect he had earned over the years slowly began to crumble apart as this behavior continued and he became the joke of the town. He learned the hard way that it takes years to build trust in a community, but only seconds to take it away. Eventually, the community began to ignore "Cray-Bo on Avenue Fo." Even the owner of the camp politely explained that his outbursts were scaring the children and that he could no longer be allowed to direct choir. The phone calls for piano lessons stopped, too, as did the welcomes from his aunt's assisted living home. His fellow brothers and sisters within his congregation were willing to help with an exorcism, which they could claim later to be a part of, but not to sit and lend him an ear. Other than Gloria and Pastor Martin, the only people who continued to visit him was the Hispanic woman with her new tattoo of an angel fish on her shoulder. His best friends of forty years and his neighbors, some of whom he'd babysat when they'd been in diapers, began to whisper about his offensive episodes, but offered no consultation or compassion. A once local hero who'd saved little Tiffany's life from a house fire was cast out of the circles of support he so desperately needed.

Once committed to Northern Lights, Mr. Jenkins became a forgotten neighbor, father, and friend; no one came around to visit the person he'd once been, and this included his only daughter – who had also forgotten that, sometimes, even fishermen needed free fish.

Buck's heart bled for people like Mr. Jenkins, who protected his mental fragility by assuming another identity. The other staff members called it good versus evil, but Buck never saw it that way. So, as Buck made his way to the craft room where he'd been called to break up a disturbance, he thought about the gentle man who'd broken down and accepted an alternate personality other than his own. He thought about Mr. Jenkins' ten years at Northern Lights, and wanted nothing more than for the two men to live as harmoniously as they could in the same body.

MEET SAMUEL

When Gloria arrived at his doorstep in the Buckeye State, it was a typical, quiet May evening for her father. He answered the door in a fake silk pajama set with his reading glasses on top of his head. She already knew that, before he'd been interrupted by the doorbell, he'd been comfortably reading his paper and watching the nightly news with his cup of decaffeinated coffee next to him. This had been the routine for years and would probably continue to be his routine until he was eighty because that's just the kind of man he was – predictable. It was also the reason his wife had left, but some people just preferred their routine, and that was okay by her. After they hugged in the foyer, she followed behind him as he walked the best he could with his slightly bowed legs to his favorite recliner in the living room. The surface chat was light and wonderful, but they skirted around the reason she was there until she specifically brought it up. It changed the mood in the house completely as Mr. Jenkins cleared his throat and got up – without saying a word – to refill his coffee cup.

When he returned to the living room, he had a steaming cup for each of them. Once he resettled in his recliner, Gloria could tell that he'd been crying, as was evidenced by a red hue in the whites of his eyes and a puffiness that hadn't been there before.

"Dad, I know you don't want to face this, but we can do this together. That's why I'm here. We just need to talk about what's going on...with the outbursts. I'm hearing the rumors even where I am in college, Dad, and if you need help – I want to help." She nervously scratched at the skin on the back of her neck and carefully sipped the coffee that she didn't want.

"I know. I know. That's why you're here. Appreciate that, Gloria. Really do. You know, I'm a grown man..." He trailed off as he choked back tears and bit at his lip, which was beginning to quiver. He removed the reading glasses from the top of his head to set them aside, allowing himself a moment to clear his throat before he began again. "I'm a grown man who is healthy and has lived a good, honest life. Worked hard. Prayed hard. Did what I could to make people around me happy, but I don't know what's happening. I black out, do bad things that I don't remember and hurt people that I love with my words. Almost scared of myself, you know?"

He tugged at his ear as if he was relieving an itch deep within then pulled a brush from an end table drawer and began to nervously brush forward the top and sides of his graying hair. "Sister O'Dell at the church – you remember her, she has the big goiter on her neck and the hairy moles on her face. Well, she told me that I stood before God and everyone in the middle of Pastor Martin's sermon to curse the Lord Almighty himself. Got so heated my partials flew out of my mouth onto the center aisle." He gingerly set the brush down and sipped at his coffee to give his daughter a moment to take it all in.

Gloria's hands covered her mouth as she sat in shock, not knowing if she should giggle at the story or be horrified.

He dug his free index finger deep into his chest for emphasis. "Go ahead. Laugh if you want to, but I believe the Father is not happy with me right now. No, sir."

Gloria asked if it could possibly be dementia or Alzheimer's. Mr. Jenkins scrunched his face up, appalled that such a question should cross her mind. "Your Great Nanna Jenkins was one-hundred-and-three...still spanking me at chess and debating politics before she passed. We don't have old-timers' disease runnin' through our family tree." From the table, he picked up the brush again and tossed it back into the drawer, then grabbed his cup and muted the news report on the television. "Something is going on. Made God mad. Made somebody mad. Him or Zeus or Allah. What's that one woman...from the people with the red polka dots on their foreheads? Shiva! Yeah, that one. Musta pissed her off, too. Ain't nothin' like a woman's scorn."

Gloria shook her head, but laughed as she informed him that the polka dot people were Hindus. They both laughed, and then she got up to investigate the burning smell that was coming from the kitchen. The coffee pot had been left on without anything in it, so she turned the machine off, pulled the pot from the heating element, and set it in the sink to cool before she checked the refrigerator for something to snack on. As she bent down to investigate the bottom drawers, though, her dad suddenly appeared in the doorway, leaning with his left shoulder against the door jam and with one bow-leg crossed over the other.

"Got fired, you know," he said.

Gloria jumped at his unexpected presence, but then she returned to the drawer without looking carefully in his direction. "Who got fired, Dad?" she asked into the refrigerator.

"Sam. I told that nigga to quit being a nigga, and let that motha-fuckin' boss know that he ain't working in a mother-fuckin' sugar mill his whole life."

Gloria whipped around to see who was speaking to her in such a manner. Surely, it wasn't her God-fearing father saying that word. When she turned, though, she saw that it was in fact her dad standing relaxed and yet confidently in the doorway with a grin across his face. "Dad! Jesus Christ! What did you say?" Her heart exploded with shock as her hand grabbed at her chest.

"Stop calling me 'Dad', and Jesus ain't got nothin' to do with this." He grabbed at his crotch, which appeared to be growing under the silk he wore. "I'd say the nigga did something right with his life if you are his daughter. God damn, you are one fine piece of ass! Ooo-wee!" Her dad stomped his foot on the linoleum and laughed a laugh that wasn't his own.

The magnitude of the stories she'd heard about her daddy's episodes, she'd thought, had been embellished, but this insanity was too much for her to wrap her brain around. Gloria stepped back, afraid, and grabbed a knife from the knife rack. As she held it in front of her for protection, it shook. "What the fuck, Dad! Stop it!" Her voice trembled as fear mangled the smooth skin in her forehead.

"I'm not your dad. We could fuck. And I won't stop. What you need to do is relax your dark chocolaty-fine pussy down on this chair before niggas start getting nervous. Now, I'm tired of this bullshit motherfuckin' nightly decaf with no women to give me a blowjob afterward, which would make my whole cup of joe experience worth experiencing. You feel me? Church can suck my dick and so can this ungrateful, unproductive, judgmental, and hypocritical town your daddy likes to call home. It has packed his mind so full of shit that it's coming out of his motherfuckin' tear ducts when the man cries at night!"

The person that Gloria knew as her predictable father was not the person in the kitchen with her. She backed herself against the opposite side of the room, so she wouldn't accidently stab him out of sheer terror, and knocked over a coffee cup that had been set too close to the edge of the counter. It crashed to the floor and splashed its contents onto the cuff of her pants.

"Here I am, doing my best to keep this nigga from losing his mind, and all he can do is...Didn't I tell you to set your motherfuckin' pussy down, bitch? You can't hear? You slow?" His eyes, which were normally uplifted and honest, were strangely squinted into slits now and staring at her as if she were the one who was out of her mind.

"Dad, please, you are scaring me!" She hesitantly

grabbed a kitchen table chair and pulled it as close to her as she could, the knife still taut and ready in her hand. She thought about her purse in the other room, that was sitting on the floor next to the coffee table, and how she was going to get to it if he continued to block the doorway.

"Stop calling me 'Dad'!" he yelled so loudly that she jumped, sending tears streaming down her beautiful face.

Gloria shook and began to cry. "What the fuck should I call you?" she screamed in fear as she tried to sit down slowly, so as to not piss of the person who was standing between her and the front door. She'd watched a documentary about multiple personality disorders in her psychology class. One thing that stood out in her mind was how family members learned the value in remaining calm when introduced to an unexpected alter ego. Granted, the knife was a little dramatic, but she was trying.

He waited for her to sit down before he released some of the tension in his face. "Samuel. A nigga's name is Samuel." He seemed very proud and smug.

She cocked her head sideways as the knife began to shake uncontrollably in her hand, but couldn't help starting to cry again in the chair. Samuel got frustrated with the whole situation and left the room so that he could find Mr. Jenkins's car keys. Gloria was frozen in the chair and unable to move while she heard him going through drawers in her daddy's room. When he came back to the kitchen he was in a suit that she didn't know her daddy had owned.

"Ain't this nigga got a wallet? What nigga don't keep a set of keys and his wallet near a motherfucker? Why don't you do me a favor, mocha, and get your ass up to help me find them. I ain't fucking asking." He snapped his fingers at her as if she was a dog.

Before this demand, she'd been scared stiff to move from the kitchen chair, but now Gloria got up and immediately 'helped' Samuel search for a wallet and keys while discretely inching her way closer to her purse in the living room, with her cell phone and her own set of car keys. Her only option was to call the police. Samuel was upstairs again when she finally reached her belongings. She dug through the bottom of her bag as the sounds of a man she didn't know rummaged through shirts in an upstairs closet. Then she dialed the local police station number, which she'd had memorized since childhood.

The dispatcher, an old high school friend of her dad's, answered. Gloria's voice was shaken as she pressed the cell phone to her ear, making it burn into the side of her head.

"Mrs. Amicy, it's me, Gloria Jenkins."

"Well, hello, Gloria! Didn't know you were in town. Everything alright, sugar?"

"It's Daddy." She looked back to assure herself he wasn't in the room while the sounds of wire hangers scratched across the bar they hung on.

"Oh Lord, not again. What is it this time? Where you at, sugar?"

"What? I'm at his house. Send someone right away. He's gone crazy," she tried to whisper into the bottom of her phone as she turned away from the hall and stepped deeper into the room, still pretending to search for a set of keys.

"Uh huh. Sure thing, sugar. Listen, he's all talk and full of shit; he won't hurt a fly. Kind of suave, though. I got to meet him the last time we booked your daddy. Got a foul mouth on him, don't he?" When Mrs. Amicy laughed, you could tell she had been a smoker for years by the way phlegm bubbled and popped within each heave of her chest. "Uh huh, maybe I would have gone to prom with Samuel, had he been around in high school – if you know what I mean." Winded, she managed to laugh again before she got back to business by clearing her throat and catching her breath. "I'm sorry, sugar; I got a car on their way. Listen, your daddy flew over the coo coo's nest after saving that little Tiffany. He's been this way for almost a year. When he comes back, just ask your daddy to sign some paperwork, so you can get the money your grandmother left him. That way, you can get him some real help. Your daddy was a good man, but God can't help him now; the man needs drugs. Real strong drugs."

"Jesus!" Gloria said a little too loudly. She didn't remember Mrs. Amicy being this bold. Frankly, it was a bit too much to handle. Her manicured nails scratched at her forehead when her father startled her by unexpectedly walking into the living room. "Jesus ain't got nothin' to do with this."

A shot of artery-bursting blood shot through every vein in Gloria's body before she slowly turned to see which man was standing behind her in the archway. The hairs on the nape of her neck stood on end when she saw her daddy standing with the suit pants on and a different shirt: the maroon one he hadn't worn since his anniversary the year before her mother had left him for a white guy.

"Where we going again?" Her authentic father tugged at the collar of his fine shirt. "It's late. Don't want to miss my shows, you know. Where did I put my readin' glasses?"

Mrs. Amicy chimed in from the cell phone, "Oh see, is

that your daddy? He's back, ain't he? Always predictable. Want me to call off the car?"

"Yes, ma'am. Thank you for your time." Gloria then hung up on Mrs. Amicy to have a conversation with her dad, who was obviously unaware of the hell she'd just experienced with Samuel. "You know what, Dad? We should take a drive. You can put comfortable clothes on," she lied.

At twenty-three years old – the age where most women are worried about finishing college and parties – Gloria made the awful decision to drive her dad to the local hospital to have him admitted on the behavioral health ward of the ninth floor. After a short explanation on the way there, he didn't resist like she'd thought he would; rather, he cried in the car. Three days later, by police escort, Mr. Jenkins was taken to an institute in Columbus where, months later, he was officially evaluated and diagnosed with Dissociative Identity Disorder – DID.

Gloria spent nine months working out legal issues and obtaining access to his money. By February of 2006, she began supporting him with it in a permanent home. Northern Lights was a new type of mental health facility – a lovely institution on a vineyard.

Mr. Jenkins wasn't bitter, really; he knew it was for the

best, even though he didn't get to walk his daughter down the aisle later that year or be there for the birth of his grandson. For her part, she tried to keep connected by sending photos of her progressing life, and even visited on his 60th birthday, but she was busy with her new family in a suburb surrounding New York City. Communication with her dad boiled down to the yearly birthday or Christmas cards, always with a JC Penny photo taped inside. Unfortunately, it got to the point where he watched his grandson become a boy through yearly school photos. She wanted to be there for her dad, but she also wanted things to be normal – and they were not. The distance helped her cope with her father's disorder.

In his ten-year residency at the Northern Lights vineyard, Mr. Jenkins had come to enjoy making the annual ice wine. He looked forward to Saturday card games with German twins who couldn't stop laughing. All of which was fine with him. He liked the idea of being able to have these routines and speak to doctors about his alternate personality without judgement. But he missed his daughter, missed his grandson, and hated his disorder for ruining his life.

Samuel's hatred for his institutionalized life was at an entirely different level. He despised Mr. Jenkins and Gloria for putting him in the nuthouse.

If it hadn't been for his girlfriend in the institution, he would have left. His girlfriend was the only thing keeping his hot temper at bay most of the time. Otherwise, he was amped enough to instigate fights with a homosexual brute nurse named Buck for catching him in the middle of a blow-job in the community craft room.

"How can you be a nigga and think it's okay to pull a bitch away from another nigga's dick? What's wrong with you, motherfucker?" Samuel didn't bother to put his erect penis back into his pants as he turned with his hands in the air like an angered baboon to face the orderly.

Buck, who'd pushed him away from a woman on all fours, was forced to use his deep man voice – albeit that it was still fluttery and wrapped in a southern-accented bow. "Stand back, Mr. Samuel, so help me God. You cannot engage in sexual activities with other patients, and you know it."

"God has nothing to do with this. Ain't that right, baby?" Samuel wiggled his hard dick in the air and moved forward again toward Belinda Jayne Beckler, who was still on her knees with her smeared red lipstick and her long blonde hair dangling over her shirtless body.

Buck put his hand firmly on Samuel's chest to prevent

him from taking another step. His stature was more than a match for the host body of Mr. Jenkins, who was slightly bow-legged and of average height, even if his alternate personality thought he had the physical ability to take Buck down.

Belinda, a twenty-seven-year-old bombshell, had poised her mouth open and closed her eyes in anticipation of his penis, but was now rudely restricted by another unwanted man who was not on her dick-sucking invite list. "Buck! God dammit, he is my boyfriend! Why don't you leave us alone, for Christ's sake?"

Samuel hushed her as politely as he could to address Buck in a man-to-man type of whisper – regardless of his naked lower half. "Nigga, listen to the girl now. If you weren't such a butt pumper, you would feel another man's desire for his woman's pink mouth to wrap itself around this throbbing love stick. Now do a nigga a favor and walk away, lock the door behind you, and mind your own motherfuckin' business!" Samuel turned to Belinda again and pushed his hips forward in a second attempt to reach his girlfriend's mouth, but the hand on his chest and the locked arm that was preventing yet another blowjob were not budging.

"Mr. Samuel, put your penis away before I call for more security. Ms. Beckler, you know the rules and yet you continue to break them. Young lady, you have symptoms of destructive behaviors and hypersexuality. Did you take your pills today?"

"Yeah, the libido killers? Shit, Buck, you are my libido killer!" Belinda pushed her hair behind her head onto her back as she stood from the craft room floor with crushed dried noodles embedded into her knees. She mumbled as she brushed them off. "Go ahead and call security. It will take Arthur an hour to get here. The man needs to retire already, Jesus."

While Samuel zipped his pants and yelled obscenities, Belinda sat down in a chair with her arms crossed, completely unconcerned with the smeared lipstick around her lips or the cool craft room air brushing across her nipples. Buck's emergency phone rang in his pocket. Belinda, pissed that her fun was completely ruined, pouted like a child. "Why are you even in here, Buck? Aren't you supposed to be getting some old ladies high right about now?" The phone rang again. "Just go before Samuel gets really angry or, worse, the host comes back. Shit, that man is boring, old and crotchety. I wouldn't suck him off if he paid me." She looked over to her boyfriend, who giggled while rubbing his crotch and winking back at her.

The phone rang again before Buck finally dug it out of the same pocket where he kept his Carmex and cosmetic mirror. Belinda just looked at him while he listened to the person on the other end, and then she quietly said, "Just go. I'll calm him down for you." She licked her lips and crinkled her nose with a squeal of excitement before she jumped up from the chair to push Buck toward the door, although he was already headed that way. "I'll lock up, so you won't get into trouble." Then she shouted to Samuel, "Baby, he's leaving! Bring your anaconda to Momma!"

When Buck was completely pushed into the hallway with his ear still glued to the phone, she locked the door and skipped over to a craft table that was scattered with scraps of paper and used staples. Samuel helped hoist her onto the table, where they could finish what they started.

BUCK OF ALL TRADES

Keeping up with the security and administration of medical marijuana was only a quarter of the stress in Buck Lynn's life. After the craft room incident, and after safely getting Hilda and Ute Schmidt into the smoking room, somewhat on schedule, he briskly walked back to the front desk where his half-sister Lydia was in-processing a new Hispanic client. His blood still boiled from all the distractions and hindrances in his routine. Only a man who took pride in his job became distraught over a schedule setback, and so he wished Lydia shared his work ethic. She cared about her job, but she wouldn't go out of her way to accomplish her daily tasks.

The initial real excuse for putting in a good word for her had been that he couldn't keep up with his daily tasks and be the intake clerk at Northern Lights. Admittedly, if he'd had to swear on his momma – despite the family feud over their biological father's military survivor benefits – he wanted to know his half-white sister out of sheer curiosity. Both were legitimate reasons anyway, in addition to the fact that he was overloaded with responsibilities at Northern Lights and couldn't keep up. Now, though, after she'd been an hour late with her reminder call for medication, he wondered if bringing her onto the staff had been a good idea...especially when he saw the way she was looking at the Mexican standing at the front desk.

Buck had to interrupt the unprofessional connection between them so that he and Lydia could get back to work. When the Mexican looked at him, he was enamored; his eyes were beautiful and sparkling, but Buck remained professional when addressing him. "Excuse me, sir. Ms. Lydia, may I have a word with you, please?" His sweet voice was polite and melodic as he ticked his finger at her to gesture that she should come to where he was standing. She excused herself from her post and followed him down the corridor for privacy.

There was something extremely feminine about him as he connected a loose, massive clump of keys back onto his belt via a D ring and swayed his last few steps before spinning as if he was on the catwalk, making his final photo opportunity pose. His hand flicked into the air before resting at his face, his index and middle fingers pressed to the top of his forehead like a fag's version of a dramatic fainting with an unnatural backward flex. His lips puckered in frustration before he popped his mouth and tongue, then placed his free hand on his hip. Lydia knew he was mad, but she had never seen him this frazzled before. Before he could begin his on-coming, nagging speech, she apologized. "I'm sorry, Buck. I just forgot to call," she tried to explain.

His eyes were wide and bulging as he stared at her, then held his finger up to shush her. "Don't want to hear it. I have had the most atrocious day, and God bless your heart, you just made a simple mistake, albeit a severe one in the medical community. What shall we do about this? What shall we do?" He tapped his index finger to his lips as if to denote deep thought. He then looked over Lydia's head to the hot Mexi-can guy who was now speaking to a bible-thumping patient at the front desk. "Lord and baby Jesus, bless the rest of my day. Get her away from him. You can tell me what happened later. Here, unlock the Schmidt twins from the smoking room in twenty minutes, but lock this tin up now before someone takes it. Has the new kid seen the doctor?"

"Yes, he just left the office. He's cleared, and can have room 19. I've already paged for an orderly to escort him. Buck, I'm really sorry about not calling..."

"Mistake. Got it. Do not let it happen again. I'll take care of escorting the new guy, and you just put this box away and let the twins out. They should be much calmer. Oh, make a note in Ms. Beckler's file, too, please and thank you very much, ma'am."

"My God, you caught them again? I don't think they even try to hide it anymore. Geesh." She crossed her arms and turned her body to catch a flirtatious glimpse of Ignacio when she felt him staring at her ass from across the room.

Keeping his voice down, Buck tried to redirect her attention in a hushed voice. "Keep your panties on. We do not have sex with clients, and you do not know what he is here for. He could be a serious case for the clinical wing."

Having forgotten about the specialty clinic that was literally positioned at the far corner of the mansion, Lydia admitted that he was right. The security checked in with the main area, but the guards always returned to the corner. Buck pulled out his Carmex and applied a thin coat of the clear wax to his thick black lips, then popped them together before putting the tiny jar back into his pocket.

"Can you grab me his file, please? I am not walking near Mrs. Koontz or she will tell me the whole story of Sodom and Gomorrah for the sixteenth time, as if Momma never dragged me to church every Sunday! Nobody got time for that!" Buck snapped his fingers, but his hand was down to his side and pushed slightly behind his leg so that no one would see his moment of flamboyancy. He always tried to keep it professional.

When Lydia returned with a fresh, crisp manila folder that was lined with forms and signed documents clipped to a clipboard, he waved the new patient over with a calm and intentionally composed motion. Then to Lydia, he said again, "We don't know his reason for being here. Remember that."

YOUR ROOM

Ignacio, directed to follow the orderly, smiled as he walked to him. He was as tall and big as a man could be, but when he spoke it was strange indeed. His voice was extraordinarily deep, but it was also sweet, and there was no other way Ignacio could describe it.

"Mr...Cheese? Mr. Nacho Cheese?" Buck tried to read the name that Lydia had crossed through and hand-written "Nacio" above. He reread the text several times, but could hardly believe that someone would name a child 'Nacho' – especially if their last name was Cheese.

Ignacio corrected him, "Nah-see-yo in English, and my last name is Chey-yez. It's actually Ignacio, but white people...non-Hispanics, I mean...have a hard time saying it, so I just shorten it." He winked, but felt like an asshole after doing it.

Buck flipped through the paperwork again, this time carefully looking at the name. "I apologize, Mr. Cheese. Would you please follow me to your room, sir?"

Ignacio smiled at the innocence of the man's second mistake. Buck turned to walk ahead of him. His hips swayed as he walked down the hall while speaking about the building. He missed seeing the stranger's dimples appear as he smiled and tucked a lock of curls behind his ear.

"I'm Buck Lynn, the head nurse here at Northern Lights. The first three days of your stay here will be a part of an evaluation period. We ask that you first speak with your doctor before you sign up for any therapies. There is a schedule of mandatory consultations that you need to participate in before we can begin your journey to recovery. Meal times are posted on the inside of your door to your room, which is...room nineteen. A pretty clean and quiet room, if I do say so myself, Mr. Cheese. There are other rules and things you should know about this facility, but they are all spelled out for you in a packet on your bed. We will have to lock up your things in a locker at the end of your bed until the evaluation period is over, and we do apologize for this inconvenience, but it is for everyone's safety here at Northern Lights. There is a lending closet where you can get essentials and hygiene products by the back library in the morning. A map is also provided for you in the packet..." Buck continued to talk, sway, and flip through the clipboard full of papers as he gave the briefing that he had effortlessly given so many times before. He spoke through it so fast that Ignacio had a hard time picking up the details, in between keeping up with the walking pace of a man whose gate was practically longer than he was tall. He wasn't going to say anything about slowing down, though, because he wasn't a chump. He was a Mexi-CAN. Ignacio giggled to himself at the thought.

"Are you okay, Mr. Cheese?" Buck Lynn seemed frustrated as he stopped his walk and turned to look down at the new client, who was giggling with the most adorable dimples on either side of his brown cheeks.

"It's Chey-ez. Two syllables. I'm sorry, just tired from the long drive. Please continue." The stranger had corrected the orderly, but was surprisingly accepting of things, considering that he had lived with name-botching his entire life.

Buck spun around like a diva to finish his speech as they continued to walk closer to Ignacio's room. "We are a different kind of facility here. We are a less institutionalized environment than others because we believe in the power of self-promoted happiness, although we do utilize precautions, such as our newly installed keyless locks." He touched a keyless push button pad under a passing door to point it out as he continued his brisk walking pace. When he reached a door with the gold numbers one and nine affixed to the outside of it, he stopped. "This is nineteen. The keypad is for staff and the traditional key and lock is for you. Don't worry; no one will come in unless there is a serious issue – a health or safety concern."

He used the key to unlock the door and held it open for Ignacio to walk through. Once inside, Ignacio scanned the room to welcome the simple and yet cozy set-up that was already comfortably lit. The room was about the size of your average American hotel room, with one queen bed, one nightstand, and an inset closet with hangers. Unlike with an average hotel, the hangers were permanently attached and, rather than a lamp on the nightstand, the lighting was provided by updated, recessed lights in the ceiling and two more in the wall above the bed. It wasn't nearly as bright as a hospital triage room, but certainly set to a level where you could relax and then fall asleep. As the stranger took in the details of his room, Buck opened the lockbox under the bed, which was also affixed to the floor. "Mr. Chee-eese, this box is for your bag. I would recommend pulling out a clean pair of underpants at least before I lock it away. You won't be able to open this for three days, minimum. It's a security thing. Until then, there's the lending closet I mentioned, with used clothing items, and the staff takes care of laundering. Everything is in the pamphlet." His voice, was pleasant, honest, and welcoming – which hardly matched his build and intimidating physique. The southern spin on his words made each one sound sincere. Ignacio obliged his request without saying a word. Buck watched him pull out the recommended underwear and zip the bookbag shut before he locked the box and stood up to explain the lighting situation. "You will find that there are no light switches in the rooms."

Ignacio scanned the walls and saw that these were indeed oddly missing.

"They are preset to this level throughout the day and will begin to dim at 10:00 P.M, until they are about the brightness of a candle in the room. This is also a safety feature, as well as a gentle reminder that bedtime is 10:30 P.M. If for some reason you need to adjust this schedule, please see the front desk."

Buck took one last look around the room to see if he'd missed anything. He patted his pocket where the jar of Carmex was tucked away, but refrained from pulling it out for an unnecessary reapplication; it was just a habitual check to make sure he was being professional. As he walked to the door, Ignacio asked where the restrooms were and, apologetically, Buck answered his question while handing him his room key. "The men's wash room is down the hall, across from the craft room. It's equipped with three shower stalls, three toilets, urinals, and three sinks. There are no locks on bathroom doors. Don't forget the lending closet, too. Some items can be signed out if you need them, but everything else will be provided by your sponsor. It's all in the packet. Welcome to Northern Lights, Mr. Cheese."

Buck shot him a smile and then nervously rushed out of the room and into the hallway, quietly mumbling as he wiped beads of sweat from his upper lip. He ran back to the craft room where he'd left Samuel and Ms. Beckler, which he'd almost forgotten about, what with the distraction of the new guy's dimples.

INTERESTING CONFLICTS

When Buck arrived at the craft room door, he peered into the window as he pressed out the code which unlocked the keyless entry. Ms. Beckler was re-dressing near the craft table and wiping the now faded lipstick away from her face, but Samuel was gone. When Buck opened the door, though, he saw that Mr. Jenkins was mumbling near it while desperately trying to zip up his pants. His red eyes were shameful. "Tell this harlot – be gone! How many times do I have to go through this, Buck? I 'pacifically asked you and the staff to keep her away!" He shook uncontrollably as he worked at his zipper to regain some of his dignity.

Buck's lips had barely separated enough to begin speaking when Belinda yelled with her hands on her hips, "Oh shut up! I was about to orgasm when Mr. Holy-roly-poly asshole woke up and ruined my cum. You couldn't have waited one more minute? Jesus Christ!"

Angered that she'd used the Lord's name in vain, Mr. Jenkins shouted back, "Jesus ain't got nothing to do with this!"

He finally tugged at the zipper just enough to rip through a tangled clump of hair and close his pants. Then he stood up straight in an attempt to wipe the dripping sweat from his brow. "I told you, harlot, that this is rape! Can't use my body without permission and I am the owner of my body! It's a violation and an abomination to think that my alternate personality is your boyfriend." He tugged at his ear which was ringing and slightly painful. The whole thing was giving him a headache. He pointed fiercely at Belinda with an accusing, damning stiffness. As his anger escalated, spit flew from his mouth. "You are insane, woman, so stay away from me – I rebuke you!"

Buck stepped between the man's horizontally erect finger and Belinda to once again calm the waters between them. "Sir, calm down. Mr. Jenkins, I have done my job. I pulled Mr. Samuel away from her and he used choice words with me before lunging...um, *ya'll's* penis into her mouth, which puts me in a predicament because it was kind of consensual – even though it's still against rules. We will deal with her for obliging your alter, but you have got to help us out here with him. Sir, when ya'll get around each other...excuse me, when *he* gets around her, he is a bull."

Buck stepped in to Mr. Jenkins' space to gain some privacy as he hushed his voice. The smell of Belinda was all over him. "Now I know you do not want to hear this, sir, but I believe the two may be good for each other in a weird way. They calm each other, and Mr. Samuel's outbursts aren't as frequent. And let's be honest, sir – despite your protests, you seem happier after ya'll's visits."

Mr. Jenkins cracked the slightest smile, but then it faded and he yelled around Buck's chest to the beautiful, soft woman by the craft table. "Temptress of the devil! Put her in the far corner – she's a rapist!"

Belinda rolled her eyes. She crossed her arms over her breasts that were pushing the limits on the buttons of her shirt. Buck shook his head. "Sir, we are not going to put her in the clinical wing for consensual sex – well, technically, it was." He followed up with a lot of reassuringly positive things to clear the air between them. Then he politely escorted Mr. Jenkins out into the hallway with a reminder that the lights would dim soon, and the suggestion that he take a nice hot shower before bed. Mr. Jenkins agreed that this would be beneficial and, slowly, he sadly walked his bowed legs toward his room for some towels and shower shoes.

When Buck turned to give Belinda a good scolding, she was standing four feet from him with her arms still crossed, trying to watch the actions on the other side of Buck's chest. Her eerie smeared lipstick across her mouth caused his muscled frame to jump in his orthopedic nurse shoes.

"Ms. Beckler!" he yelped.

"Call me B.J.," she insisted with a whore-red smile that might have looked lovely, had the lipstick stayed within the parameters of her lips. She winked at him as if he hadn't caught the meaning of her preferred nick name.

"Ms. Beckler, I know you are infatuated with his alter, but ya'll cannot continue this relationship, and frankly, I am tired of repeating myself. You are torturing that man." Buck pointed down the hallway in the direction where the good Christian man had walked seconds ago.

Belinda waved her index finger in the air and rolled her neck with pointed sass. "That man is a pain in my ass. The one I was fucking is not that asshole. Crazy people get horny, too, Buck Lynn!"

Buck sighed. Realizing the situation was about to get heated, he pressed his index finger and middle finger against his forehead in frustration. When he flexed them into an unnatural backward bend, this simple motion seemed ten times more feminine than it was ever intended to be. Finally, he shook his index finger in her face and put his free hand on his hip like a true queen would – because even his stance on professionalism only lasted until a blonde bimbo like Belinda swirled her finger in his face. "Listen, missy, if you really cared for Mr. Samuel, you would make every effort to appreciate his host, who happens to be the primary and dominant personality! Then, maybe, one day the three of you could learn to live harmoniously. I just pray that the Lord bless your heart in another facility far from my aching head, though, because you drive me batshit."

Buck straightened himself up again and looked around the craft room to ensure that no one had seen him lose his composure. "Unfortunately for you, I must add this to your never-ending log, and I am going to suggest the doctor take another look at your pill dosage."

Belinda tried to open her mouth to speak in protest, but Buck put his finger to his own lips and closed his eyes while he shook his head no. She didn't say a word over his unspoken request for her to be quiet. "You know I am right, Ms. Beckler, and you also know that these infractions will kick you out of Northern Lights despite your uncle's monthly checks, so, ma'am, be nice to people."

Belinda huffed and puffed as she ran her fingers through

her long blonde hair while rolling her eyes. She adjusted the crotch of her pajama bottoms then, realizing that sex fluids were still uncomfortably drying there. She excused herself coyly to take a shower at the other end of the hall.

"Wait, Ms. Beckler. We received a new client today. After today's shenanigans, you will be watched, so leave him alone! Being nice doesn't mean harassing other patients for sex."

She turned around in the middle of the hallway. "New dick? Well, if anyone is going to watch me shower, could you make sure it's that new orderly, Charlotte? I like the way she subconsciously licks her lips when I am around. Can I tell you what I did to her last week?" She walked back to Buck, ready to tell her story even if he didn't want to hear it.

"No, ma'am. Lord Jesus, Ms. Beckler, I am locking this for the night and going home." He turned his back to her and put in the code for the now emptied craft room, then waited for a ticking noise before attempting to walk away.

She continued without much of an effort to hush her vulgar words. "I stuck my finger in my pussy and smeared it on the wrist of my other hand, and then I pretended she had a loose eyelash and wiped it away so intentionally that wrist was right next to her nose!" Belinda was smug.

Buck was disgusted. "Have you no shame?" he scolded as he tried to hide his horror underneath a steady stream of professionalism. After the beep of the locking mechanism chimed, he put his hand gently into the middle of the woman's back and nudged her with respect to her room, which was four doors down from Ignacio's. Belinda never stopped chattering.

"Dude, she smelled it! I mean, took a good whiff, then smiled at me! Oh Buck, she has some nice titties – I can tell through that shitty orderly uniform you guys wear!" As she got more excited, her voice went up in pitch, and Buck knew that soon this one sign would turn into a fiercely raging desire to fuck anything with a pulse. With knowledge of her previous episodes, he knew exactly how to handle this situation.

Buck immediately called Lydia at the front desk to deflate the escalating hormone walking next to him. He intentionally made no effort to hush his tone. "Please note in Ms. Beckler's file: reevaluate dosage, mandatory escort, and leave a message for Charlotte to see me when she comes in for her shift tomorrow."

Belinda's jaw dropped as she stopped dead in the middle of the hallway with her stiff arms jutting straight down to the floor in a tantrum. "I fucking hate this place! If my boyfriend wasn't here and I had a place to go and you fixed the fucking cracks in the sidewalks, I would leave!"

Everything was moving too fast for Buck's built-in southern timing, where things ran at a slower pace. But the benefits of his upbringing included his ability to throw back insults within seconds. "Ya'll need to start focusing on rehabilitation for your disorder and stop sucking the dicks of men who don't exist." Buck's jaw dropped, and his hand immediately slapped over his lips in an attempt to shut himself up. His cheeks began to fill with blood as he blushed with utter embarrassment; he had been raised around too many of his God-fearing aunts and a mother who praised the Lord on Sundays for such words to spill from his lips.

"Oh my Gawd, Buck Lynn, did you just 'read' me? I think professional, uptight Buck just let his guard down to – read me!" She squealed with laughter as her head shook, making her long locks of hair jiggle and bounce. "That was better than our stupid one-day-a-week open admittance – and you know how much I love the newbies!

An unexpected door opened four doors down; Ignacio poked his head out of his room to see what the commotion was. The two of them looked at the floating head peeking out of room nineteen.

Belinda turned back to Buck to quietly address him in a suddenly reserved, almost embarrassed manner. "Is that him? Oh, look at his hair. He is cute! Are you looking at his dimples? Did you see his dimples?" She turned and walked over to the new guy to introduce herself without regard to possible implications from Buck as she shook Ignacio's hand through the crack in the door. Buck could hear her apologizing for the noise and giggling as she walked away a minute later, intentionally swaying her body in case the Mexican guy was still looking. She was happy with herself and felt sexy, too, until Buck regrettably informed her that she still had smeared whore lipstick all over her face and smelled like sex. Of course, he used better and politer southern words to describe it, but he was certainly thinking those words.

When Belinda had finally tucked herself away in her room, Buck walked back to the main hall and front desk. He had yet to check up on the twins and make sure the tin was secured before he could begin doing his nightly checks and finally go home. Even though a majority of his time was spent at the facility, he truly loved his work. A bonus, of course, was that helping the residents paid the bills; it was both financially and personally rewarding. Sadly, his love life had taken a toll for it in the past because he had opted to stay the night in the staff room for various reasons and emergencies. His partner at the time just hadn't understood his undying dedication to the mansion, and neither did his half-sister, who had left on time after locking up the pot tin and letting the twins out. Yes, she did what was asked of her, but the keys were sprawled out as if they'd been thrown onto the reception desk and the light was still on in the smoking room.

Buck's own finesse with the things he was responsible for displayed an undeniable compassion for the facility. Lydia's lack of pride had to have been something she'd inherited from her white half, because his mother and their father didn't act that way.

After securing the keys and turning off the light, Buck ran through the list of his nightly checks. He somewhat forgot about his terrible day and the many proclamations he'd made about not getting paid enough. He was sort of happy to be there, no matter what.

After he secured the front door and initiated the security cameras, he felt the pride he'd been taught to take in his work. And as he heard the twins cackling from some far corner of the building, he thought how true it was that every day was an adventure here at Northern Lights, and how every person was there for their very own reasons.

MAGGIE KOONTZ

Maggie Koontz, twenty-five-year-old resident of Northern Lights, had always been small for her age; malnourished children usually are. Almost an image of Snow White, she had dark chocolate brown hair and blue eyes that were complimented by a natural red coloration in her lips – beautiful, had she been a healthy weight. Her arrival at Northern Lights had come months before Ignacio's, and her story was just as strange.

In the beginning, her young parents considered abortion because they knew, at 13 and 15 years of age, they could not take care of a baby, but their families insisted that God would make things right if they led Christian lives and asked for forgiveness for the sins they'd indulged in.

They tried, but desperately failed.

Her underage parents didn't exactly intend to neglect her, but they lived in squalor and could barely afford to keep the lights on – let alone heat the trailer every time she complained that she was cold. Not that they ever heard her complain since they were usually working minimum-wage, low-end jobs in a one-light town that they lived outside of and regularly stole power from. They put Maggie in school long enough for her to learn a few things, and then pulled her out when educators and board members began to ask about her tiny frame and why she never ate a proper lunch. As a result, she became shy to hide the fact that she had gaps in education – she didn't understand some words or concepts that others clearly understood.

Despite her learning disabilities, Maggie worked hard and, along with prayer, overcame her circumstances to earn her high school diploma. She also worked on being more social by getting involved in a local church youth program where she sang hymnal solos in the choir. A year later, the nineteen-year-old, blue-eyed beauty was married and lost her virginity to the choir director who was only a few years older than her.

The young couple was happy together, and equally yoked in faith under the eyes of the Lord. He loved her even after he caught her swallowing paperclips, slowly and me-thodically, from a fresh box of one hundred. He confronted his beautiful wife about it, too, only to learn she had done it for as long as she could remember, but didn't know why.

She also confessed she had been indulging in eating one un-cleaned pebble a day from a fish tank in an office next to her cubical at work.

Together, they prayed.

The Lord took her urges away for about five days – be-fore she began to deeply desire the taste of the change in the bottom of her purse. She secretly scrubbed a few pennies and dimes with an old toothbrush, meticulously dried them under the hand blower at work, and placed them in a sandwich bag which she then tucked away in a zipped side pocket of her work blazer. Her excuse for this was that the clean change was supposed to serve as a reminder of the toxins she had been putting into her body. She'd come up with the lie as she was drying the coins, and polishing them just a little be-yond dry with a paper towel. Yet, for the love of her life, she tortured herself by letting the sixth day pass without eating the change, as he had requested and prayed about her habits. Even as the coins clinked and ticked inside of her blazer like a tempting metallic jingle, she struggled, but remained true to her word.

On day seven, the Lord must have rested. She inevitably couldn't hide from the truth of consumption, no matter the power of prayer. While her husband slept, her brain throbbed over her compounded craving for the shiny metal objects that she had somewhat successfully set aside. The desire to eat grew stronger and more uncontrollable. Trying to push it aside while she rested in bed and stared at the ceiling was next to impossible, and it almost made her desire stronger. These guilty thoughts made her mouth water while she struggled to keep her hands away from pleasing herself. Part of the connection had always been the smell and taste of minerals within each item, but there was also a deeper, unexplainable emotional attachment to the items that she wanted to fill her belly with. Secretly, there was an element of sexuality to eating coins, but Maggie never understood it.

Coins and pebbles were satisfying, but they were not the only non-edible items that she consumed. Paperclips and change held their own special taste and texture in comparison to wall hanging nails and the random keys she collected. Metal was a buffet of flavors for her, and each item was a little entre. Her diet also included buttons, dirt, safety pins, thimbles, sand, and a myriad of other inedible and non-nutritional items. When she consumed them, she experienced the same relieved sensation that smokers had to feel when they lit their first smoke of the day. She was proud that she'd never picked up that nasty habit, though.

For the next four years of marriage, she lied and hid her destructive eating disorder. At twenty-three, however, she became careless and came close to hospitalization for numerous bouts of severe constipation and sharp abdominal pains. Each time she was taken to the doctor, though, she refused treatment, declined x-rays, and persuaded her husband that she just needed a good laxative.

While convincing herself that cutting back on swallowing these items was her first step to recovery, she was inadvertently channeling her compulsions into other obsessive-compulsive behaviors. On any given day, anyone could have stopped by Maggie Koontz's home and eat from the floor if they desired, it was so clean. After work and on weekends, she couldn't control her new-found desires to clean. When the bathroom was spotless and the major items in her kitchen had been scrubbed inside and out, this including the coils on the back of her refrigerator, she began to remove unnecessary items from her home because she felt they collected dust and harbored germs.

Six-and-a-half years into their marriage, her husband discovered that his lovely home was missing every curtain, but he didn't initially panic. He figured Maggie was washing everything or spring cleaning, but then she never put them back up – even months later. It wasn't his favorite look for the inside of their home, but he was okay with it as long as the blinds were in place. With that compromise in place, Maggie went on to remove all knick-knacks from tabletops and books from shelves so that she could donate them to the local Salvation Army, so that he actually commended her rather odd gesture – as it was for the greater good, and in line with being a good Christian...despite his home's newly stark appearance.

More months passed, but her compulsion didn't stop. Finally, Mr. Koontz had to draw the line when he came home to neatly organized boxes of artwork, tapestries, antiques, photos, and other wall hangings that were surrounded by naked walls and discolored paint in the spots where they had once hung. Now the home they had built together had become a shell of what it once was, and he was no longer comfortable living in a house that appeared to be tidy enough to sell.

He confessed his concerns to his wife, again, and together, they prayed for answers.

At 2 A.M. one Sunday morning when Maggie was twenty-five years old, her husband caught her for the last time – eating the dirt she had been collecting from her cleaning sprees out of a torn-open vacuum bag on the living room floor. She'd separated the lint and hair into neat piles that she disregarded. The remaining sand and smaller sediment from the bottom, she was scooping into her mouth with the knife she'd used to open the bag. With the lower half of her face riddled with sludge and her red lips peeking from beneath it, she tried to explain herself through heartbreaking tears.

As she cried, she tried to breathe normally through the dirt and spit that was filling the spaces between her teeth. According to her, God had come to her in a dream in the form of a bird. It was black and white in coloration and had a long tail with shorts wings. It squawked to her about seeking refuge in a place of healing. As she begged the Lord to explain what that meant, it flew away. She told her husband that she'd been up for the next hour on their home computer, researching what it could possibly mean. When she came across the homepage for a behavioral health facility, it all made sense – and yet, it upset her to think that God wanted her there. She didn't feel it was where she belonged and, to make it worse, she didn't understand some of the words on the website. That had been when she'd lost her composure and ransacked the house for something to 'eat' – which was how she'd ended up on the floor, shoveling vacuum cleaner dirt into her mouth with a knife.

Maggie's tiny frame slumped next to the pile of hair on

her left and the half-eaten dirt at the bottom of the vacuum bag on her right. The kitchen knife used to slice open the bag was shimmering next to it as she continued to cry and talk with muddy saliva and darkened teeth, all of it looking very reminiscent of what one might have seen oozing from a zombie's mouth. "I went to the office to think, and then, I knew I had to go to this place and let Him lead the way back to salvation, but I feel like this is a test and I am Abraham, conflicted with killing my only son." She sobbed, spraying black sludge onto her husband's bare feet.

"Am I then Isaac, the son you were told to kill?" He took one slow step away from his wife.

"No! I interpreted His message as leaving you behind, so I may save myself and our faithful union." She lost composure and began breathing heavily from her mouth that spewed bits of wet dirt onto their clean floor. She then buried her face into her hands and cried so hard that she began to hyperventilate.

Her husband, in fully buttoned top and bottom pajamas, dropped to the floor to sit across from her and placed his right hand on her left shoulder. "Then why do you cry at God's plan?"

Into her hands, she mumbled, "I don't want to go." She

struggled to take a breath from the cracks of her fingers so that she could look up to her husband with her blue pools of sadness. "But then I knew I had to, so I took my ring off to give it back to you and explain everything after waking you, but..." Tears continued to fall down her face, and then past her mouth and cherry lips that were caked with dirt. A new wave of hysteria overwhelmed her as emotions distorted her next sentence. "But I didn't make it out of the office, and I ate it. I ate your ring!" She succumbed to the new bout of squealing and tears as she threw herself backward onto the floor in total submission. Dirty face and all, she lay there, arms spread, asking the Lord and her husband to forgive her.

He moved the half-eaten bag of dirt to the side and slid the knife under the nearby couch before lying next to his wife to stroke her arm in comfort. "We should pray for strength."

Together, they talked between piles of hair and half-eaten vacuum waste in an empty house, void of personality and children. It was a sad, uncomfortable place where the extent of their affection was a stroke on her arm between wiping a few tears away with the sleeve of his pajama shirt. The filth around her mouth remained there as they prayed.

The next week, she admitted herself into the acclaimed Northern Lights behavioral health facility in upstate New

York. Upon her arrival, the young receptionist behind the desk was welcoming. Maggie was pleasantly surprised with the friendly and happy atmosphere the mansion provided, too. Two chatterbox twins helped ease her fears. While Maggie was talking to them, the clerk interrupted to explain that she was new and that she had to get clarification on some procedural things. Maggie was patient as she continued to chat and laugh with the twins, who insisted she meet another patient who was a man with her same beliefs.

Meanwhile, a tall orderly came to the desk in khakis and a white scrub top to make a call from the phone at the desk, and then left. A huge bundle of keys, that were attached at his hip, swayed with his walk. Maggie immediately felt that the Lord had led her to him, so she could free him from his obviously homosexual lifestyle, and so she knew she would take it upon herself to speak with the nicely built man at every chance she was allotted in the future.

By the time the lovely attendant gathered the paperwork and walked over to the waiting area, Maggie had had quite enough of the German twins' insane laughter. She politely excused herself to follow the receptionist into a cozy office that was filled with books and antiques. The beautiful clock behind the woman's desk was particularly wonderful with its detailed woodwork. Maggie immediately tried to wipe a few items off with her monogrammed hanky, even before Mrs. Reed invited her to have a seat.

"Welcome to Northern Lights. I'm Jill Reed. My husband and I own this facility. My apologies, but what is your name again, please? I've seen so many clients today." She respectfully offered her hand for a shake, but Maggie was busy dusting the things on the woman's desk and was barely audible when she spoke her own name.

Jill pushed away a file from the top of another to see her name. Then Mrs. Reed watched her for another second with an opened hand, but finally continued to speak when she realized that Maggie was far more interested in dusting than formal introductions. "The prescreening doctor has informed us of your situation. That God told you of this place. But...Mrs. Koontz, the Lord almighty does not pay earthly debts. There is a process here." Jill picked up her pen to write. Her strawberry blonde hair with its random silver streaks had turned completely grey over the years since the grand opening of the mansion, but she maintained an appropriate shoulder-length that was fitting of a first lady.

Maggie stopped dusting to sit, and grabbed the arm rest of the chair with her ringless hand. Jill opened the correct folder with her name at the top and began writing notes while Maggie spoke.

"I eat things like keys, dirt, paperclips, nails, pebbles; you get the idea. I've been doing it all my life and I don't know why. I've asked God to help me, but I believe my faith isn't strong enough, and that's why He is testing me and sending me here, away from my faithful husband to be healed by your medicine."

Mrs. Reed put her palms together in a motion of prayer and rested the tips of her connected index fingertips on her lips. She tried very hard to seem professional and sincere. "Mmm hmmm, I see. Maybe there is something we can work out."

Maggie blinked.

Mrs. Reed corrected herself and reiterated, "We don't accept checks from God, although we do allow free practice of your faith in this building as long as it doesn't interfere with the positive emotional and behavioral progress of others."

After Maggie blinked again in silence, Jill restated her point. "You can do Bible study here."

The clock on the wall chimed at the top of the hour. Jill, a little frustrated with how things were going, finally suppressed her desire for an answer fitting the situation. A smile began to change the harshness of her age lines around her mouth. She wrote some things down on her notepad and flipped through a folder she'd already reviewed. "No suicidal tendencies or aggressive behaviors...some mild learning disabilities that you overcame on your own to get your high school diploma – good job on that, by the way. Okay, there may be another option we can look into to provide you treatment." She pushed her chair away from the desk and picked up Mrs. Koontz's file to tap it on the table before she stood. "Pro-bono...that means free. I'll make some calls, so I think you will be fine. Meanwhile, we already have a room for you."

Maggie simply shook her head as Mrs. Reed's smile intensified.

Three months later, her eating habits were controlled with a diet rich in iron and with a daily vitamin C tablet for absorption. A steady turn-around time on open-admission day patients allowed her to spread the word of God, too, which made her very happy and improved her socialization skills by proxy. She'd particularly enjoyed the antics of the Schmidt twins since learning of their disorder from her group sessions and their conversations filled with laughter in the vineyard. She felt a kin-ship with them, but it was only because she didn't understand their backhanded humor and the sarcasm communicated through their smiles.

The nickname they gave her, Kaput Koontz, actually meant 'broken', but Maggie thought it was cute. No one clarified the meaning to her because she was a genuinely nice person, and breaking her spirit was the last thing anyone wanted to do. The twins also played on her educational level by hiding behind their heavy accents to call her Kaput Cuntz. Her ignorance of this fact made her a happy woman... until the Mexican arrived. He had only been at the facility a few days when he disrupted her improvements without ever knowing of his impact on a tiny, malnourished woman with a strange eating disorder. The man was completely unaware of his influence, in fact, but she still blamed him for meddling with her healing progress. As much as she found issue with the Mexican, though, she never let on that it was a problem and went about her days like she always had.

***

During one of Ignacio's initial welcoming group sessions that all patients were required to attend, Maggie was the first to begin the introductions. Proudly, she explained the dream that had led her to Northern Lights, a glowing smile on her face.

Maggie, now twenty-six, kept her composure despite Belinda's rude stomping of her feet. She clutched at her crucifix necklace as she wrapped up her story with a concluding statement about being lucky enough to spread the word of God.

When it was the new guy's turn to speak, he introduced himself and then rubbed his sprouting facial stubble to soothe his itchy new growth and spoke directly to Maggie. "I think the bird was a Magpie." He looked around at all the eyes staring back at him with confusion. The room was silent with wondering where he was going with the comment. He continued, "In your dream, the bird is called a Magpie. It scavenges and hoards small items. I guess it chatters a lot or something, like a crow. I learned about it in college."

It was suddenly awkward and tense in the group. Everyone stared as Ignacio grew uncomfortable, wondering if he should have said anything at all. He'd never imagined that something like his knowledge of a bird would make everyone so uneasy.

Belinda seized the opportunity to blast her semi-annoying voice into the still room. "That's fucking hilarious. How fitting that God sent Maggie a hoarding, chattering crow!" She flipped her blonde hair behind her back and crossed her long athletic legs with a smug, close-lipped smile. Her eyelashes fluttered unnaturally.

Ignacio felt terrible and tried to ease the tension with a calm tone as he addressed everyone in the room, making sure to hold a second's worth of eye contact so they knew he was sincere. "That's not what I said." Then he stared down Belinda with scrunched eyebrows while he shook his head in disbelief at how she'd twisted his words.

The gold cross pendant was Maggie's only comfort. There were two tiny red gemstones at the tips of the arms, but she preferred touching the smooth center. She pulled a piece of gum from her pocket. Everyone stared at her to see if she was going to say anything, but she balled up the foil that surrounded the gum and shoved it into her pocket as if her intent was to trash it later.

Ignacio tried to be apologetic to the group, "I didn't mean it that way. I was just pointing out…"

Belinda interrupted him as her ears began to burn, "That Magpie talks too much and hoards shit." Then she laughed so loudly that it made the therapist's eyes blink as he jerked his head back. After correcting her inappropriate behavior and regaining control of the room, he allowed the Mexican to have the floor again because, like Ignacio, he knew that the new patient's words hadn't been meant the way they'd been taken.

Ignacio looked to the therapist for reassurance and a cue that it was acceptable for him to speak again. He finally addressed the room, "I apologize; it was just an observation. I didn't mean…"

Maggie folded and smashed her first stick of gum into her mouth. Ignacio's voice trailed off as she closed her eyes to pray for him before she blurted out the inappropriate feelings in her heart. She fought the desire to violently rip the cross from her neck to eat it in front of everyone. Thankfully, Mr. Jenkins rushed into the room a bit disheveled, which distracted everyone at just the right time. She needed her Christian friend in that moment and God must have known.

"I'm so sorry, everyone. 'Parently my alter was having an argument with Buck Lynn again," he said as he sat in an empty chair next to Maggie with a finger in his ear.

The therapist looked at his watch while Mr. Jenkins jiggled his eared finger to stop the ringing inside.

When the ringing subsided, he leaned over to Maggie to quietly ask, "Sister Koontz, you look lovely today. We still on for Bible study later?" His breath smelled of cigarettes – most certainly smoked somewhere by his alter and probably the reason he and Buck Lynn had shared choice words.

Maggie relaxed to politely respond, "Brother Jenkins, I would love that, as usual." Her hands dipped into her pocket to dig for the balled gum wrapper that had fallen into the deep corner. She just wanted to feel its jagged edges over her fingertips.

The therapist resumed the session to give Ignacio an opportunity for a second self-introduction, which he reluctantly took.

Meanwhile, Maggie rolled the jagged wrapper between her fingers as she fantasized about the foil – hard at first but getting softer, had it been nestled inside of her mouth like she desired. She thought deeply about how she would suck the remaining gum flavor from it without compromising its shape. Her tongue flicked around at her teeth and cheeks, pretending it was physically there in anticipation of her intent to do it later when no one was looking. She noticed more saliva building up in her mouth as she stared at Ignacio, portraying active listening, but intently focusing on her hidden oral activities and the foil ball in her pocket which she now gently rolled in mini-circles with the pad of her middle finger.

The motion sent a rush up her hand and arm, then down

the right side of her chest to the center of her body where it pulsed. Although she missed her husband terribly, their usual missionary style lovemaking didn't allow for the thoughts that were currently flowing through her head. Defiling a stranger with no connections seemed less offensive than asking her husband to bite down on a huge ball of softened foil so that she could sit on it and ride his face. Ignacio was new and without guilty connections, so she projected onto him and imagined shoving a palm-sized ball of foil into his mouth to stop him from talking as the others faded to black.

With freedom to imagine her fantasies, Maggie nudged him gently to the floor, where she saw herself lifting her ankle-length skirt, exposing dainty legs, and then squatting to take a polite seat on his face. She dreamed about how careful she would be while placing herself just right before she let her full body weight, which wasn't much, rest there. After gyrating for quite some time and getting herself close to orgasm, she eventually stood over him to slap his moistened face, with her cross dangling uncomfortably close to his eyes. In an effort to breathe, he swallowed the ball. She smacked the other side of his face and he obediently stuck out his tongue to show her that it had indeed transformed itself into a shiny new metal tongue – hard and cold when forced to be, but flexible upon his command.

She immediately scooted down and fitted his erect metal tongue inside of her, and rolled her hips with fierce intention. As she got closer to orgasm again, the shell of human flesh on Ignacio's body became copper, platinum, and gold with silver-specked eyes. His clothing became tailored tinfoil as his hands shifted into delicately welded iron grates. She simply let her fantasy progress into sex with a metal man. She imagined many positions that she'd been too afraid to try with her husband. The dreamlike, robotic Ignacio continued to give her pleasure as her eyes began to water from her own self-gratifying thoughts that made her toes burn and the center of her body burst with satisfaction.

A strange aftertaste of spearmint began to infiltrate her palette before she was stunned awake by the human flesh and bone of the real Ignacio, who was attempting to dig out an obstruction from her mouth.

A wad of foil was packed to the back of her throat, but the sticks of gum the foil had once covered were tossed to the floor next to her seat.

Mr. Jenkins pushed the stranger away from his friend. "Skuse me, she don't know you, son. Mrs. Koontz, are you alright? Looks like you had an episode. Spit it out, Sister

Koontz. That's right, calmly...don't choke." He held his hand under her chin to catch whatever fell from her airway as he tapped her back.

She pulled out pieces to set in his hand and then tried to push out the majority of it with her tongue. The therapist rushed over with a trash can just as Mr. Jenkins reached out to dump the wad of foil into it and then wiped the minted saliva onto his jeans. "You okay now? Breathe. You just kept shoving it in, Sister; it was like you wasn't you anymore. What happened?"

Belinda was quiet for once, simply taking in the orgasm she knew Maggie had just experienced.

BELINDA JAYNE BECKLER

Belinda Jayne, nick-named B.J., was a Florida-born, blue-eyed beauty who was always a clean child. Her parents were boastful of how neat and orderly she kept things in her room at a young age. They never had a complaint when Belinda's cleanliness transferred into self-initiated weekly chores around the house. Concern only developed when, as a young teenager, she let the weekly chores become daily tasks that lasted well into late school nights and prevented her from completing homework or engaging in normal social activities. Eventually, Belinda's disorder got out of hand and it went much further than her just being a girl who liked a tidy home. If her parents hung a towel improperly or turned a Campbell's soup label the wrong way, she would self-destruct – she'd rip out her hair, shave off an eyebrow, or burn her leg with a curling iron.

In her senior year, instead of going to prom, Belinda began treatments with a doctor to dig up the potential issues which might have manifested themselves into such an Obsessive-Compulsive Disorder. Her parents supported all aspects of getting their only daughter healthy again, and after nearly a year and a half of therapy, she was cleared to begin college in New York at the age of twenty.

In college, she was a late entrance student due to issues with her disorder among other things. This had prevented her from starting school with her peers, but everyone felt that it was best for her to get a handle on her dysfunctional life before it affected her for good.

Mr. and Mrs. Beckler were elated that their daughter's disorder seemed to be under control after treatments, though, so it was a triumphant time for her parents. Each believed the young woman had subdued her OCD to a manageable level, even if it wasn't a complete conquering. At least her life was functioning with some parallels to normalcy. For instance, she joined a debate team and took an interest in being an advocate for gay and women's rights, speaking on the quad's grass about equality for all and justice for hate crime victims. Within these activities, she made friends and a few enemies, which everyone agreed was healthy and completely on track with college life. She learned how to adjust to common turmoil in a positive way, which further developed her coping skills – and it showed in the way she finally began presenting herself to the world.

In her second year of school, she met a boy who was a transfer from a nearby college, and together they fell in love. At twenty-two, she lost her virginity to him after a lovely date of wine and candles while everyone else was parading around in painted-on school colors, screaming for their home team to win the night's football game. She was maturing into a beautiful young woman, strong-minded and headed in the right direction...but it only takes one link to break in an already weakened chain before the weight of the world crashes to the floor.

That's exactly what happened.

Her boyfriend met another virgin, a freshman studying chemistry, and he courted her the same way he'd courted Belinda – with a gentle approach, trust, honest-seeming lies, and self-gratifying intent. The bastard chased innocence, simply enough; in college language, he was known as a 'purity puncher'. The kind of asshole that sought women who'd held on to the most precious thing they could possibly give a lover...just so he could take it. This mind-boggling character threw Belinda into a whirlwind of sadness and self-destructive behaviors all over again. She had worked so hard to normalize her life and he destroyed it without blinking. To expose her vulnerability to him was not easy and when he crushed that trust, he crushed her. Only this time the folds of despair became much more permanent. Her parents noticed the dramatic changes even from their phone conversations, and decided to drive from Florida to New York to be with their daughter in her time of need.

She appreciated her wonderful parents and how they'd handled her disorders over the years, so she was elated over their upcoming arrival and ecstatic to see them – despite her state of mind – until she heard the news from her uncle, that a tragic car accident somewhere in Georgia had taken her parents lives. This epic tragedy sent an already spiraling young woman straight to the depths of hell on earth. Cleaning and the desire to keep things orderly was a way for her to control her environment. She tried to revert to her old ways, but the more she tried to gain control of her world through cleaning, the further into depression she fell. In her darkest moment, she devised a plan to commit suicide by doing all the things she had refrained from trying in her youth.

Her logic dictated that she would party like a rock star before she succumbed to her forever sleep. Although, when she told people about her plans, she omitted the death part since it would have snuffed the party vibe.

Belinda meticulously set up a weekend where she could

party with anyone via alcohol, pills, cocaine, and ecstasy. Word of mouth was enough to draw in a small crowd with serious intent, although lots of students had been bragging that they would be there. The seedy ones who actually showed up were comprised of everything from Goth kids to top scholarship students. She remembered most of it as things progressed, but by the 18th hour, things began to blur together. The next thing she knew, she was in the local hospital looking at her Uncle Tom through swollen slits around her encrusted eyes. "Am I dead?" she managed with a painfully swollen throat that far surpassed any common flu symptom she had ever known.

"Did you intend to be?" her uncle asked.

Belinda turned her head away from him as best she could to avoid answering the question, but it was just like admitting her plan – as if she had screamed 'yes' at the top of her lungs in response to his question.

"I'm really sorry about everything, Belinda. But I'm here for you and, when you are released, you can stay with me for a while."

She was embarrassed at first; however, during her few days of recovery in the hospital, she realized that cleaning didn't give her the control she needed in her life...but the sex did. She would always have control over her own body, she realized.

At twenty-two, Belinda Jayne Beckler transitioned almost completely from one disorder to another. Her case was highly unusual, as a result, and she required specialized care. Luckily, Uncle Tom was a wealthy businessman who lived about an hour from the college she'd been attending. He'd been around when she was a child, but when he'd made it big, he'd moved. Belinda had been thirteen when the yearly Christmas visits had become the only time of year when she saw him. They were familiar with each other enough to be comfortable, but estranged enough for them to each carry their own sense of uneasiness when she brought all her belongings to his luxurious home.

In an attempt to continue treatments for Belinda, Tom hired a specialist so that she could cope with the loss of her virginity, her first love, and of course her parents' untimely deaths. The therapist conducted home visits three times a week while Tom was at work.

Tom also scheduled his longtime maid and landscaper to come in on the days when Belinda was not with the therapist, just to keep an eye on his fragile niece while they worked. He didn't want to take the place of her parents, but he tried

so hard to help her in any way that he could. His heart had always been huge, and he wanted to spare no expense when it came to her welfare. No child deserved to go through what she had been through.

For B.J., the whole situation worked out perfectly, if not in the way that Uncle Tom had intended.

The landscaper, a Polish guy in his fifties, was a closeted transsexual. Belinda keyed in on his sexual vulnerability and began giving him genuine presents of women's clothing. She encouraged him to wear them for her during their Tuesday and Saturday rendezvous in the tool shed.

The maid, a pudgy and insecure woman around thirty-two years old who also befriended Belinda, confessed that she was a virgin because she hadn't met the right man During their heart-felt conversations on the maid's brea Belinda shared her woes of losing her virginity to the p ty puncher in college. Once a sense of trust was establi between them, the maid gave in to gentle touches and to lovemaking on a piano that Uncle Tom never played.

Having sex with the maid and the landscaper al Belinda control over her body again and gave her a she'd been told she had to regain by her bald thera was astounded when Belinda intentionally confesse

appropriate behavior to deliberately see his pants swell – as confirmation of her newfound power. When he clearly explained that this wasn't what he'd meant by her getting control over her body, she went into full seduction mode.

He who had been loyal to his high school sweetheart began a sexual affair with Belinda – after much coaxing from his patient. Guilt-ridden, though not enough to end it, he eventually allowed this to continue. When her typical week was finally full of sexual adventures, she began to show improvement. Her Uncle was clueless, but impressed and very happy with her six month stay as they began to develop a closer relationship. But when the Christmas holiday approached, Uncle Tom's staff invites to a party made for a very sticky situation.

When the landscaper unexpectedly brought his new fiancé, Belinda was crushed. She tried to sabotage their relationship by informing the woman that her future husband wore woman's clothing. But the woman wasn't thwarted by this, and simply giggled as she stuffed another piece of summer sausage into her mouth. Unbelievably, she winked. "I know. It's kind of kinky, right? I love it," she said.

Moments later, the maid arrived alone, and Belinda immediately took her coat, courteously rushed through in-

troductions, and latched on to her arm as if they were best friends. The maid looked amazing and was happy to see her. Together, they walked to the library unaccompanied, and this was where Belinda tried to engage in a quickie, but the maid shyly allowed only one sweet kiss before telling her friend that she'd finally met someone. Belinda pretended to be happy, but she was seething in anger. Adding fuel to her fire, the maid's boyfriend arrived moments later. When there was a free moment, Belinda pulled him aside to maliciously exploit the virgin's truth while everyone poured drinks in the front room.

His response was one of shock. "Wow, a thirty-two-year-old virgin!" He'd had no idea. His large brown eyes looked worried and intense as he sipped his imported beer.

Belinda was finally happy with where this seemed to be going, and saw hope of continuing her femme fatale relationship with the maid.

The boyfriend took another rushed drink of his beer in the kitchen with perplexed, scrunched eyebrows and a worry that showed in the wrinkles in his forehead. "She's waiting for the right guy. Am I right?"

Belinda was smug as she adjusted his tie in a hidden attempt to seduce him while nodding her head yes as her blonde, cascading hair bounced against the middle of her back.

"Well, I waited until I was twenty-seven and then I married the love of my life. When she died, I never thought I would share that with anyone again – you know, being in my thirties now. Thanks for telling me. I have a whole new respect for her." He patted the top of Belinda's shoulder like someone would pat the head of a dog and then walked to the living room, where the maid stood with the landscaper, his fiancé, and Tom, who was prepping everyone to toast.

Alone, Belinda was left to sulk in the kitchen over her defeated plans of sabotage. She didn't want to join the festivities, and pouted for a while before finally leaning against the archway while she watched everyone laughing with holiday spirit. Her green dress sparkled as her arms crossed over her buxom chest and she peered upon the group that was beginning to huddle around Tom's huge, lovely black piano. Her uncle waved her over to have a drink before he played a few merry tunes on it, like he was hosting a scene in some 1980s chick flick where everyone sported turtlenecks and bad Christmas sweaters.

Bitterly, Belinda forced herself to join the party and, once she was tipsy enough to forget her anger, she was finally able to have a wonderful time. Her new stress, however, was that she wouldn't be able to see the cheating shrink until after the new year, and with apparent love in the staff's air, she would also lose out on four sex days a week with the transsexual and the virgin. All her control was once again being taken from her.

Frustrated, she felt that the only thing to do was to turn to her uncle – not for help, but for sex. With her moral compass completely gone, she didn't even wait until the guests were out of the home before she attempted to seduce him in the hall. In fact, they were still refilling their glasses and emptying their bladders between jovial bouts of genuine and drunken laughter. Tom, of course, was completely horrified with his niece's vulgar actions. He immediately locked himself in his study and called in some big favors, to not disturb the guests. Within hours, on Christmas Eve, Belinda found herself in the back seat of a white limousine that was headed to a nut house upstate. Her instructions were to admit herself, and to know that the bills would be taken care of; it was as simple as that. She was being given no other choice and, with nowhere else to go, she did what was asked of her.

However, as bad as everything had been and how out of control it was all becoming, she did not feel that it was worthy of institutionalization – because mental instability had become her normal. She had only ever known OCD, and then recently the generous leap to sexual addiction.

At Northern Lights, as a result, she fought treatment... but after a month or so, she became accustomed to the cleanliness and the structure of "established" life – as she called it. Falling in love with another patient helped her transition, too, even if it was with the alter persona of a man struggling with multiple personality disorder; otherwise, she would have left. Beyond the love, though, for the first time, Belinda felt a sense of peace at Northern Lights, and so she didn't exactly want to leave it or the love of her life.

But then the Mexican arrived, and there was something about him that stirred things up in the facility and in her loins.

DISTRACTIONS

During his first night at Northern Lights, Ignacio did not notice the automatic dimming that the black orderly had explained would happen at ten o'clock. He was entirely too exhausted from the drive and had barely had enough energy to brush his teeth, let alone observe any gentle dimming of lights. In fact, after an odd interruption from Belinda – who smelled of sex with an odd hint of strawberries – he fell asleep on the bed in the brightly lit room, completely clothed. His second night at Northern Lights, he did notice the dimming as he prepared for bed, once again exhausted from his eventful day of intake therapy and scheduled mealtimes, but the dimming was actually calming. His pants and shirt hung on the fixed hangers to air out for another day's wear while his crumpled underwear lay sadly on the floor near his foul-smelling tennis shoes. As he walked into the room, though, he noted to himself that although it wasn't exactly tidy, it was better than his grandmother's massive clutter.

He shut the door behind him and then ran and jumped onto the mattress like a child before settling happily between the clean sheets. It had been somewhat stressful, getting to know the layout of the huge mansion and attending his first mandatory group counseling session, which had clarified some of the true colors of the clientele in the building – they were crazy, and obviously there for legit mental disabilities. This conclusion had come to him after his witnessing of the Bible-thumping Mrs. Koontz shoving gum foil into her mouth until she nearly suffocated before their afternoon lunch. He felt guilty when he thought about his own faked mental state, compared to the truly debilitating disorders of the others, and how, for years, he had manipulated the system into paying his way through life, for the rest of his life. But the guilt quickly faded, and he was soon enough smug with warmth at the genius idea as the second iteration of dimming lights calmed the room; once again, it proved itself a wonderfully relaxing change from his Abuela's humble and yet hoarded home.

The price of his comfort seemed to be relinquishing sanity and reason, a few times per year, to keep money coming in. The additional self-admitted 'vacation' in an institution solidified his supposed mental state, so far as he saw things. He shrugged off any worries when he thought of how simple his plan was.

Although his ultimate goal was to find his mother, who'd

reasonably enough been institutionalized after insanely trying to kill her entire family, this place offered him a break
from his search and a break from meager means. The years
of lies, faking symptoms, and acting his way through tears
and bursts of anger were being rewarded, in a sense, with
automatically dimming lights in a mansion surrounded by a
beautiful vineyard, and so it was totally worth it. Even though
his antics and thoughts had blossomed from a genuine concern, he was now proud of his endeavors and his so-called
hard work to get to this point. He wondered if his mother was
in a place as nice as this now, and even giggled at the thought
that she, too, could have faked it all to gain the luxuries she'd
never before been provided.

Ignacio shook thoughts of his mother out of his mind. He
ran his hands and fingers over his brown skin and down his
tight abdominals under the 800 count sheets with the thought
of pleasuring himself. He certainly felt comfortable enough.
Verified by the welcome packet on his bed, he knew that he
could orgasm anywhere in the room and the government
checks would pay to have Northern Lights staff clean it. He
smiled, which pushed the dimples in his cheeks inward as he
began to stroke his genitals.

A few seconds into the process, though, he jumped when

an unexpected knock at his door startled him. He threw off the blankets and grabbed a pillow to cover his naked middle as he scurried to the door. Back home, there was a nearby baseball bat for such unexpected visitors as could show up in Abuela's shady neighborhood, but here there wasn't even a peephole through which he could inspect the hallway. Carefully, with the pillow covering his private parts, he cracked the door open with a foot wedged at the bottom. Habitual routines were unnecessary, but the foot wedge seemed appropriate.

He blinked profusely as the light from the hallway stabbing at his pupils. "Yeah?" he asked quietly, squinting one eye as if this would help him see the uninvited guest.

Her voice was sort of high-pitched and annoying, but strangely seductive when it came, though he wouldn't have thought the qualities could all go together if asked. "Belinda Jane, remember me? You can call me B.J. if you want. Can I come in for a second?"

She stood in the hallway wearing a long grey terrycloth robe, red flip-flops, and a towel around her hair that smelled of fresh strawberry shampoo. Without the makeup and fresh sex smell surrounding her, she was much prettier than he remembered from their first encounter. Her blue eyes batted at him and then looked down the hall to check for unwanted witnesses. When it was clear there were none, she flashed open her robe to expose perky pink nipples surrounded by flawless alabaster skin. She'd fashioned nipple adornments from re-shaped paperclips that linked in a chain across the center of her chest. Before Ignacio's eyes could peer elsewhere, she closed the robe. He felt his erection press uncomfortably against the pillow, but didn't exactly know how to handle the situation. As a man, the answer was to pull her inside, but as an insane man, he needed to think of his money and why he was really there.

"You better go," he said, hesitantly.

Belinda pushed at the door before he could close it, which threw him off-balance. She was a quick little devil. While he was stumbling backward, she slid into room 19 without his permission and witnessed the pillow accidently falling from his grasp. Naked and vulnerable, he regained his balance against the wall as Belinda stood in awe of his never-before-seen, fit physique wrapped in Mexican brown skin. The glow of light made them both look as if they were covered in amber warmth. As she pushed the damp towel surrounding her head to the floor, she kicked off the cheap shower shoes she'd worn and dropped her robe in one seamless motion.

Ignacio immediately grabbed his exposed body, which was swelling to full capacity. He watched the bombshell before him slowly back into the wall on the opposite side of the room, with slow, slinking steps, as the paperclips shined and glimmered in the ever-dimming light. It was obvious that her backward steps were intentional and calculated to sway her chest just right so that the crafted adornments shown like laced platinum. Once she was up against the wall, he could see her groomed pubic hair glistening with wet excitement. She stood there then, waiting for him to make the first move as if she was shy.

Trying desperately at first to cover himself, he finally gave up to let her see just what she was getting herself into by being in his room. It was almost a last chance warning, but it backfired. Impressed, she exhaled with choppy releases of air. Her blue eyes widened with anticipation before she regained her wind and continued breathing deeply enough to fill her lungs to full capacity. The two of them stood in animalistic form, ready to attack. To facilitate the mating decision, she tugged at the makeshift jewelry. It stretched her nipples as she pulled at the linking paperclips with her thumb. "I can smell your erection," she said confidently. "The cameras in the hallway are on rotation. It's an old system – go figure.

What kind of damage do you want to do before they scan this hallway again?"

As she asked the question, she gently swayed her hips left and right. She released the link to let the paperclip chain dangle freely between her breasts.

Ignacio could no longer look a gift horse in the mouth and push it away. He needed to be a man. He reached across the space between them to grab the chain. He ripped it quickly from her delicate skin. It pinched sharply at her nipples, but only offered short-lived pain. He lunged forward and spun her around by the shoulders as he pushed her face against the wallpaper. This position forced her into a submissive arch, but she knew how to angle herself to appease him. Her long, wet hair sprayed across her back while other strands hung at her face and slapped at the wall. She tried to be quiet as she felt him touch her backside, but moaned and prepared herself for whatever he was going to do.

Ignacio couldn't look her in the face, so he pushed his tip between her clean buttocks as he held her neck. With his other hand, he wrestled with his manhood and masturbated with its tip buried comfortably between her cheeks. He made sure, however, to never enter her body. He'd always had trouble finishing and, although this embarrassed him, it made for interesting sex. She tried to push herself onto him, but he deflected with his strong arms by holding her back.

His hand slapped at the bottom of her skin with each stroke. She could feel him swell before his orgasm finally erupted. She exhaled hard enough to produce moisture on the wallpaper. Then he released the pressure to her neck in order to smear his fluid on the backs of her legs. Her body rocked back and forth in a perceived shared orgasm.

Ignacio smelled her strawberry-scented shampoo again before he told her to never visit him again. She couldn't respond verbally as she tried to calm herself, so Ignacio spun her around and asked her politely to pick up her things. She simply did what had been instructed of her without question. "I'm here to get help and you are a distraction. Open your mouth and stick out your tongue."

On the floor to collect her balled-up towel, she looked up immediately to display her pink tongue as instructed. She felt a wet oozing down the sensitive inner part of her thigh as he spoke, and he wiped the tip of himself down the center of her tongue as he squeezed the last of his orgasm out. He grabbed the towel that held the scent of her shampoo and untwisted it while Belinda remained on her knees with her tongue hanging out. He helped her stand to her feet then and gently wrapped her in the robe with his orgasm still between her cheeks. Like a gentleman, he knelt to help her into her cheap flip-flops while she used his shoulders for balance. When he stood again, Belinda was still completely silenced by the bizarre way this adventure had panned out, and still savoring the taste of him.

"Don't distract me again." He looked into her stunned blue eyes and shook his head yes to show her that it was okay for her to respond. Belinda shook her own head yes as her tongue wiggled and flicked at the roof of her mouth. She shuffled out of his room a different woman. The powerful temptress of seduction had been duped for the first time.

Ignacio closed the door quietly and didn't bother to watch her shuffle four doors down to her own room. Instead, he leaned against the inside of his door while rubbing at the stubble on his face and laughing to himself. The way he saw it, the state had basically paid for that sex-capade to happen. Quietly, he repeated 'I'm the man' over and over again as he danced a jig from the door to the bed, where he wiped himself off onto the underside of his comforter – knowing full well that the staff would change his bedding tomorrow. Then he randomly assigned notes to made-up lyrics as he sang aloud while tucking himself under the blankets.

I get money. From the government.

Bitches lick my dick. Don't get a cent.

Blame it on my mom. Crazy Juana, no?

Was she really loca? Nobody knows.

Why'd she start the fire? With her other hoes?

Who cares? I'm on vacation, fucking blonde buttholes.

The automatic lights, finally on their last iteration of the night, dimmed to a soft candle-glow as he massaged his testicles and fell asleep as happy as he could possibly be.

***

In the morning, Ignacio was abruptly awoken by the big black orderly, who flung the door open and rushed through the doorway in a panic. Buck was breathing heavy while his eyes darted all over the automatically lit room. His deep yet sweet Darth Vader voice boomed into the quiet space. "Mr. Cheese, are you okay?" The southern accent smoothed over each bass note.

Groggy but perfectly fine, Ignacio sat up in his bed to answer the man while he rubbed at his eyes as they kept adjusting to the sudden scare. "I'm good. What happened?" His voice popped and sounded rough with sleep.

"Well, Mr. Cheese, you missed breakfast, and your first individual appointment with the doctor! Charlotte practically beat down your door when you didn't answer. Lord, you are lucky she is new here." Buck trailed off to reset his tone, then put his hand on his hip before his anger escalated to a point of no return. "What do you have to say for yourself?" he asked, the chap stick on his thick lips glistening gently under the lights.

"Listen, man, I guess I just slept in. I'm sorry." Ignacio wiped some crust away from the corner of his eye and yawned.

"Well, sir, shower up. In case ya'll didn't read your information packet, today is open admittance. The one day of the week we open our doors to the public. Charlotte can reschedule your individual session for this afternoon." Just as Buck was about to walk out of the room, he turned to inhale intentionally. His nostrils flared open to deeply inhale in the strawberry scent that, although faded, was still there. "Lord Jesus. I hope your visit last night was brief and uneventful. If Mr. Samuel catches wind that your room smells like out of season fruit, I won't be able to call security fast enough! You hear me?" His eyes bulged to emphasize the seriousness of his statement.

Ignacio scrunched his eyebrows and refrained from saying anything that could get him into trouble. Suddenly, he felt like a child. "Got it. Thank you. Oh, and it's Cheyez. I just... well, you keep calling me Mr. Cheese, and its Chay-yez," he politely corrected from his bed.

"Mmm hmm, that's what I said." The orderly closed the door behind him and called the front desk to report his findings to Lydia. Ignacio heard him tell her that the situation was under control, just beyond the door, and that she should put another note in Belinda's file, whatever that meant.

As he got out of bed completely naked, Ignacio couldn't decide if Buck was being sarcastic or was genuinely confused about his last name. The southern accent of the orderly seemed to level anything negative he may have meant, but... well, c'est la vie, a new day had begun, and Ignacio was anxious to visit the showers.

After visiting the lending closet for shower supplies and cloaking himself in the same clothes he'd worn the day before, he made his way to the front reception desk with a new attitude. There was only one more day to go before he could open the foot locker at the end of his bed. Meanwhile, Lydia was busy speaking with an older woman who wore faux fur around her neck and a matching hat atop her styled hair, so he meandered over to the bay window where the Schmidt twins were giggling profusely.

"Velcome to the vonderful Northern Lights bonker-haus again, young Mario Lopez vis da dimples!" Ute shouted as she stood from her window seat to rush him with a grand hug that came complete with bouncing boobs which slapped together with her every move. "Oh, the things my sister and I vould do if our physiques...BOOM! POW!" She thrust the pudgy lower half of her body into his thigh as Ignacio looked around in embarrassment.

The fake fur lady looked utterly disgusted. Lydia smiled, but snapped back to professional mode in the same second the rich lady looked back at her.

Hilda laughed as she walked with a slight waddle over to her equally fluffy sister and Ignacio. "My Got, Ute! You look like a humping hound; the Pug, you know, vis the eye-balls vich pop out! Young men don't hump Pugs unless they smell like strawwwberrriesss!" Hilda giggled and covered her mouth to pretend like she was concerned about knowing his secret, but she was only interested in witnessing his reaction as she winked at her sister without discretion.

Ute's eyes opened wide as her mouth dropped into an elongated 'o' shape before she hunkered down and covered it in an attempt to hush a laugh that had been about to explode onto his Mexican shirt. The two elderly women giggled and scurried with heavy steps back to the bay window as if they were kindergarten girls who'd just exposed a secret on the playground. When Ignacio followed them to get clarification on what they'd just said in a quiet, private manner, the twins' laughter amplified and bounced through the grand foyer, once again disrupting the ongoing conversation between Lydia and the fur coat woman.

He tried to explain himself to them quietly, but the sisters cut him off before he began. The dominant one of the two, Ute spoke first with a really bad impression of the former president, Bill Clinton. "I did not have sexual relations vis das voman!" She threw her head back as her mouth seemed to unhinge so that her loud, heavy laughter could release itself from the center of her body. She tried to contain it, but it was always futile with this disorder that rendered her permanently euphoric.

Ignacio smiled hard, pushing his dimples to the surface of his cheeks as he watched her stand and wobble back and forth, mocking the former President's southern accent in a terrible rendition of his deep manly voice.

As she paced, though, she continued babbling while she

jiggled her large boobs to emphasize her point. "Und like I didn't give Mr. Jenkins a blow job two years ago. Und Ute didn't service Mr. Jack Reed in das vineyard and Kaput Koontz didn't put something new in her mouth with Charlotte last veek. Nobody is looney here, just horny." She shimmied while winking at her sister with an obnoxiously large smile.

"Are you serious?" Ignacio looked around the lobby, guilty of smiling at such information, to see if anyone else had heard their epic voices spilling ambitious rumors.

"Nein." Ute shook her head no. "But it makes the Northern Lights bonker-haus more interesting, doesn't it? Und so das thisss." She pulled down her shirt then, exposing a long line of old wrinkled cleavage that was sprinkled with age spots, the effect being reminiscent of a matriarchal elephant about to stumble away to die in peace. As Ignacio was about to turn his head out of blended respect and disgust, he noticed a hidden pewter flask jutting angrily from the middle. Noticing his attention, Ute invited him to have some wine later before the lights dimmed to talk about some more things that didn't happen on the vineyard. He graciously accepted with a wink before excusing himself to speak with the fresh-faced goddess at the intake desk, and on his way, he shivered off the image of those old tits cuddling a liquor flask.

Lydia was wearing a white button-down blouse with a sassy red handkerchief around her neck to match her lipstick and earrings. She'd chosen a white lace bra to support her average breasts, but the darker complexion of her skin contrasted, possibly intentionally, to emphasize the appearance of a see-through top. The first thing he did was to open the conversation with a compliment on her attire, in response to which she lightheartedly poked fun of his two-day-old t-shirt and jeans. He reminded her that his foot locker should be open the next day and smiled hard to display his clean-shaven dimples.

"I can't talk too long, Ignacio. I must attend to the desk and the open admittance people; high maintenance bamboozlers if you ask me. They are worse than the Schmidt twins sometimes!" She crossed her arms over her supposedly unintentionally see-through shirt and looked around to see if anyone had heard her before she leaned over the upper portion of her intake desk to whisper. "Rich folk check in every week, stay for three days or so to talk about how stressful it is to be rich. They eat grapes, pick apart the renovations of the mansion, and check themselves out when it's time to go back to work on Mondays. Bullshit if you ask me." She pulled back into an upright standing position behind the desk with her arms still crossed over her chest. "I heard they somehow write it off on their taxes, too, essentially making this a paid vacation!" Her eyebrows shifted into a high arch as she froze in this sassy position for a moment. Ignacio figured it was to emphasize her distaste for dishonest rich people, but all it did was highlight her beautiful light brown eyes.

"They do that?" he asked as he tried to look like he was sickened by the thought of people taking advantage of the system. His hope was that she didn't see his true intentions via the contorted look on his face and his unintentionally dodgy eyes.

Lydia channeled her black southern stereotype as she popped her tongue and lightly tapped at her mixed hair instead of itching it. "Well, that's what I heard."

He flashed his dimples to charm the pants off Lydia next, but also inadvertently shifted his penis into a more comfortable position...which she ignored. The rich, fur-toting woman did not, however, think it was remotely in good posture, and gasped as she waited for an orderly to walk her to a room. Ignacio ignored her, looking around instead.

Jarring Ignacio from his prior gaze, which had been trailing the twins, Maggie Koontz suddenly appeared next to him at the desk to ask Lydia a question. She was embarrassed and had a difficult time saying hello without lifting her eyes too much from the floor. Still, she addressed Lydia without issue to ask where her brother could be and if Mr. Jenkins had been looking for her for their apparently impromptu Bible study. Then, oddly enough in unison, both she and Ignacio asked Lydia what room the rich woman was staying in – with intense interest. Taken aback by the abrupt transition, Lydia's chin jerked into her neck. "Four. Room four. Why?" Her eyes ping-ponged back and forth from Ignacio to Maggie as her lip curled at the edge like she was impersonating Elvis.

Maggie said with deep concern, "You can't put her in four. That's Mrs. Cleary's room. She'll get really upset if you touch her rock collection. That woman can't touch her rocks."

Lydia was surprised that Maggie was privy to that personal detail at all. "How do you know she has a collection? Anyway, she was released yesterday afternoon. Cleared. Not that I had to tell you that. You should go, Maggie." She was trying to be polite and more professional.

Maggie grabbed her pendant and rubbed the red jewels on the arms of the gold cross. "I'm a vessel doing the Lord's work. I do talk to other patients. Has my husband called?" Maggie changed the subject nervously and retreated into a more submissive posture as if she had done something wrong.

"No, ma'am. No messages today, I'm sorry," Lydia replied factually.

Ignacio asked a mirror of the same question to reroute the tension between the women. "Did my grandmother call?"

Lydia tilted her head and scrunched her eyebrows together in confusion. She looked back and forth between Maggie and Ignacio as if they should know what she was about to say. "Personal calls are a distraction from your healing goals. It's in the brochure, Ignacio, and, Mrs. Koontz, you know this."

Clearly upset at this unintentional mistake, Ignacio inquired further in order to hide his mistake as he crossed his arms defensively. "You don't allow personal calls here?"

It was obvious to her that Ignacio hadn't read the material that had been provided, but although she was used to patients dismissing their reading material, she was a little surprised at his forward tone now. "Whoa, slow your roll," she told him. She uncrossed her arms to put a hand up at chest level to warn him. "I see where you were about to go with that and I don't like it. We don't prevent personal calls here; we just don't encourage them. Northern Lights nurtures personal healing. You need to read your information sheets. It's all in there."

Mrs. Koontz walked away with that, hunched over like a

guilty dog to avoid the situation and to prevent further questioning of why she'd wanted to know where the rich woman was staying.

After a moment, Lydia smiled at Ignacio to change the vibe between them. He smiled back, and they shared a flirtatious moment now that they were finally alone, unwatched and yet standing in the center of the main area. She leaned over the desk again after re-crossing her arms. "You know, I always wanted to learn Spanish. Maybe you could teach me a few things after my shift ends. Would you teach me? Six o'clock right here?" She bit at her red-stained lip that matched her scarf and dangling earrings.

His grandmother had always told Ignacio that devils and harlots adorned themselves with this sinful color of red. Her elder voice echoed through his ears, but he shook it off to accept Lydia's invitation because she was clearly no harlot. "This is a distraction from my personal healing, but I'm willing to make an exception." He winked.

By the time the clocks in the main hall and Mrs. Reed's antique-filled office had chimed seven, Lydia and Ignacio were fully engaged in passion, hidden in the corner of the twins' smoking room. They were pretty sure no one had noticed how they'd slipped into the room, but there'd been excitement in the idea of getting caught as they'd rushed to strip.

Ignacio was extremely careful not to make noise or lose his balance as he held her body around his. The moment was brief, but for Ignacio, it held more passion then he had ever experienced before, and he was glad that he had not engaged Belinda in such an intimate way. Ignacio didn't notice how Lydia rushed through redressing as they reset themselves back to a neutral state as if nothing had happened. He giggled as he kissed her red lips one last time but she quickly backed away then escaped the camera's timed view. Although this experience had touched him on a deep emotional level, his egotistical, masculine nature was amused at the fact that he was getting paid for busting a nut in the 'nut' house once again. He relished the afterglow with a mumbled song while turning the corner of the hall to his room. In the cameras transmitting back to the security room, it was apparent that he seemed a little too bouncy and light for a mental patient.

I get dinero from the state of New York.

Harlots hug my dicko. Something, something dork.

I am Nacio. Everyone should know.

On a paid vacation, sexing chocolate holes.

QUID PRO QUO

Maggie waited until the old lady had been there for three days before inspecting her foot locker. She had been watching the rich woman settle into a few routines before attempting to race between the timed cameras' views in order to gain access to her quarters – an act she was very familiar with playing out. As she waited for the woman to exit room four and head to the craft room, Maggie peered upward to the small black bubble jutting down from the ceiling. When the cameras automatically changed position, a sparkle of plastic shimmered from the metallic parts within their core; this was her cue.

Maggie took a deep breath and scurried to the keyless entry keypad, immediately punching in the access code she'd memorized from a safety inspection that had happened months prior. Thanks to the previous tenant's clever rewiring of the recessed lights, Maggie had been able to catch a glimpse of the opening digits as she'd happened to pass by. Buck had to open room number four with another orderly and two electricians in order to correct the rewiring and clear it for safety, and in the commotion, the last thing on Buck's mind had been protecting the code he typed as Maggie walked by, clutching the crucifix around her neck. She valued and praised the impeccable timing that God had presented her with. The numbers were bits of gold-leafed information wrapped in a neat, miniature bow.

She thanked the Lord in prayer as her underdeveloped fingers keyed in each number. When the access code was verified by the system, a green light appeared, and a metallic click was faintly heard. She opened the door just enough to slip her tiny body through the crack and then disappeared inside as smoothly as a vampire would have floated in rather than walking.

With no time to waste, Maggie knelt before the foot locker at the end of the bed and pulled a kinked paperclip from her pocket. After gingerly working it around in the hole of the lock, she heard a beautiful click ring through the silence of the room. Maggie's nipples hardened with excitement as she pulled the lock down and opened the lid. There wasn't much to rummage through since the woman had only planned to stay for four or five days, but in the locker, was the fur coat, a huge black bag that seemed to be made of some kind of reptilian skin, and a book entitled *How the Rich Stay Rich*.

Maggie grabbed the black bag, unzipped the inside privacy pocket that most purses have, and searched it; she found one pack of estrogen pills and a vibrating bullet.

Out loud, she accidently said, "Lord, is that all people think of around here – pleasures of the flesh?" Disgusted, she tossed the items back into the pocket and zipped it closed to continue searching the main body of the bag after wiping her hand onto the comforter. From a found wallet, she pulled out six-hundred-and-eighty-two dollars and twenty-four cents. Maggie stuffed the twenty-four cents into the bottom of her shoe before continuing on to pocket a dolphin-shaped money clip, a tiny safety pin that had used to hold the price tag inside of the purse, a random key, and a large gold ring with two tiny emeralds. Six-hundred-and-eighty-two dollars in paper money went back into the wallet. She held the reptilian bag by her ear then and shook it once or twice before placing it back into the footlocker. At the last second, rather than securing everything and leaving the room as usual, she decided to check the pockets of the fur coat. In it were items that were just as useless to her as the paper money; lint in the left pocket and thin leather gloves in the right. She began folding the coat exactly how she'd found it...when in the middle of a fold, a hard object slid across her hand from a hidden pocket that was deep within the breast. After pulling it free from the satin lining, she found that a tiny, curvaceous ladies' pistol had appeared, complete with ornate embossed etching on the grip that shimmered back at her.

In amazement, Maggie shifted it in her hand for a second before removing the bullets and stuffing them into her bra. With quick thinking, she pulled open the front of her pants and panties to nestle the gun as best she could next to her body. After placing it there, she secured the locker shut. As she stood to leave, the cold trigger of the gun nudged itself against her clitoris and she jerked forward in guilty pleasure.

Ignacio stood at the closed door with a face of hidden accusation.

Maggie jumped out of her skin and choked on her screams to prevent anyone from hearing. The gun in her underwear pushed forward between her legs as she instinctively clutched at her cross and slumped into a blameworthy stance displaying saddened Snow White features.

"What are you doing?" Ignacio inquired. His voice had cut through the stillness of the room like a knife, making Maggie's blood feel as if it was infused with micro-daggers ripping through the inside of her veins. The instant image of his fantasized metallic face flashed before her eyes and faded into the realization that he was in fact covered in skin made of human flesh. He looked less seductive than the metal man from her secret fantasy.

Stumped at first, the only thing she could manage to do was confess to taking the change so that she could eat it later. She unsuccessfully tried to hide behind the simple announcement, as she made no mention of stuffing an object into her crotch – that, she hoped he hadn't seen. Her dark chocolate brown hair and blue eyes created a very innocent yet haunting beauty, and she begged him not to say anything about her stealing the change...but he walked to her and stopped when his face could look down at hers. Her tiny frame and organic red lips would have been lovely, he thought, had she taken the time to maintain them.

"What did you put down your pants?" he asked as quietly as he could while hovering uncomfortably close to intimidate her.

"Nothing. Listen, there is money in there. I'll open it for you, so you can have it if you promise not to tell." She looked up into his big brown eyes in desperation. "We only have a few minutes left before the cameras turn this way again." Her voice was small and panicked.

Ignacio grabbed her crotch to feel the barrel of the gun.

She jumped and squealed in shock, then tried to hush herself from the paralyzing fear of being caught and the simultaneously stimulating sensation of the gun's rigid edges against her soft tissues.

"Get the money." Ignacio was bewildered about the fact that the Bible-thumping Christian would resolve to do such a thing as steal and act as she did, but if he could get a little something out of her need to eat metal, he would gladly do so.

Maggie rushed to the box, picked the lock again, and returned to Ignacio seconds later with eighty-two dollars that she crumpled into his hand, hoping he hadn't seen the money she had left behind. "We can't be in here." She forcefully spun him around and pushed him to the door, where they both slipped out and walked to the dining hall as if that's where they'd been headed all along – with the exception to their act being Maggie, who was walking a little slower than usual. She looked up and over her shoulder to the black bulb in the ceiling that clicked in their direction. The camera picked up a smile in the corner of her mouth that was only there for a split second.

They were quiet at first, but as they got closer to the dining hall, Ignacio was the first to break the silence as softly as he could. "I must confess, I was in there to do the same thing.

Thank you for the gift. Maybe we could help each other in the future." His attempts to smooth over the literal facts were something to be applauded in case someone overheard.

Maggie didn't catch the hidden meaning, though. "Listen, I am a married woman who is completely in love…"

He interrupted as soon as he could. "What? No, not sex – I meant I can get you things if you get me money. We could be a team."

"Stealing is against God. I do this to survive and to eat, and therefore I can be forgiven if I truly mean it in my heart… which I do." Her worried eyes were sincere as they passed by the many doors and hallways.

"Whatever helps you sleep at night, sister; I just want to save my money for a ring for someone. I believe I am falling in love."

"You haven't even been here a week!" Maggie yelled in a whisper through her teeth as she looked around suspiciously. Together, they entered the dining room and then they each picked up a tray while falsely smiling at the servers behind the counter. She felt compelled to ask Ignacio to attend the next Bible study with Mr. Jenkins, but she knew he would decline.

As they selected items to place on their trays, she tried

to do something kind to counteract her acts of sin and sinful thoughts in room four. She pulled the ring from her pocket and smashed it into the sweaty palm of his unsuspecting hand. She didn't want to give it to him, but she could tell that he was serious about the whole ring idea and, really, she just wanted him to leave her alone. The ring was a strange, yet kind gesture just as much as it was a disgusting payoff. She leaned into his space to prevent others from hearing. "It's big enough to fit a man, so you can get it resized when you get out of here. How are you paying for this place if you can't afford to buy a ring, though? Scoot down."

Ignacio took a quick look at the ring before dropping it into the pocket of his fresh jeans and grabbing a side dish of mash potatoes. It was beautiful and simple and perfect. "Well aren't you nosey? You were going to eat it, weren't you?" He could not believe how someone could want to eat a non-edible item when he was staring at the fried chicken in front of him, and the cheesecake he would eventually grab at the end of the line and happily consume. Thinking of food had suddenly made him very hungry, so he began putting a little more on his plate than he normally would have. Sadly, the thought of going back to his grandmother's hoarded house to eat stale items washed over him next. With clarity, conviction, and focus, he said, "I'm declared mentally disabled by the state of New York. I'm sponsored."

"Well, I'm a pro-bonobo case," she said smugly, not realizing how incorrectly she was pronouncing the term. Ignacio smirked while she continued. "I don't have money, either, and now you don't need money for a ring. No more deals to be made here."

Maggie began to walk away, feeling very clever, but he grabbed her arm with just enough pressure to stop her in mid-stride. "Don't make this difficult," he said. "I'll never tell anyone about your thievery if you get money for me. You can even watch me send it to my grandmother who's living in squalor. I swear, it's for her." His beautiful brown eyes were earnest, but Maggie saw something beyond his sweet dimples and neatly combed hair that seemed sinister.

"You've got the devil in you. Let go of my arm!" she again yelled through her teeth while shaking her arm to free it from his grip. "I don't know where squalor is, but I'll do it for the innocent souls you have tortured now and in your future." Then she waddled away like a pregnant woman, or rather, like a woman with a gun between her legs.

He flipped her off when she wasn't looking and smiled again when she was.

TRIUMPHANTLY TRAPPED

Clinically, alters and hosts of people who suffer from Disassociative Identity Disorder are normally oblivious of each other. However, Samuel and Mr. Jenkins were something of a classic Dr. Jekyll and Mr. Hyde case – aware. Samuel, the alternate personality of Mr. Jenkins, didn't see himself as he was: a mid-sixties, bow-legged, church-going piano player. He felt strong and wise and healthy, unlike the image he saw when he looked into any mirror. He repeatedly complained to his girlfriend, Belinda, about 'that old fucker' adversely affecting his appearance since they were one and the same. Reflections of the physical form that Mr. Jenkins had dominated for over fifty years were used and tired. The confidence of Samuel felt this reflection should match the lion that roared within. Despite smoking and drinking, Samuel believed he would have been in good shape if he'd been the only personality occupying the one frame. To Belinda, he proclaimed that his host was a pitiful lost cause who wasn't surprised with the current rental situation. His exact words were much less refined: "This nigga should be thankin' me for putting some youth back into his soul and gettin' the spunk out his dick! It's nigga maintenance."

To Mr. Jenkins' credit, he relentlessly tried everything from drugs to exorcisms to free himself from waking up in undignified situations. Though unsuccessful, it never thwarted his desire for freedom. A failure merely meant longer periods of duality while he planned his next attempt. There was no chance of harmony in one body with two distinct personalities. Moreover, beneath their solitary skin, Samuel and Mr. Jenkins were twice as bitter as time moved on.

Their opinions on picking grapes as "alternative therapy" fell right in line with their constant opposition.

According to Mr. Jenkins, harvesting grapes at Northern Lights was one of the most pleasant alternative therapies. He enjoyed being outdoors as everyone busied their hands with the task and looked forward to the guided therapeutic conversations. It opened the doors to releasing the tension in his head.

Samuel felt this "alternative therapy" was really slave labor that doubled as one serious libido killer.

Unfortunately for them both, the season to pick grapes for ice wine fell within the rental space of Samuel.

Just over a month after the Mexican's arrival, Samuel begrudgingly suited up for the cold weather – all the while cursing the safety vests they were required to wear. He knew it was simply to track everyone. He then followed orderlies, therapists, and Mr. Reed to the appropriate vines. During the block of instruction, Samuel popped a few cold grapes into his mouth to tantalize up some desire for the juicy bursts of chilled perfection. He mumbled under his breath, "Fuck ya'll. Niggas eat grapes, too." While darting his eyes over the group, he noticed Maggie Koontz rolling a grape in her own mouth. As she shifted it from one cheek to the other, her cross pendant shimmered, and then she smiled at him. Her smile indicated that she thought his body was occupied by her Bible partner. Just as he was about to destroy her with words, though, he noticed a shiny metal object poking haphazardly from the pocket of her red coat. This alone stopped him. The safety vest had tightened the coat appropriately so that it pushed the foreign object to the top of her pocket for easy viewing. Samuel sidestepped in order identify the object. It pained him to smile back as if her face was a friendly and familiar to one.

Maggie stepped to him and whispered under the cover of Mr. Reed's briefing. "This is my first time being in a vineyard. I'm excited to be a part of this process, although the end result is wine, but I guess it's okay because they drank it in the Bible." She winked. Samuel didn't give a fuck, but he forced his head to nod in agreement.

He sniffed as his nose began to run, then sniffed again to stifle a barrage of degrading comments that were boiling in his throat. He faked being agreeable while she continued to whisper. Thankfully, she turned for another grape just enough for him to clearly see a gun. He was genuinely shocked, and popped another grape in his mouth like frozen candy. It appeared to be a small vintage metal pistol that was carved and etched at the grip with ornate designs. He tried to bite down on the thawed portion of the grape, but then cursed Mr. Jenkins for the tooth he needed to fix. He winced and balled his fists up.

How and where had she acquired this item, and why would she have it on her now? Although these questions burned at his brain, he knew that Magpie, dumb as she was, wouldn't share information with him, Samuel...but if he played nice, softened up his posture, and tried his best to sound easygoing and polite without cursing, she would squeal like a pig. "You know you can't have that in your muth...pocket," he whispered in his best reenactment of Mr. Jenkins. Then he added,

"The Lord is watching you. Why don't you give it to me, so you won't get into trouble?" He swallowed the grape in his mouth and tried to look trustworthy as he sniffed several times. A massive shiver shook him as he inhaled more chilled air. He tried to overcome the cold by standing a little taller, as if this would help.

Maggie thought about his words and bounced her eyes back and forth over his face. Somewhat frightened, she looked up to his average stature. "The cold drains the snot right out don't it? My ears hurt too do yours? Sure, Mr. Jenkins, I have tissues." She said just to get closer. Her head dropped low as she whispered, "It's been a burden. Would you throw it away for me?"

Samuel whispered 'yes' as quietly as he could.

Maggie discretely tucked the pistol deeper into her pocket with one finger. Then, unexpectedly, she plunged her hand past the vest and coat into the top of her shirt. The material moved and stretched beyond its intended capacity. Samuel was baffled, but refrained from talking by chewing and rolling more cold grapes around in his mouth. Finally, she pulled three bullets from her bra and held them in the palm of her hand for him to see. Her breath, visible to the eye, blew on them like dragon smoke. They rolled around with her movements before she curled her fingers and shoved her tiny fist into his coat pocket to deposit them without asking permission. She told him that one must have fallen out and asked him to get rid of the bullets that she had been hiding for weeks. Transferring responsibility of the rounds lifted the weight of the world from Maggie's shoulders. If he had them, she couldn't eat them.

Samuel fumbled with the bullets for a second and then zipped the pocket for better security. He never looked around to draw suspicion to his actions; instead, he calmly continued pulling grapes from the vines like a professional. Frankly, he was stunned that it had been that easy and didn't really know what to do with his excitement as he faked being unaffected. His mind, however, became fixated on the pistol still hidden in Maggie's deep pocket. Plans began to formulate as to how he would obtain it, either through a polite request or violent apprehension. There was something funny about the latter of the two options. His devious thoughts weren't cut short quickly, as he kept on plucking many cold bundles and moving down the row of grapes like a robot.

Meanwhile, Maggie's eyes darted over and through each row to scan every person as they talked amongst themselves and put their carefully selected bundles of grapes into their baskets. No one was looking, no one cared, and everyone was popping an occasional grape into their mouths. When Mr. Reed walked past them to move into an untouched section, she made sure he was beyond earshot before asking if Samuel had seen Lydia. If this was her attempt to avoid suspicion, it was a terrible one. What could have been disguised as general concern for another person sounded as if she knew for a fact that something was terribly wrong. Her instincts were usually correct when she became worried, too, and it definitely showed in her face and her hushed tone. Samuel thought for a moment, and then realized that he, too, had not seen the receptionist for a few days. Then Maggie swarmed in with the rumors as if this was the reason she'd brought it up to begin with, and he immediately judged her in a way he was unfamiliar with. Although she claimed to be a fundamental Christian, she sure did a lot of things that were hypocritical and against the Bible – information he'd surely obtained via his host's brain and not his own.

Maggie grabbed at her cross. "The twins told me Lydia left today because she's pregnant. Nobody knows if it's the truth." she blurted quickly. Her eyes widened and became smug, but she shook her head disapprovingly and pretended to be troubled by this while asking him to pray about it later.

Samuel, forgetting to maintain his cover, giggled when he joked that he wasn't the daddy. Then he literally bit his tongue to prevent any more identity clues from spilling out. Being yin and yang with his alter had its perks sometimes, and he wanted to preserve it. Maggie giggled, too, as her dainty hand covered her guilty smile. She then placed it on his shoulder before telling him what a good and honest man he was, despite his disorder – which was exactly how she felt about herself. Samuel had a vision of slapping Snow White's face so hard that it spun her tiny frame to the ground for that comment, but she was a strange asset in so many ways, just as long as he was polite. So, instead, he popped another grape into his mouth and let the icy juice squirt all over the back of his teeth as he bit down through the pain. He sucked in cold snot before asking her how the twins had come upon this information.

"Well, you know how the twins are; they are everywhere. They listen to stuff through their laughter. People assume they are in their own world, but it's like being a fly on the wall. Ute told me that. She thinks I am dumb, so she thought I wouldn't know what that meant." She bent down to put a few bundles of grapes into her basket before jutting upward again to whisper loudly into Samuel's face. "By the way, I looked up 'kaput' on the library computer. It's German for broke and useless. They think I am kaput Koontz!" She slinked back to the lowest part of the row to pick grapes as if she'd said nothing at all then, making the transition extremely awkward.

Looking down upon her crouched position, he said, "You. I mean, we, can pray about that later, too." He swallowed his pride and tried to maintain an act of innocence which was literally making him sick to his stomach.

"Oh, you are so thoughtful. Yes, we should, and I should pray about this need to gossip, too, but I'll tell you one last thing then before God heals me of it...the twins heard it from Lydia, who was not so quietly telling Ignacio that he was the father. They must have, you know, done it right after he got here, because he's only been here a month! And they call us crazy. Okay, I'm done. Lord give me strength." She lifted her hands to the sky and then circled them downward into a position of prayer as she shook her head into her delicately connected fingertips. There was an awkward pause, and then she placed some more bundles of grapes into her basket without skipping a beat.

Unable to bend anymore due to a new knee pain, Samuel stood straighter as his eyebrows hit the top of his hairline and he plucked bunches of cold grapes from the upper portion of the row as if he was an android on autopilot. What was unsettling was the thought that Ignacio had sex with her. The thought of them together baffled his brain. Lydia always seemed overly professional to him. In the next random moment, though, he happened to look right down into Maggie Koontz's beautifully hallowed white face as she placed her boney index finger over her mouth, shushing confirmation of their unified thoughts.

For the first time, Samuel liked this idea of being a "super nigga spy"; it was empowering. He was stuck in this body, but honestly, he was triumphantly trapped.

MAN OF CHANGE

In the first month of being at Northern Lights, Ignacio had done his best to be exceptionally friendly with the staff at the Northern Lights behavioral health-mental facility...or, the wacky shack, as some called it. Ignacio knew it was of utmost importance to maintain good standing with the owners and clients who had permanent homes within its walls. This ensured that he could admit himself again in a few years' time – according to his plan. He felt the facility was like a borderline resort atmosphere, minus the crazies and the people who were faking it.

Sure, he had made a mistake with the blonde bombshell, but he was a young man – locked, cocked, and ready to rock. He was hardly to blame. He would have dealt with the error in his own way, too, but she'd become metal to a magnet that couldn't be repelled no matter how hard he tried. Their one-time bedroom rendezvous had put her in a permanent state of horny that she could only satisfy with secret fantasies. Samuel, her boyfriend, had confessed man to man that he almost couldn't keep up with her recent demands for anal.

Ignacio had listened to his tales of sexual woes on the rare occasions when the alternate personality had sought him out. He was just glad that Samuel didn't know her sexual appetite had originated with him, and that, regrettably, sometimes the smell of strawberries made him hard.

When the bombshell had approached Ignacio thereafter, it had always been for one more secret session. Temptation had been strong in those first few days, too, but there was something about Lydia's caramel complexion and unique style that he desired over any physical orgasm that Belinda could have given him. It was unfortunate for her, but Ignacio had stood his ground against yet another sexual adventure – reminding her that her offering herself to him was simply an unwanted distraction. He reminded himself that the goal here was to get a break from pretending to be insane and to secure his monthly disability paychecks; getting lost in her advances would surely ruin everything he'd set up.

He'd held out for the right person, finally giving in to physical desires with Lydia, the sexiest receptionist he had ever known and the apple of his eye since the second he'd seen her. There was an unexplainable familiarity with Lydia from the beginning – an instant connection. Their experience in a dark corner of the smoking room had clarified that he should never give in to the smell of strawberries ever again. Though he understood her reason for backing away was because she didn't want to lose her job, he was certain their connection was strong.

Holding on to the idea of love, he'd wished daily that it would happen again...but it never had. She never afforded time alone together, even if he planned it. But now, a month into his stay at Northern Lights, Lydia said that she was pregnant – and Ignacio's mind was utterly blown into a million little pieces. Was she joking? He had to replay their experience in the dark in an unsettling mental loop to understand what had gone wrong. The only thing he regretted during their passionate time together was leaving things to chance by assuming that, when he'd unleashed himself from his jeans and she'd directed it with her hands into her body, she'd known what she was doing. He'd ignorantly presumed she was on some kind of birth control.

Dumbfounded that a one-night stand could end this way after weeks of his hoping for a relationship, he slowly picked the scenario apart as he relived it from memory – only to hear those three shocking words in an unfortunate coil of repetition. *I am pregnant.* He'd been calm when she'd said it through the laughter of the twins at their bay window, but numbness washed over him now as he remembered staring with confusion at her red lips over the words that had transpired between them. The rest of her speech was made up of mumbling with unrecognizably high and low tones that were much like the background noise of a television on low volume. Something in his mind told him this wasn't the truth, but he never asked. He was shocked again when she touched his shoulder to echo that she was also leaving Northern Lights to deal with it.

How could she have used those words without blinking? Something about it wasn't settling well in the confusion of his head. But if she knew his façade it wouldn't make anything clearer other than the fact that they were liars together.

He wanted to tell her that he was falling in love with her and that everything would be okay, but he was a patient at Northern Lights and she didn't know the truth. He certainly wasn't going to expose himself to her in the front lobby of the building, with those nosey twins listening at their bay window.

So, he'd lovingly given her time to sort out everything. But she would never return to duty at the front desk. He'd stopped waiting for her when the ring he'd bartered from Maggie Koontz seemed to be endlessly rolling around in his pocket as a sad reminder of where his emotional state had been headed even before she'd disappeared.

Ironically, the person who eased the pain the most wasn't one of the counselors or therapists who were happily getting paid to do just that. It was Buck Lynn, the southern orderly with a fascination for keeping his lips moist. Everyone, including Mr. and Mrs. Reed, agreed that Buck Lynn practically ran the mansion, and now Ignacio felt like he understood why. He was the 'go-to' guy for everything at the vineyard. So, it was no surprise to anyone that Ignacio sought his advice from Buck, as so many others had done before him.

Gay, obnoxiously tall, and southern were his identifying traits, but if given a moment to understand him, anyone found that his compassion was genuine for every client – yet, he maintained his professional responsibilities as a head nurse and an unofficial part-time security guard. The respect that he'd earned within the facility was pretty standard across the board, too, no matter if Sam said negative things about him or pushed his buttons. The average person did not come across a man as well-rounded as him very often, either. Everyone was lucky to know such a kind soul. He was funny when he was relaxed, serious when he needed to be, and persistent at the appropriate moments. In previous years, Jack and Jill

Reed had rewarded him with select wines from their personal collections and gifted him etched metal certificates that were presented on fine wooden placards. He'd been grateful as usual and humble about his place at the facility, but deep down, he already knew his worth was invaluable to them and so many of the staff members. That's why he'd stayed then, and it was why he still stayed now, even though some days working at a mental health facility became incredibly intense.

However, without the ability to develop real friendships among the clients, lack of fraternization did present itself as a work hazard and as a direct path to loneliness. His half-sister's sudden interest and help at the front desk had been a blessing in disguise. Her timing had been impeccable after a horrible break-up he'd suffered through, and her desire to build a relationship with him had been just what he'd needed to pick himself up again.

But when she left, it was so sudden that it was hard for him to cope with the silence in their apartment after his shifts. She didn't even take all her belongings – just two bags, and one photo of him and their dad before he'd run off and married her mom, the white lady. On the undusted portion of the table, where the framed photo had once stood, she'd placed a note that promised she would return the original after making a copy. Tragic as it was, Buck couldn't really do anything but consider her ambitious youth as a part of the dramatic decision to leave. A lot of unanswered questions plagued him, so when he and Ignacio began talking, this was a key point of interest.

At first, when they had a moment to chat, the conversation tended to boomerang back to Lydia and her unusual disappearance. Both men were affected by it, but neither would divulge just how deep their personal ties were in the whole mysterious situation. Ignacio was five weeks into his therapy at Northern Lights when he and Buck began to discuss the facility in general and how they'd ended up there, along with bits of gossip from their days inside of it. Buck slowly began to appreciate Ignacio's realistic sense of humor, longer hair, and stupid dimples that everyone loved so much. Having a friend in Northern lights made for pleasant working hours, and he noticed a great sense of pride returning to his personal work ethic.

Six weeks into Ignacio's time at Northern lights, they shared lunch together every other day in the cafeteria, which led to discussions of outside interests and future dreams in between dirty jokes and talk of building fantasy football leagues. Their friendship bloomed into a brotherly bond, and yet there were hidden secrets they kept from each other. Ignacio didn't speak about Lydia, and Buck never talked about his most recent past relationship. Those were boundaries that neither wanted to knock down.

By the time Ignacio had been at Northern Lights a grand total of eight weeks, he and Buck were on a first name basis – although, around others, they maintained a professional boundary. It had to be this way for obvious reasons. The only person to witness the deeper level of the relationship was Ignacio's doctor. During a counseling session, she struck an emotional chord while attempting to discuss the VHS tape of the Cheyez incident. When the doctor persisted with what Ignacio felt was an irrelevant question, it triggered a belligerent outburst. Buck calmed the situation before it escalated; however, it was not necessarily in the capacity of Northern Lights security.

Before Buck had entered the room, Ignacio had been screaming with his hands up in the air like an alpha baboon. The doctor who was scrunched down in her chair knew she was beyond her scope and had pressed the hidden security button mounted under her desk.

"Why does everyone ask me about my feelings when I watched the fucking tape? Why doesn't anyone ask about my mother's feelings? You should have seen her god damned face! Where were all of you concerned assholes when she was fifteen? Bitch, I told you about the fingernails stuck in her face – the moons! Fuck the moon – I wish I could light that bitch on fire! Get me out of here. Open this piece of shit door before I kick it the fuck down!"

He tried to kick at the door, but the security button triggered a locking mechanism within it that was only to be opened by staff. By the time Buck arrived, Ignacio was standing on the back of a chair, pulling down a painting of a night sky over a body of water with a sailboat in the distance and, of course, the moon.

"Stop asking about the tape!" He whipped the painting at the scared counselor like it was a rectangular Frisbee. "Stop asking about the tape!"

Buck's baritone shout only stunned him for a moment before he jumped down from the chair and charged at the door. Buck aimed his Taser without hesitation. "Sit down, Mr. Cheyez, before I pull on this trigger long enough to make your grandchildren have seizures."

"Get out of my way, Mr. Lynn!" Sarcastically, Ignacio wiggled his head at the formal use of names. Then he rushed Buck so quickly that the Taser flew out of his hands before he was stumbling backward. Buck quickly rebalanced himself and, in one impossible move, wrapped his arms around Ignacio to restrain further movement. There was no room for Ignacio to twist his body away from Buck's firm yet somehow gentle embrace. Ignacio yelled about feeling pain and tried to thrash free, but Buck's strength was more than a physical force. The suppression of his emotional eruption suddenly became an intensely intimate moment between them.

It seemed as if Buck's voice was sincere, calm and assuring, but the kind of concern he projected through his words came across as a plea. "Isn't that what you are here for? We will take care of you. That's what you are here for – shhh…" He lowered his tone before continuing. "I will take care of you." He looked over to the doctor, who had a white-knuckled grip around both arm rests of the chair she'd hid behind. Her eyes had witnessed more than a rescue. "We all will."

Buck's words pacified the anger that burned within Ignacio. Although his face was buried in Buck's chest, it was as if he could finally breathe. He relinquished it all in an exhale that weakened his knees. Depleted, Ignacio slumped and gave in to a deep cry that purged his mind. He was letting the compassion of this man carry the heavy burden of his mother's weight.

Ignacio moved his ear to Buck's heart. He let the beat of it drum away his anger. They stood together until Buck loosened his grip. His eyes glassed over with tears made up of something other than sadness or pity. His heart beat with much more than adrenaline. His body swayed to sooth his friend with movements representing love.

That was when Mr. and Mrs. Reed ran into the office to check on the doctor, along with an older security guard, with the intent of sedating Ignacio. But, Buck told them he would personally escort the young man back to his room rather than relying on further drugs. The older guard spoke with the Reeds at that point, and then they simply gave him permission – after all, it was Buck.

PINKY SWEAR

It was never Ignacio's intention to befriend people at Northern Lights, and certainly not when it came to a staff member with whom he should be strictly professional. However, he and Buck had one thing in common that brought them together, and her name was Lydia. They spoke of her in restricted conversations, and then as Ignacio's relationship to Buck blossomed, the subject slowly became an unspoken closed door. It was suddenly possible to consider that Lydia's disappearance was a blessing in disguise. It brought two people together and formed a friendship that was beginning to fill the holes in the men she'd left behind.

They continued living without answers to their questions. Sometimes not knowing the awful truth allowed people to move on despite the ties that bind. There was a certain kind of irony in the way life replenished itself at Northern Lights.

No matter the hidden circumstances, Buck and Ignacio naturally gravitated to each other. It opened the doors to happiness for both friends – something that each had forgotten existed.

Their conversations, no matter how simple, brought joy into their lives. Like the time Buck brought in a small plaque he'd received from the Reeds during his fifth year there. He spoke proudly of the bonus that had come with it and how he'd spent the money on a whitewater rafting trip. He shared his amazing adventures with Ignacio, who appreciated his story and the way he told it.

"I would offer to take you once you get out, but your hair would get wet, Ms. Priss, and I don't know how to braid," Buck harassed him. Ignacio used choice words as he laughed and went on to giggle through racial stereotypes about swimming. It was always the little things that bring the most joy.

As the bonding continued, Ignacio heard many stories from Buck, both funny and heartwarming. Most of them held a compassionate element that reminded him of his grandmother. He realized that Buck was more than a staff member or even a friend. He was a wonderful human being who really took pride in helping others. This quality was admirable, and Ignacio repeatedly told his buddy just that.

"I mean it, man. That was fucking nice. I wish someone would have done some shit like that for me when I was fifteen. You listened. You cared enough to actually listen." He choked back the lump in his throat and pushed himself away from the lunch room table. He watched Maggie dump what appeared to be a full plate of food in the trash and walk out of the dining area. Distractions were good when he felt too emotional.

Buck shook his head as Ignacio returned his focus to the conversation. "Naw, anybody would have done the same." The keys attached to his hip clinked as he dug into his pocket for the Carmex.

Ignacio, obviously touched by his most recent story, pressed on the best he could as the lunch crowd bustled around them. "That's just it, man – no, they wouldn't. Not only is that a great story, but you are humble about it, too. You have a good heart, fucker. Take a compliment." He shook his head in an attempt at composure, then inhaled deeply and exhaled into a smile.

After moisturizing his lips and tucking the container away, Buck leaned his shoulders over the table. He spoke in a low tone, forcing Ignacio to lean in, too, so that he could understand him. "Are you messing with me? Tears? Get it to-gether, girl – I'm the gay one here, but *you* are acting like it." He pointed to Ignacio and circled his finger around his head, then retracted it while smacking his lips together. Ignacio, lingering in the smell of his lip balm, laughed so hard that tears began to well in his eyes. Buck laughed harder.

After wiping away moisture from the outside of his eyes, Ignacio said, "I haven't laughed that hard in a minute. Hey, bro, do you have a boyfriend outside of here?"

"What do you mean 'outside'? You act like I never leave," Buck said in a small attempt to change the direction of the question.

"Seems like you are always here...come on, you know what the hell I mean. You're such a cool guy. I'm just wondering." Ignacio shrugged and took an oversized bite of his noodles.

Buck sat back in his chair and folded his arms over his chest. "You know, I don't really care to talk about that personal stuff."

While chewing, Ignacio said, "I told you I wiped my ass with my hands once because we didn't have toilet paper, and you can't answer the fucking question? We're bonding." Then he wiped his mouth with a napkin.

Buck didn't move his arms, but his head turned to face the serving area. "I'm not indulging you in the lunch room of my working environment." He shook his head and then looked back to Ignacio, demanding he change the subject.

"Damn, you are suddenly wound up tight. You need to get laid. What about the prep cook? He is a handsome queen." Ignacio lifted his chin to the door of the kitchen and raised his eyebrows several times.

Buck was disgusted, and immediately turned his head in the opposite direction as if he would be sick from the thought of it. Then he leaned over his tray again, directing his soft-ened voice at Ignacio. "I would not sleep with any man in this facility, so just stop." He thought for a second, then circled his finger in the air to clarify that he was speaking about everyone at Northern Lights. "Sex isn't just something ya'll can just give away." He sat up and took a sip of his water without breaking eye contact.

Ignacio wasn't sure how to react to this, and rather than thinking about what had just happened, he said the first thing that came to his mind. "See, you have standards. That's what I like about you. So, are you going to answer the question?" A part of him wished he would have shoved another fork full of noodles into his mouth instead of pushing, as he felt imme-diate regret after speaking. There was an uncomfortably long pause before Buck spoke again.

"I need to speak with Mr. Jenkins about his medication anyway, so I'm going to go." Buck stood up and began placing his cup and silverware on his tray. He seemed to be deep in thought.

Ignacio, recognizing the pain he'd caused, grabbed at Buck's forearm. When he did, the muscles jerked inside. Ignacio's pinky finger rubbed at Buck's skin in gentle, subtle sweeps. "I'm sorry. I didn't mean to hit on such a sensitive subject. Please sit down." He let go of his friend's arm when Buck looked around to see if anyone had noticed. Ignacio looked around, too. Belinda had seen the gesture from the opposite side of the room, but not in detail. Ignacio folded his hands on his lap and tucked his rogue pinky under stronger fingers.

After another staff member walked behind him with her tray of food, Buck whispered, "It's apparent that I am getting a little too comfortable during our lunch breaks. This is my fault."

"Maybe we need privacy for our deeper man to man shit. I'm your friend now, and I enjoy getting to know you, all about you. Could we meet in the craft room after your meeting with Mr. Jenkins? We can talk about toilet paper and swimming instead." Ignacio knew this would get Buck to smile, and it did. Then he added, "I'll teach you how to braid hair. Every Mexican knows how to do that shit." He flipped the bottom of his hair backward and laughed.

Buck shook his head. "Sure. It's completely against my personal work ethic, though, and I may cancel."

Ignacio held his hand up. "I can see you struggling with the thought of you having fun on duty, but I'm the fucking awesome exception." In this moment of friendly egotism, there was joy.

"Go to group, you idiot," Buck said, and then he walked away happy.

BROTHERLY LOVE

On the three-month anniversary of Ignacio's admittance, Buck snuck his brother by proxy a Mexican dish that he'd made himself from an online recipe. It was in a plastic container that he slipped between two clean towels which he then hand-delivered to Ignacio's room. Buck, a man of rules and discipline, would never do this for someone who wasn't a friend about to be released, but he felt sure that no harm would come from this one-time charitable dish of deliciousness.

When he finally made it inside of Ignacio's room without anyone taking notice, he stood at the door to share the surprise that was balancing on one hand between towels. "I know ya'll are doing your final evaluations this week for release, but I wanted to do this for you because you are a really good friend. Ta da!" He pulled the top towel off to reveal the dish as he lifted his moisturized lips from ear to ear. His heart racing with excitement, his eyes twinkled with elation as Ignacio's eyes ignited upon seeing what it was. Ignacio immediately grabbed the container to lift the corner for a wonderful first sniff. His face relaxed with a smile as he took in a long deep breath of rice, beans, chicken, spices, and other ingredients; he had missed that smell of delicious food from home.

"Thanks, man. It smells wonderful! I can't believe you did this yourself." He backed up to the bed to sit on its edge as Buck held out a plastic knife and fork set for him to use – because he always thought of everything, and this occasion was no different.

Ignacio knew it would never be as tasty as his grand-mother's home cooking, but it was the thought that counted. He set the lid on the comforter and began taking big bites after offering some to Buck, whose face had softened with pride. "Oh, I ate too much as I was cooking it, so I need to watch this figure or it will go straight to my ass. I never knew Mexican food was so good!" his deep voice boomed through a soft southern accent. He put his free hand on his hip and flipped the clean towels over his shoulder with a gently fem-inine motion.

Ignacio shoveled the dish into his mouth as he unsuc-cessfully tried to compliment the cook while food spilled out from the edges of his lips. Eventually, he gave up and just shook his head up and down while displaying an upward thumb. After finally devouring the contents of the container, Ignacio wiped his face on the back of his hand as he joked about having a beer to finish out the meal.

Buck, in all his infinite wisdom, pulled two imported bottles from the waistband of his pants. "It's probably a little warm from my body heat, but surprise! I figured, since I have been breaking the rules with you, I might as well go all out. Seriously, you tell anyone, and I'll have to kill you."

Ignacio smiled at his comment, but was taken aback at the glimpse he'd gotten of Buck's defined stack of abdominal muscles when the man had lifted his orderly shirt to retrieve the bottles. They compelled him to make a comment as he wrapped is hand around the chilled neck of one beer. "Damn, man, what work-out video are you watching? That shit is insane! I'm toned, but I couldn't get definition like that in my gut if I paid for it. There is steel under all of that cotton candy." He twisted the cap off the beer and swigged it hard before belching.

Buck joked, "It's a black thang." Ignacio rolled his eyes before they laughed together as each drank from his own bottle. Then Buck joined Ignacio on the edge of the bed.

When the alcohol neared the bottom of the bottles and the joking began to taper to an end, Ignacio confessed to

Buck his appreciation for everything. "Thanks for the food, man. The beers…" He held his bottle up and tapped Buck's in a simple toast. They both welcomed the clicking noise as a reminder of better times outside of Northern Lights. "Some days here were rough and you were there for me. No, no, really. It wasn't just your job, man. You made sure I was okay and really cared about me as a person, no matter what. I want to officially recognize that. You know. Maybe after I'm out, we could get together some time. I'd kick it at a gay bar with you."

"Why would I take you to a gay bar?" Buck pretended to be sincere as he let his deep voice roar through a softly southern, melodic tone.

Ignacio laughed and slugged his buddy's arm. "Shut up. Thanks for everything, though; I mean that shit from the bottom of my heart." He looked over to Buck again, who was suavely shaking his head as if to say, 'You're welcome' without saying a word.

Buck was deeply touched, but he wasn't about to shed a tear in this awkward moment in front of his buddy. He swallowed the last sip of beer to hide the fact that he was choking down unmanly emotions and looked downward to stare at the carpet. It was no secret, though, that he was sad to see his friend go.

Ignacio set his empty beer bottle on the floor and called Buck's name. When the security guard turned to answer, Ignacio reached out and pulled Buck's beer-flavored lips onto his own. Both tightened every muscle in their bodies when the physical link between them created indescribable bursts of energy. Ignacio gave Buck a moment to relax before engaging in a harder and more passionate kiss, sliding his lips over the Carmex that covered Buck's.

Buck was lost in the moment and let it all happen, as it felt so right to be kissing with such devotion. Their lips softened, yet pressed firmly into each other's as they began to breathe heavily through their noses in a biological display of swelling arousal. A heat began to wrap each of them in its warm embrace as the kiss continued to develop into something more than instant gratification. When Ignacio slipped the first gentle tongue lick into Buck's mouth, it seemed to awaken him from a surreal fantasy that he'd secretly wanted more than anything. With wide, apprehensive eyes, though, Buck pushed Ignacio away with his two massive hands. Their lips unlocked with an audible wet pop before he asked, "What the fuck are you doing?" while wiping saliva off his mouth with the back of his hand. He repeated, "What the fuck are you doing?" in a whisper, as if someone could hear from the hall.

For a second, Ignacio was still trapped and hovering in the moment with transferred Carmex glistening around his lips, and eyes that had transformed into something so seductive that he was barely able to see through them. Not even the shove backward had pulled him from the trance he was in. Then, as clarity began to sweep over the glassy raw state of stimulation in his face, he was suddenly aware of what he had done and felt uncomfortably embarrassed. His hand immediately covered his mouth as he wiped and tugged at his lips with eyes as big as saucers. All he could manage to say was 'shit' over and over again in awkward repetition while Buck gathered the contraband he'd brought in in preparation to leave.

When Buck reached the door, he whispered forcefully through his perfectly aligned teeth, "I like you and I know that you already know that, but I am not your experiment, Ignacio! I'm going to go before this gets any more uncomfortable than it already is."

"I'm sorry, man. I never...that...like that..." Ignacio pleaded with him, even while still incredibly insecure about what had just taken place, but he stumbled over his words like he was stumbling through a massive pile of hurricane-whipped thoughts.

Buck angrily tried to contain himself the best way he knew how by attempting to turn on the professionalism that always pulled him out of sticky situations. After gingerly shoving the empty bottles back into his pants, he stood up straight at the door, holding the towels and container like a proud waiter. "Believe it or not, this is not the first time this has happened to me," he lied. "This is after all a mental health facility and I have been a little too accommodating with this friendship. I apologize if I led you on. We can forget this happened and move forward so you can focus on your upcoming release." He turned to reach for the door handle, but Ignacio called out his name to stop him. Buck held his position for a moment more to at least hear what he was about to say, listening without turning his head to look at his friend.

"I don't want to forget it, man. You ignited something in me and I feel whole for the first time in my life." Ignacio didn't dare approach Buck because he was so nervous, but more horrified at the thought of possible rejection.

Buck removed his hand from the door handle to hold up a long, firm finger, which stopped Ignacio from saying anything else as he bit the inside of his cheek with closed eyes. The muscles in his jaw tensed and hardened. He took a few steady breaths to look at Ignacio, who was now standing helplessly at the edge of the bed. His hair swirled in different shades of darkened waves, highlighted by gleaming light. His dimples, barely noticeable under the sad face he projected, didn't distract from his heartfelt brown eyes. His lips, still swollen from their shared kiss, begged for another. Buck inhaled deeply, and then, with conviction, said what Ignacio needed to hear and not what he wanted to hear. "You're not gay. And I don't want to lose my job."

Buck rolled the container between the towels and walked out of the room before Ignacio could respond.

What he'd thought was sadness when Lydia had left without a trace wasn't remotely close to the deep devastation that sank into Ignacio's soul when Buck walked out of the room. All he could do was submit to the rejection on his bed and try not to cry as a longing he had never felt before warmed over him in wavelike motions from an unknown internal source. He inevitably succumbed to the knot in his throat and shed some much-needed tears before trying again to pretend he was a real man, toughened by life. A week away from release, a sane man was broken.

BEND OR BREAK

Ignacio struggled with his sexuality though he tried regaining control of the things he thought he knew. Once he discovered unexpected comfort in Buck's presence and feelings it was like a page in a storybook that he couldn't unread. The only hope for relief was his upcoming release. He found solace in the bittersweet idea of going home.

It was merely days before his official discharge was to take place, when Ignacio's therapists extended his stay – indefinitely. Just when he'd thought he could leave the turmoil of conflicting sexualities, he was blindsided and trapped in the very place he'd initially been free to leave. Between the researcher's notes and the counselors, it had been decided that he needed more therapy; therefore, his release was being denied. They could do things like this when you were sponsored, a downfall to the lies that had gotten him there. The other patients used colorful words to explain it – calling him a government-funded wacky jack – and Ignacio didn't argue. He'd spent years convincing others that he was crazy so that he could find out the truth about his mother, and the fact was, it had worked...and now he was beginning to believe his own lies. Maybe he was insane.

This was the pivotal moment where Ignacio began to break, and while inside of a converted mansion on a vineyard. He rubbed his eyes profusely as if he had an uncontrollable tick. His inner monologues became mumbles and conversations that the other patients thought were meant for them. Something was troubling him, and everyone saw his indescribable change from being in control to – not. What should have been a happy, uplifting time of release had gone horribly wrong, but none could have guessed the truth of things. Even Maggie Koontz began to pray for him during her Bible study sessions with Mr. Jenkins.

Ignacio didn't want to admit or acknowledge any kind of homosexual tendency. Especially since he had never in his life thought himself gay or held any interest in a lifestyle that was so unfamiliar to him. If gay people knew at a young age, shouldn't he have known? His brain couldn't wrap itself around this concept, that he might be finding out now, and consequently shut down every time he tried to understand it. Like when a computer went into sleep mode after idling for designated minutes.

It was five days after he and Buck had shared their first

kiss when Ignacio began to black out. At first, he thought he was just tired, as he'd felt less and less rested. Then he began to doze off and wake up on the other side of rooms. Increasing emotional outbursts invaded his peaceful moments. He found that his anger was barely under control during civil conversations.

Samuel was the one who discovered that the Mexican could no longer maintain his composure when provoked. Of course, he was never one to have a civil conversation.

They were in the lobby when Ignacio engaged in his first physical altercation. It happened to be the day when he'd originally been supposed to leave Northern Lights. What onlookers heard was Samuel shouting first. His bowed legs spread more than shoulder-length apart to create a more intimidating stance. That was the intention, at least, but his average height and average frame didn't lend themselves to the idea. He didn't realize that his ego was far more powerful than his posture.

The other scattered patients remained close to the perimeter walls. The centrally placed welcome desk – recently occupied by a new, gangly, pimple-faced clerk – was filled with two orderlies ready to intervene, but one of them was close to retirement and didn't want to make a move unless it was absolutely necessary, which slowed them both from reacting. Meanwhile, Ignacio, matching Samuel's average height, stepped forward into the space of this mental patient who was currently occupied by his highly aggressive alternate personality.

"Faggot..." the alter taunted him.

Ignacio swung his right balled fist so hard and fast that, if you weren't paying attention, you would have missed it. Even the onlookers were stunned. When his knuckles met the left side of Samuel's jaw, the force of it popped open his mouth and shot a set of partials across the lobby. They flew through the air in what seemed to be slow motion. Ignacio, the other patients, and the orderlies behind the reception desk watched the teeth finally land in a potted geranium next to the bay window. Then Ignacio felt dizzy, and a sudden opaque hue blanketed his eyes. Those trying to keep their distance were embarrassed for Samuel, who whipped his head back to its neutral position while fondling the empty spaces with his tongue. Some onlookers cupped their hands over their own mouths in shock while others inhaled air through their teeth.

Just as Samuel was about to say something in the dramatically intimidating way that he favored, Ignacio swung again, this time in wild anger and with a high-pitched scream as he missed completely. It felt as if Samuel had taken two steps back, he was so far from the mark. The swing put a spin on his body that caused Ignacio to lose his balance, though, so that down he fell in the mansion lobby, crumbling clumsily to the floor like a fainting harlot.

Samuel kicked him, then bent down to antagonize him with words that came pushing fiercely through the gaps between his teeth. "Ya did thith to your mothafucking thelf, bitch." He bent down further, hovering over the Mexican who was now in a defensive pose on the floor with his wild curls covering his eyes. Samuel slapped the back of his ashy hand across Ignacio's face so hard that it whipped his head sideways.

Spit initially spewed out of Ignacio's mouth from the impact, but his lips began to ooze blood as he lay there embarrassed to move – feeling small, angry, and out of control... like he was losing his mind. The truly unfortunate part of this whole situation wasn't the pathetic and almost whimpering person he had become, either. It was that the lies of his illness, or of his falsified mental state, had caught up with him three-fold. He had acted many kinds of crazy for the sake of a monthly paycheck, but this was the first time he truly felt the insanity at all, let alone deep within his core. Through watery

eyes, he scanned the room for familiar shoes. He hoped beyond belief that Buck did not witness his loss of composure.
His concern for his love was in deep conflict with the projected assumptions that Buck alone had put him in this position,
but he couldn't help that. He didn't want to give in to loving
a man, either, but it was happening, and it was breaking him
down in a way he'd never expected. Dizziness came and went
in waves before he finally closed his eyes to make the world
stop spinning.

The surrounding patients and staff near the walls began
whispering to each other. The pimple-faced clerk behind the
reception desk pushed an emergency button, unaware that it
would call for the very person Ignacio didn't want to see.
And even though Ignacio had no intentions of getting up, the
orderlies were ending the fight with restraints.

Mr. Jenkins, an innocent victim of his disorder, cried as
they clicked the wrist cuffs into place, and then he walked
shamefully wherever they led him.

The witnesses zipped their eyes from him to the clerk
that was biting his fingertips before ending their stares with
Ignacio, the sissy Mexican who was crying on the floor. The
display of violence they'd witnessed was clearly just the tip
of the emotional iceberg.

WAR & PEACE

A few days after recovering from the fight, Ignacio's blackouts were taking over in longer durations. He kept his secret hidden even from Buck. However, at Northern Lights no secret was completely safe, and sometimes insanity was the way secrets got discovered.

In the bedroom mirror, Belinda brushed through her long blonde hair as she fantasized about sex. Her prescribed pills were not effective at curbing her appetite for it, like the doctors claimed they should. As an addict, she thought about her vice nonstop between fixes. Soothing herself from her addiction usually produced obsessive compulsive behaviors which tonight had manifested in repeated, long strokes of her hairbrush. Standing in front of the mirror, her blazing bright blue eyes were catatonic and emotionless. She stared back at her reflection as her hand pushed the bristles into her hair and then pulled down. It was three in the morning, nearing the hour when the cameras in the hallway swung back to record their designated lane. Between spins, the area outside of the bathroom was not monitored. And beyond the door, she could hear muted footsteps which she assumed were from her boyfriend, seeking a late-night blowjob. When the footsteps passed, and the sound faded, she curiously pulled herself away from her mesmerizing reflection to inspect the hall and its occupant. Down it, she discovered Buck Lynn, the muscle-bound, insanely tall orderly who was gliding as quietly as he could over the carpet to the Mexican's room, where he then used his master emergency key to gain access.

Her heart pounded with excitement as she peered through the cracked bathroom door, eyes growing wide with the thrill of catching this secret moment. She could smell Buck's intentions in the air, his desires swirling past her nose now. Sex addicts could sense when others felt desire just as accurately as if they had a glowing neon sign above their heads...not to mention that there was proof of his feelings in that single entry into a room. If it had been business related, he would have brought another orderly. She shook her head, then closed her eyes and inhaled the smell of Buck's sex which had a faint scent of wet iron.

She looked at the camera's position and then, with one hand, held the door open an inch more so that she could stare more easily toward room 19. Her pulse beat in her ears as she slid her other hand down her lace panties and nestled her fingers between her folds. She began teasing and rubbing as she watched the stillness of the hallway and the door that hid so many indiscretions. Memories of her moment with Ignacio warmed her body as she recalled the finesse it had taken to pleasure her without penetration. Her imagination went wild as she fantasized over the things that were going on behind the door now. Belinda focused, and fully engulfed in the throes of her sexual addiction, she teased herself in anticipation of seeing Buck's assumed afterglow.

Never peeling her eyes from the door, she rubbed until her panties were soaked and visible shining lubrication glistened between her thighs. When the door to room 19 finally opened, she allowed herself to burst with orgasm. Just as expected, Buck exited the room disheveled, but smiling and relaxed. He took one step away from the door before patting his uniform pocket and then returning to room 19 to quietly knock. His deep voice mumbled as Belinda's knees weakened. Buck waited in the hall for a moment more, and then she witnessed Ignacio handing him the master key and sharing a kiss in the archway. Belinda swirled her fingers again with different pressure and came again as she watched the two men kiss with an emotional passion. It was clear that their sensitive connection was much more than she'd given it credit for.

***

The next morning, she tried to share the gossip with her boyfriend, but he was gone, dispersed from the body of Mr. Jenkins – who was engulfed in Bible study with Maggie Koontz. They were in their usual corner booth of the dining hall flipping through biblical pages. To make a scene, Belinda stomped her feet and waited for him to acknowledge her presence. Mr. Jenkins invited her to join the discussion of Ecclesiastes. Maggie, uncomfortable with the intrusion, reverted into silence for the duration.

"No, I don't want to join your stupid fucking study group. I want to speak to Samuel!" She was livid as she held her angry stare on Mr. Jenkins. Floating lights danced across his face as a burning heat intensified within her ears. Had her boyfriend been there, he would have grabbed her breasts without regard to other occupants in the dining room. She blinked profusely as she scanned this man's face for any sign of him.

After pushing his reading glasses onto the top of his head, Mr. Jenkins looked up from the word of God to address her in a very calm manner. "Told you a million times to stay away from me. Million times. You're a godless woman…"

Belinda rolled her eyes. "For shit's sake, Mr. Jenkins.

Blah blah, I've heard this speech a million times is what has happened a million times. I hate you. But we are all a big fucking family and I need to speak to my boyfriend!" She slapped her palms on the table in front of him, which flipped over his empty paper coffee cup.

It was not her words that made him uneasy, but the wind from the force of her tantrum turning his Bible page unintentionally. He looked down, visibly upset now, and turned over a page to reset his Bible. She moved her face to within a foot from his to look him in the eyes, still in search of the man who loved her back. Extremely uncomfortable with her encroaching position, Mr. Jenkins backed into his chair as best he could even as the blast of strawberry-scented shampoo tickled past his face.

"Ms. Beckler, I rebuke you. Step away or I'll call Mr. Buck Lynn to escort you out." He pushed his hand outward, making a motion as if he was parting the red sea without touching her.

"You will do no such thing!" Without thinking, she swooped into his space, cupping his cheeks with her hands specifically to shout in his face. "Samuel, you listen to me and come the fuck out!"

Mr. Jenkins squirmed and backed away, falling into his

chair again. His glasses fell from his head to the dining room floor and spun on their spectacle glass a few times before stopping in the middle of a square tile. Mr. Jenkins grabbed Belinda's hands to pry them from his face. "Don't work that way, Ms. Beckler." His strength pulled her tiny wrists from his aged cheeks without effort.

"Fuck you, Mr. Jenkins, and fuck you, too, Magpie!" She viscously tugged at her blouse, causing one button to pop off and another to strain. She reached into her bra then to pull a breast out of the opening in the shirt. "You know I don't need your Jiminy Cricket guilt trips, so just save it." The vulgarity of her shaking the breast by her nipple satisfied her frustration. Her eyes were focused on Mr. Jenkins as she haphazardly returned it to the cup of her bra after another moment, but the floating lights intensified. "I'm in love with a crazy person! This is what I get. Jesus hates me! Don't say a word, Maggie Cunts...I know what you are about to say." Belinda closed her eyes tightly in an attempt to dim sparkling illuminations that shined all the brighter, the angrier she became.

Mr. Jenkins was utterly appalled. He grabbed at his heart while inhaling deep breaths and suddenly there was an intense pain in his ear.

Rather than become preachy, Maggie attempted to calm

her lost soul with promises of trust and her ability to keep secrets.

Mr. Jenkins scowled at Maggie and shook his head. "Oh no. I won't stand for this insanity. You need your pills. I'm going to get Mr. Lynn." He grabbed his glasses from the floor and stood up to leave.

Belinda stepped aside as the body of her boyfriend pushed past her. She rubbed at her eyes, but it only rekindled the dancing embers obstructing her vision. The shell that walked away from her was void of the man she loved as he stomped away with his bowed legs.

Maggie unexpectedly shouted, "The world needs more people who will listen! Sometimes you just need to listen, Mr. Jenkins! What happened to free fish?" Then she went quiet again. Mr. Jenkins looked over his shoulder to his friend. He wanted to return to her, but the situation was too much for him to handle.

The open Bible made Belinda uneasy, so she closed the book and then pushed it onto the seat Mr. Jenkins had left open. After taking a seat, she nervously bit at the inside of her cheek and shook her leg up and down, which vibrated particles of salt on the table. "I'm not crazy; I'm just horny and I know sex. Ya know what I mean? I can smell it, and

I smelled it the other night when Mr. Squeaky Clean Buck Lynn walked out of Ignacio's room. Yep, you fucking heard me...Buck and Ignacio." She canted her head to the side to emphasize the names, then flipped her golden locks behind her back. "What you got to say about that, church lady?" she yelled as she rubbed her eyes. Then she threw her hands in the air like she was giving up on being mad, giving up on Samuel, and submitting to relinquishing the information that was weighing her down.

Maggie wanted to touch her cross necklace to rub at its golden texture, but it was missing, and instead was settling rather nicely at the bottom of her stomach.

Belinda yelled, "Jesus Christ, you ate it, didn't you? Your necklace! Your favorite necklace." She gestured in the general area of where it should have hung.

Maggie's voice was small, as usual, and extremely distant. "I guess I did. If your sin is that you are...the way you are all the time, mine is that I am hungry all of the time."

Within the kitchen came a loud crash from a stack of pans that toppled over. Everyone looked to the commotion and a few patients set their silverware down to clap.

Belinda returned her head to the table and shrugged.

"Whatever helps you sleep at night. Call it hunger if you want to, but you swallow nasty shit out of guilt. You are guilty about everything, for fuck's sake!"

As the clapping died, the servers began to talk about who'd knocked over the pans. They were nudging each other and laughing as they continued to serve food to patients and other staff members. It was as typical as any other facility that served food – except it wasn't. Maggie, offended with the cursing and accusations, filled her thoughts with a healthy dose of reality. "And you sleep around to fill a void of self-love!" It was a guilty pleasure to express that in such a damning way, as it was not Christian-like to cast judgment. However, it made perfect sense.

Belinda, compelled to push back on the edge of the table, was shocked. She felt she needed to brace herself from the imaginary blast of hate. She looked around and was comforted to see that no one in the lunch room had heard or cared. They were focused on the pans, the servers, and their own private conversations. The truth of it made Belinda unexpectedly laugh out loud as she slapped the table with one hand and wrapped her other arm around her stomach. Maggie did what she could to stifle her embarrassment.

After catching her breath, Belinda said, "Shit. We have

it all figured out, don't we? Guess we don't need to be in a loony bin anymore." She acted like she was speaking to the owner of the facility then: "Uh, Mr. Reed, we don't need to be here anymore because we just realized that we are self-loathing women...I for one use sucking dick to fill a void, and she eats weird shit in lieu of dealing with her guilt. It's all oral. Are there pills for that?" She giggled just a little too hard at her own joke.

Without understanding, the only thing Maggie could do was remain quiet. Belinda laughed harder because they were having a moment together for the first time, but mostly because she thought Maggie was such a dumb bitch.

***

Walking briskly, just the best he could with his bowed legs, Mr. Jenkins thought about the young blonde woman who had been harassing and stalking him. The hallways at Northern Lights were long with French-tiled floors, but the Reeds had taken the time to lay beautiful carpet runners for noise reduction when they'd transformed the mansion into an institution. The calmness of it helped. Although angry over the abuse he'd taken from Belinda, Mr. Jenkins looked down as he walked over its plush weave to appreciate the patterned design as it moved under his feet. It seemed to take his mind off Belinda. The thought of sleeping with a woman other than his beloved wife, even though she'd run off with some white guy from Tulsa, was repulsive – especially Ms. Beckler, who disgusted him with her loose history. What made the situation worse was his inability to recall anything about her other than a flash memory of her nipples and his penis nestled between them. He asked Jesus to forgive him in so many of his nightly prayers, but thanks to his alter's relationship, this was the violating memory he had of a woman he barely knew.

With a fast and angry pace, he felt the carpet pattern and colors blend together as his vision began to blur. As he headed to the far corner of Northern Lights, a familiar chain of events began to happen that he desperately wanted to stop.

He pressed at his ear with the palm of his hand. "No. No. Stay back," he said as he walked faster to get to Mr. Lynn. His head hung low as he stomped forward like a horse-worn gunslinger disheveled from the desert sun. "Devil. I rebuke you." He shook his head to refocus and tried hard to stand proud and straight. While blinking frantically, Mr. Jenkins reached out in front of him to steady his wobbling legs. Shooting points of light floated around the hallway like angry summer lightning bugs. A burning sensation warmed the insides of his ears then, which muffled Ute Schmidt's voice asking if he was okay. "In the name of Jesus…" he began, but he never finished.

An edgy voice mumbled back, "Jesus ain't got nothing to do with this."

Mr. Jenkins turned the corner, looking up to another hall that looked the same as the one he'd just traveled. At the end of it was a modern double glass door that was monitored and locked by an electronic security system. It was out of place for the architecture and period style mansion, but had been custom-ordered by Mr. and Mrs. Reed. Beyond that was a locked second door with a simple key entry, the door marked 'Clinical Staff Only'. Mr. Jenkins called out for someone to help him as he fought back the urge to sleep. He was angry about something. He tried to remember what it was as he pushed forward, his feet heavy and tired.

The elderly plump German woman with euphoria giggled as she ran down the hall, whipping past him toward the secured glass in an effort to help him seek aid. She banged on the glass and pushed the emergency button nearby while laughing and looking back down the hall to Mr. Jenkins, who was trying to steady himself. Ute shouted for help through laughter and a thick German accent, but Mr. Jenkins's world was fading away while his alter intrusively pushed his way in.

"We have to work together, motherfucker. Don't you get it?" Samuel's voice was piercing and stern as it pushed its way up and out of Mr. Jenkins's vocal cords. "Your harlot ex-wife is off sucking white dick in buffalo country. She ruined your life, nigga, but we got our own white pussy now, man, so it's all good!"

Ute, witnessing this self-conversation from just 30 feet away, laughed harder and prepped herself to take a seat because she was utterly out of breath. "Someone is coming! Whooo, und zey sink I'm crazy." She gave an unseen, dismissive wave to the black man talking to himself down the hall before she crossed her arms over her huge sagging breasts and slid down the door to sit on the floor against the glass barrier.

"Don't do this to me, Samuel. I'm a God-fearing man. Leave me alone. Quit using my body for foul acts," Mr. Jenkins pleaded and slapped at his head.

"Quit being a bitch!" Samuel growled just before a Hispanic person jumped out of an intersecting hallway to block his path.

"Who's the bitch now?" Ignacio yelled as he swung his fist, which was aimed at Samuel's cheek. It contacted his left ear instead, causing him to swirl and lose balance with an instant ringing in his head. He bent awkwardly sideways as he fell to the floor.

Ute, in as much shock as Mr. Jenkins, lifted her hands in the air as if she was a fan in a baseball stadium witnessing the World Series. She never got up from her seated position, though, as she was too old for such reflexes anyway. Instead, she wrapped her arms around her belly and let herself tilt onto the floor in hysterics.

Samuel seemed to disperse with the blow. What was left was a bewildered sixty-two-year-old, bow-legged man with a bleeding ear who was lying near the baseboards of the clinical wing. Ignacio backed down the adjoining hallway with a sway in his hips. As he ran his fingers through his hair, he gave a warning in a voice that was much higher than his own, "Leave my fucking son alone, pinche!"

Ute was confused, and didn't make a sound of response for the first time in her life.

Mr. Jenkins closed his eyes and prayed through the pain of his throbbing ear. For a split second, he wanted Samuel to come back so that he could deal with this; after all, he was the stronger personality. Sometimes, he thought his alter was someone he wished he could be. Then an image of Belinda's breasts flashed across his eyes. This revolting picture reminded him that he and his alternate personality would always be two different people.

BUSINESS

Mrs. Jill Reed's office, filled with books and antiques, had a cozy feel and was decorated intentionally to seem inviting for potential clients. Every move she'd made over the past eleven years, while running Northern Lights, had been made from a business and marketing perspective. She genuinely cared about the clients, too, if not to the extent she presented – and there were concrete reasons for her strategies. She knew that personal investment in client history was not her job. Her job was to provide optimal care in a premium facility – the first of its kind. It was easier and much more efficient to hide behind the walls of being a businesswoman. Additionally, the mental health issues that plagued her own family history would interfere with the goals of the Northern Lights mission, to provide alternative therapies for optimal living. She couldn't risk bonding with anyone involved, for fear it would derail the entire operation. And so, her logical brain usually concerned itself with the financial aspects of running the business and nothing more.

Jack, her husband, just wanted to run a successful vineyard. This was how he pushed their history with mental illness out of his daily life. To be honest, he didn't care how it was taken care of, so he let his business-savvy wife hold the reins on the numbers as long as he could get his hands dirty, profit from the enterprise, and forget.

They hadn't exactly set out to run a business this way, but the couple was hardened by the fact that they had to be, and because some of their clientele were bull-shitters. Point blank. Anxiety, obsessive compulsive disorders, and depression were merely secondary diagnoses in a long list for most of their long-term patients. The others just wanted to stay in the mansion and vent about a recent divorce, but this paid bills. The Reeds justified their strict financial policies and liberal methods of therapy as ways to scam the scammers. Unfortunately, within their facility, there were a dozen or so seriously ill patients with disorders ranging from Anorexia to Psychosis. Some of them had been to the restricted far corner otherwise known as the clinical wing – the wing that everyone knew of but conveniently forgot existed. Regardless, none of these people were criminally insane or a danger to others...if they were contained and undergoing treatment. Samuel was the first aggressive patient who'd spent time there.

For years, the biggest asset to Northern Lights had been

the Schmidt twins, sponsored by the German government in exchange for surveillance footage and notes on their rare disorder. Never mind how strange and fishy the whole situation was; Jack and Jill Reed were getting paid to house two very hard workers. By managing their disorder, the couple was getting paid for free labor. Only in recent years had the twins slowed down – with the help of age and very strong pills. The monetary value in the twins living at the facility was in the fact that their stay was paying most of the bills.

Another paycheck for the Reeds was Mr. Jenkins. He was funded by a large inheritance that he could have lived quite well with, had he remained a Christian hometown hero and nothing more. His daughter, Gloria, had set up automatic payments that Jill dumped directly into the employee payroll. His alter, Samuel, would have been angry to find out that his host was essentially paying the bills of the head nurse who frequently prevented him from sexual encounters with his girlfriend.

Some other patients at Northern Lights were funded in multiple ways, as was the case of Mr. Cheyez. A portion was paid for by the state, but the majority came through a private research group. Keeping up with all of it would normally have required an accountant, but since some paperwork was under the table, Jill was forced to do it alone. To stay on top of things, Jill tried to review and rotate her way through files on a regular basis. And this week, while going over the long list of patients and their financials, Jill had realized that one client's time was coming to an unexpected end. Jill reviewed her meticulous notes. After pulling the appropriate file, Mrs. Reed called for a meeting with the patient, in the office, to discuss her tenure.

The patient was noticeably uncomfortable, the minute she walked into Jill's office. She scrunched down a little into the chair at the opposite side of Mrs. Reed's desk and sat – just waiting for Jill to speak first.

Jill pulled out a notepad and a very fine pen. "Hi. Let's begin, shall we? Please state your name so I may document the meeting." She smiled and glanced at the name on a file next to the notepad.

"Maggie Koontz."

Mrs. Reed removed the file from her desk and returned it to a drawer. Then she pulled Maggie Koontz's file out and flipped through some tabbed pages to catch up with her recent history. She glanced behind her desk to a beautiful wooden clock and annotated her name, the date, and the time on the paper. "Hi, Mrs. Koontz. How has your treatment been here with us?" Mrs. Reed forced her own face and posture to appear concerned and attentive as she held her pen ready over the notepad.

Maggie answered, "I love doing God's work here. Has my husband called?" She pulled her arms in close to her body and rubbed at the hairs on her petite forearm.

Mrs. Reed jotted a note on the paper and then smoothed her white hair back, pushing it to the back of her shoulder. Just as she was about to speak, though, the automatic, wall-mounted deodorizer sprayed a soothing lavender scent into the air – but neither woman could smell it right away. They were inhaling the scent of strawberries from a client who was no longer present. "I regret to tell you that your uncle has…" Jill immediately corrected her words. She glanced at the name on her notepad. "Mrs. Koontz, your time here at Northern Lights has expired." She watched for a reaction to this news, and then wrote on the notepad to hide her own embarrassment. It was difficult to keep the patients' files separate especially with her limited interactions. Their stories blurred together, and it was all the same to Jill, but she tried and sometimes she failed.

Maggie disregarded the error and mumbled under her breath, "I'm not cured." Her gaze cast upward to a heaven she couldn't see.

Mrs. Reed tried to sound sympathetic as she refrained from smiling at her innocence or dabbing at her sweaty upper lip. "We don't cure disorders here. We teach you tools to cope with or help you suppress...depending on the issue..."

The antique clock behind her desk chimed at the top of the hour. Jill's face immediately softened. Realizing that she was already losing her client's attention, she stopped and re-stated, "We can't cure you here, Maggie. We just teach you how to live better. Do you understand? Our goal here is to allow clients to live normal lives." The lavender scent finally made its way from above the door to her nose. Jill sat back in her leather desk chair and crossed her arms, and then after rethinking her body language, uncrossed her arms and sat forward. The leather made stretching noises as she moved. "I have already made arrangements with another practitioner for your continued care – I mean, your remaining care." She dabbed at her lip with a finger while avoiding eye contact, and then wrote more notes.

Maggie's tone was insecure and childlike. She blinked profusely. "God told me to come *here*," she begged with more volume in her voice.

Jill remained professional as she ended her written sentence with a period and then looked up from the page.

"I'm not leaving." Maggie was firm.

"Excuse me?" Jill's eyebrows scrunched together as her chin tucked into her neck.

While a nagging heat burned her ears, Maggie's posture changed into a stance that wasn't typical of her character. "I don't think you'd get to keep your license if someone knew there was a gun floating around this place, or that an employee was having sex with a mental patient."

Jill's eyes widened as far as they would go initially, and then retracted to a squinted position, visually calling her bullshit statement a bluff. Part of her had to wonder if Maggie Koontz was making this stuff up in an attempt to stay institutionalized, but she certainly didn't *need* to do that. Jill was calm as she spoke, but there was an obvious undertone of sarcasm that poor Maggie didn't pick up on. "That's a safety issue, Mrs. Koontz. If you know who has a gun, you should let someone know." Her mascara-heavy lashes flicked open and closed with false concern. She picked up the pen and added more sentences to the growing list of notes, ending it with several exclamation points.

The insecure, frail woman who everyone knew so well resumed speaking. "I know, and I feel guilty about that, but I need to stay here." She produced a bullet that she'd saved before turning the rest of them over to Samuel. She knew it had been him in the vineyard and not her Christian friend because Mr. Jenkins would never, ever in a million years have been comfortable handling a gun in any capacity. She had difficulties learning, but she was not stupid.

Jill watched the bullet being rolled back and forth in Maggie's hand, and then sat forward in her chair, resting her elbows on the top of her desk and folding her hands under her chin. "Are you telling me that someone has a weapon in my facility?"

"Yes. And I am telling you that your prized staff member is sleeping with a patient." Maggie was confident now, and yet, awkwardly...not.

"Have you witnessed this?"

"Well, no, but Belinda told..."

"Belinda Beckler? Are you kidd..." Jill giggled, cleared her throat, and then wrote more notes. When she finished, she said, "Listen, I don't follow rumors." She caressed her white hair around her ear even though there was no good reason to do so, and then she held out her hand to suggest that Maggie relinquish the bullet.

Maggie didn't move; rather, she said, "Lives are at stake.

Can you live with that?"

"If you don't tell me who has this hearsay weapon, I could have you arrested for obstruction of justice if one is found via random search." Her hand was still extended to receive the bullet.

Maggie could tell she should be offended or scared. "I'm not sure what that means, but you are probably right, and that's why I've been taking paperwork out of this office and mailing it to my husband I don't know what the German government has to do with this place or why it's full of German doctors and hidden cameras, but I believe it's a reason to shut you down. Jesus told me where to look."

Jill caught herself from choking on her own tongue by swallowing as hard as she could without showing discomfort or concern. There were many things she could have said to get herself out of this, if she'd been sure that what Maggie said wasn't true, but Maggie knew too many details! She wondered how Maggie had gotten into the office, when she'd done it, and what she'd originally been there for...and how the hell had she opened the lock box with the Schmidt twins' file in it? There was a feeling of violation and vulnerability that swept over Jill as she stared at the woman before her. Jill accidently looked back at the clock twice then. The lavender deodorizer automatically sprayed into the air again. The sound of it, like someone was opening a fresh bottle of Coke, hissed suddenly through the silence.

Jill's face burned red with anger. She was getting physically hot with the tension this whole situation was creating and just wanted to snap into a full-blown, red-headed temper tantrum. She was tired of navigating around difficult personalities and faking her way through conversations. All she'd ever wanted was to run a successful business with Jack – not this. Not to run a mansion full of insane characters. She looked behind her again. The clock was still in place; it was comforting and sad at the same time. Jill was the first to speak and look away as she tapped at her white hair and then tugged at the bottom of her jacket. "Well, I'm sure we can work something out." Jill bit at her lip to keep it from quivering.

Maggie swallowed the bullet.

Unable to remain professional after the bullet disappeared down Maggie's throat, Jill lifted the filter on her words. Her heart hurt, and the pain in her soul re-animated. "I gave birth to this place! You will not destroy it."

The beautiful antique door that Jill had purchased a few years earlier was heavy with iron handles and intricate iron designs affixed on either side. It was so heavy that it took a while for the door to completely close on its own, leaving Jill alone in the office. After hearing the metallic click of the locking mechanism, she allowed tears to pour all over the exclamation points on the notepad. In anger, she swiped the file with Maggie's name on it off her desk to the floor.

TWO SIDES OF BEING

"We can't keep doing this, Buck. It's wrong on so many levels," Ignacio said as he looked into Buck's beautiful brown eyes while lying on his twin bed in a tender embrace.

Buck's voice was deep and smooth, but his southern accent was accompanied by a sing-song feminine sweetness that exposed his orientation no matter how professional he tried to be. "Are you telling me or asking me to stop?" He gently traced his finger down the bridge of Ignacio's nose.

"I mean it. We're going to make a mistake and get caught. I don't want you to lose your job. You know? And every time you leave, I feel this horrible guilt about what we are doing... like it's wrong." Ignacio wished Buck would just admit that he knew the struggle and understood, because they had talked about it so many times before. But Buck simply sighed as if this conversation wasn't important enough to bother over, and it hurt Ignacio's feelings.

Buck felt his disappointment, of course, but there wasn't much more to say. They'd had this conversation a million times before, and yet it didn't matter how he expressed himself; they would still have the same conversation again and again because Ignacio was scared of his new-found sexuality and seriously confused. Buck knew it was something he would have to work out on his own, just as every other gay person had had to do before him. He wished he could help Ignacio through it, but the fact was that understanding one's sexuality had to come from within. "What do you want me to do about it? I can't help who I fall in love with."

"Well, once I get out of here, we can start a relationship – a real one, without you risking your job." Ignacio was hopeful, and truly meant it.

"Yep."

"Yep? Pendejo, that's it?" Ignacio was hurt by the distant and quick response, and pushed the other man's chest away with the palms of both his hands.

"Whatever you say." Buck smiled lovingly.

Ignacio pushed at Buck's chest again in a passive-aggressive tease. No matter how comfortable he felt being with him or how much loved the experienced, there was always an uneasy, sickening sensation that infiltrated moments like this. At times, when they kissed, he wanted to turn away, shameful about feeling a positive bodily reaction – even if it was a sensation as wonderful as butterflies in his stomach. He felt like loving Buck was a constant battle. "I'm not gay, man." Ignacio flicked his toes up and down on Buck's shins then, gently tickling his skin with subconscious motions. His eyes disconnected from Buck's and looked down into the space between them; a black hole that was created by the blanket covering both their nude bodies.

"So you have said." Buck pushed back the hair around Ignacio's forehead and gently kissed it. "You will figure it all out and, when you do, I'll be here for you."

"You are patient, and so good to me. I love you."

"I love you," Buck replied. "But I have to get my black ass up and do some work." He flipped open the covers, exposing their naked bodies to the room temperature as he giggled.

Ignacio tensed as a chill caught him off-guard, pulling his testicles closer to his body. "Pendejo!" He grabbed the extra pillow and threw it at Buck's back while he bent over to pull up his pants. Buck giggled again when it puffed against his cheeks and crumpled to the floor.

After saying their goodbyes and kissing at the door like they were sending each other off to war, Buck whisked himself out of the room like it was an old habit. Ignacio was once again left to wallow in his own silence as he put on the shorts that were still scented with foreplay from the true love of his life. A smile smoothed over his face, pushing out his cheeks and dimples. The smell of sex lingered in the air, as did the smell of sweat under his armpits. He grabbed his towel from a mounted rack, slipped his feet into cheap flip-flops provided by Northern Lights, and walked down to the community shower room at three in the morning to wash away the tangible guilt of sleeping with a man.

On his way down the hall, though, he heard a noise from the door to the female bathroom. His eyes immediately scanned the door as he passed, but he saw nothing and continued onward. He wouldn't have given it another thought, had Belinda stayed hidden for just a few seconds longer. Instead, though, she cracked the door open again, exposing blonde hair and one bright blue eye peering out from within. Ignacio, in mid-step forward, stopped and took steps backward to see deeper inside.

"You stalking me? I told you that we are not having sex again…"

"Fuck you, Ignacio, I don't stalk people. I was masturbating."

"Now that, I believe." His smile pushed his dimples to the surfaces of his cheeks.

She whispered, "What were you doing?" She opened the door enough for Ignacio to see that she had on a tight white t-shirt with screen printed words that were fading and peeling from too many washes, and that she wore no underwear. The pubic hair couldn't hide the skin beneath it, which was red from recent rubbing. Her masturbation story was most likely true. There was something vulgar and sexy about that. His head and body battled with the conflict of being in love with a man when he wasn't gay and finding Belinda's raw skin a disgusting turn-on.

"You and Buck just had sex, didn't you?" She already smelled their shared orgasm on his body and honestly didn't need him to verify it with words. "Come in the bathroom. I won't beg you for sex, I promise – just let me smell it," she tried to whisper.

On a subconscious level, Ignacio pinched at the towel that was wrapped around his waist. He wanted to be straight again, but Buck had flipped his world upside down and made it difficult for him to ever be the same. Maybe falling in love with a man had fulfilled something he had never experienced before with women. Even his feelings for Lydia were clearly not worthy of the label he had given them and by now he was beginning to suspect her story of a pregnancy was a lie. Buck would never lie to him. It took time to discover his inevitable physical attraction to the man which had manifested but it was real, and he knew it. The moment he'd found himself looking at Buck in a sexual way, however, he' realized that it was already too late...he was in love. This three-month battle with homosexuality has raged inside of him ever since because admitting this was too difficult. It was easier to be straight.

However, Belinda had a sick sense for the desires of others and, by asking her strange question, she'd made it seem like she was reading his thoughts. Her validation was his eyes that fixated on her pubic hair. There was a comfort and a familiarity in her body, so he aspired to have it again despite his emotional connection with Buck. It was a sign of a sad, repressed longing inside him as he stared at her, which changed the expression on his face from being satisfied on into a worried desire. It wasn't about Buck and Belinda, per se – it was confusion over whether he wanted men or women.

Belinda picked up on the unwavering perplexity running through his head. "Step in and let me help you figure things out. I just want to smell it, for fuck's sake. No harm, no foul."

For some reason, he stared still at her nude bottom half. "Did you...ya know?" Ignacio couldn't take his eyes off it for some reason, and was embarrassed that he'd even asked the question.

"Yes; all over, when he left your room. I've been watching your door for weeks."

Ignacio pushed himself into the women's bathroom after assuring himself that the cameras were aimed in the opposite direction. He wasn't necessarily surprised that Belinda had been voyeuristic. Once the door closed behind him, he thought nothing of dropping his towel, exposing himself to Belinda. There was a strange respect for each other's inner turmoil as they swayed together, she breathing him in with her arms wrapped around his thighs while he stroked her beautiful blonde hair with closed eyes. Together, they inhaled and exhaled with long and deep breaths that were calming in their simplicity.

It was as if he wasn't himself at all because he was so involved in his current actions that he almost forgot about the person he loved. The familiar feel of a woman's body was comforting. They eventually walked together into the shower area, where he helped her lay on the cold tiled floor, away from the drain cover.

Once she was as comfortable as could be, he knelt next to her and rolled himself onto the floor, gracefully scooting his body next to hers. Ignacio nestled his face close to her body. He moved back and forth through the hair to release more of her scent. As promised, she didn't beg him for sex. Belinda whispered to him, but it seemed loud in the acoustics of the shower room. "Tell me you are gay. I want you to say it."

Ignacio maintained his silence as he inhaled. He refused to admit anything by holding a neutral silence while his brain swirled in a battle of love verses sexual attraction. He repeated to himself that he was not gay as he visualized giving Buck head while Belinda nudged herself eagerly at his lips.

"Tell me who you are," she whispered again.

Ignacio, who'd enjoyed the connection without sexuality, was beginning to seethe with frustration over the tornado of emotions in his mind. Why was she doing this? Why couldn't he leave? His torment was deconstructing his mental stability one piece at a time. What he truly wanted was to once again enjoy the company of a woman, but the orderly was a new craving that pushed at his moral fiber.

Together, their inhales became wilder and stronger. He wanted to push away before things got out of hand, but instead he pulled her hips closer. Although he was guilt-ridden with images of his love flashing under his eyelids, a part of him wanted to please Belinda in every sense of the word.

Yet, how could he miss Buck so much that his heart felt twisted and heavy, when he thought he'd desired women since he was fourteen? Homosexuality verses heterosexuality...too complex to analyze when there was an aroused woman rolling her body over his face. He tried to stop himself from giving in and just breathe, but even that was twisted.

Belinda questioned him again. "Who are you?"

Ignacio thought of Buck. A guilt tugged at his heart as arousal swelled in his groin. His eyes fluttered as he batted away dancing colors of light. Belinda licked at his sensitive skin and he submitted to her kisses while distracted by his inner conflict. The pitch of his voice ascended with every moan. He was breaking on so many levels.

While his mind and body were at war with each other, a stress washed over him like he had never felt before. His heartbeat almost became too much to withstand while he labored to breathe through the rolling of her hips above his face. His ears burned as the floating lights brightened. There was a sensation of drowning, and panic which at first felt like he just needed to lift her off his nose, but this inability to breathe couldn't be relieved. It didn't come from the physical scenario he'd put himself in. It was a manifestation of an inner, repressed hurricane. The physical reaction that grew from the oncoming storm was a sick hyperventilation that pumped blood to his genitals in an uncomfortably perverted rhythm.

Then there was a sensation of something sinking in his center. Was it guilty thoughts or tormented ideas of homosexuality? A tingling itched and pinched at his nipples then as he arched his back to get comfortable. The arching of his back led to a rolling of his hips, though, and the desire for the penetration he was able to get with Buck. Ignacio gave in to pushing Belinda's hips upward, so he could shake the panic from his body. But he was experiencing the beginning of an orgasm that wasn't his alone, and his moans began to sound soprano in the echoing of the room.

Ignacio was fading into the truth of his insanity and sexuality.

Juana's personality seeped and pushed out of the body she was hiding within. Belinda repeated a demand that Ignacio was unable to hear because Juana was the one who was listening. "Tell me what a dyke you are," Belinda said. This made Juana's delicate toes curl and burn as she finally released with orgasm. It was a beautiful thing to finally be out of Ignacio's mind and into his skin.

WORDS AMONG MEN

Mr. Reed sat to watch the sun set, relaxing with his head nurse on a small bench at the end of grape row 6B. Jack found that naming conventions helped identify where the grapes were with regard to ripeness, not to mention keeping him on track with where the hell he was when he became disoriented, working all day, in the middle of his precious vineyard. It was cold enough to see breath in the air when the two men exhaled – the perfect temperature and time of year for harvesting ice wine.

Jack had never been one to sit and chat with the staff, but Buck had been visibly upset when he'd requested the conversation – and there was that special something in Buck that tugged at Jack's heartstrings. To be honest, Jack felt genuine curiosity over the stresses of this man with visibly welling tears in his eyes. Jack had to find out what the issue was – not to be nosey, but because he sincerely cared about Buck. It seemed that now was a perfect time, while they shivered on an antique wooden bench with Jack's boney butt pinching under him, cold be damned. The colorful dawn sky slowly faded to black as Buck spoke.

"Been this skinny your whole life, Mr. Reed?" Buck looked him up and down with a smile on his face as he watched his boss squirm more than a few times to get comfortable, and rubbed at his elbow that had accidently knocked at the back of the bench. Jack's Northern Lights employee coat, with his embroidered name on the left breast under the logo, couldn't hide his pencil-thin frame or the abnormally large bulge in his right pocket.

Jack knew that Buck was trying to find a way to open the conversation so that he could vent his frustrations. Usually, Buck was a bold man, very comfortable about telling folks which way was up, but as of late he had been having trouble finding his words. Jack guessed this change in personality was the result of whatever he was trying to get off his chest. He looked to his employee, a very strong man, as he pulled two mason jars nearly full of whiskey out of his employee coat. He offered one of the jars to Buck, who unscrewed the lid sipped at the rim, leaving some kind of chapstick grease on the threaded, curved edge of the glass. They drank while they chatted.

Jack entertained the silly question Buck had asked by confirming that he'd always been a tall, lean kid and that he'd passed it on to his children, who'd gotten their physiques from him along with their mother's red hair. He felt compelled to wink after the comment. After a long pause and a shared smile, he went on to say that his height and mad skills should have gotten him a spot in the National Basketball Association, even though he knew that his employee wouldn't believe him.

Buck laughed at the thought of Mr. Reed's wiry frame shooting a basketball from half-court. They raised their jars in a toast to the NBA, but the truth of it was that Mr. Reed's skills in the game actually could have put him there if he hadn't been unreasonably concerned with his asthma. Moving on from the awkward starter question, though, Mr. Reed told Buck to just spill the beans, his welcoming and open disposition shining through the awkwardness. He told Buck that he had his undivided attention, and obvious privacy, which was the absolute truth – however, in the back of his mind, Jack knew that he was on an early schedule in the morning. If his employee needed a gentle nudge to open the platform into a serious conversation, he was more than willing to provide it, as long as he rested before harvesting rows 8D through 13A and review security footage.

Buck, beginning to feel the chill in his bones, pulled the

hood of his jacket up over his head to protect his neck and ears. It was also a good way to literally tuck himself away into the guilt over what he was about to say. He placed his lip over the same greasy spot on the rim of the jar and let the liquid burn as he swallowed. Buck a man of great strength felt vulnerable and small. After he took another swig he tugged at the hood to reset himself within. He took a deep breath in preparation, and finally told Mr. Reed that he was sleeping with a patient in Northern Lights, but then he refused to say which one when Jack asked.

Jack, clearly aware of the tumultuous relationship between Samuel and Belinda, hoped it wasn't her. He couldn't imagine Buck switching his sexual preference for her – nor did he want to; however, stranger things had happened at Northern Lights. He made a note to watch more security videos later, to try and discover the identity of Buck's lover out of curiosity.

"Buck, this is a mental facility. These people are sick in the head, buddy. You can't get involved with them!" He set his empty jar down next to the foot of the bench.

Although Jack had no room to be judgmental, he next explained to his employee that he had to end it – otherwise, he and Jill would be obligated to fire him; although, at this point, he could technically have done it immediately. Buck completely understood. By the end of the talk and by the time they had a second empty jar, Jack and Buck were drunk and the sky was dark enough to call it night. Each man felt content and happy with the way their conversation was going and how well they were getting along. It was almost disappointing to know that it was coming to an end.

Alas, Jack thought again of the grapes that wouldn't pick themselves. "All right, buddy, it's been fun, but let's go in. You better sleep it off in the staff room before the wife finds out about this. When you are ready, you can tell me who it is. I like gossip, too, even though I don't admit it to everyone." Jack patted Buck's back before standing up to stretch his Ichabod Crane body. The material in his jacket made all kinds of crunching noises as his arms lifted to the heavens, pulling the bottom of it up above the waist of his cargo pants. When he was done stretching, he bent down to reach for the empty mason jars. But the second he applied enough pressure to get a decent grasp on the glass, which was cold to the touch, Buck said the name that made him loose his grip. The corner of the jar connected with the bench in just the right way, breaking it into five fairly large chunks. The tin lid rolled aside and lodged itself in the cracks of the boards below where Buck sat.

"You are fucking who? Ignacio Cheyez? Out of all the people in this place, you chose him? You know he's the craziest one in this facility! Well, I shouldn't say that...um, his alternate personality is very complex. Juana is his mother, you know? She tried to kill his family!" Jack tried to refrain from shouting, but the emphasis in his voice pushed the volume to an uncontrollable level. Realizing that it was unnecessary to use that scolding tone with his favorite employee, he paused uncomfortably to choose better words and a better tone. It only took a second for Jack to change his breathing and demeanor. "Buddy, her personality is volatile." He pulled his coat jacket down over his hand and wiped the chunks of glass into the nearly frozen grass beneath the bench. He shivered when the cold sensation permeated his cargo pants after reseating himself.

As if the shock of this information wasn't enough, Jack dared to interject, "Wait, I thought you were gay?"

Buck's booming base voice lended itself into a sweet southern accent that was fluttery and feminine. "Yes, honey, I am. I think." He tilted his head down and away with guilt at first, and then he looked to Jack, whose mind was completely blown. A strangely random wind picked up for a brief moment and pushed at his hood, exposing his beautifully fearful eyes. He didn't necessarily see Mr. Reed as his boss, but as a better father figure than his own biological dad who'd left his mother for a white woman and never looked back.

And the last thing Jack wanted to do was disappoint him, as a man or as the favored staff member.

Jack ran his bony fingers over his own face again and again, caressing his nose, cheeks, and mouth. In college, he'd learned from a body language class that this subconscious sign meant that you want to say something, or you are holding something back. Both were true as he tried to unscramble drunken thoughts from the very deep information in his head. While rummaging his hand repeatedly over the lower half of his face, he offered, "But he has split – into her." Between curses, he looked at Buck to confirm the validity of his confession. "Holy cow! You. I can't believe...Well, which one are you fucking? How did this happen?"

Buck admitted that he didn't know how it had happened exactly, but he attributed the beginning of it to when his half-sister had left the receptionist position because she'd gotten caught with Ignacio in the smoking room. As he continued talking about the incident, Jack heard Buck's voice tremble with increasing difficulties over catching his breath. A man of his strength, not just physically, didn't get rattled easily; Jack needed to console him. "Listen, I know you didn't want us to fire your sister for that, but two other patients saw them together. We had to." He stared at Buck's face, which was beginning to blend into the darkening night sky.

Buck sniffed. "I've been working here for years, Jack, and I have experienced lots of things with DID patients. I believe I have a general understanding of the disorder...but Ignacio is different. When I look at Ignacio, I see Juana, too, and to make things worse, I think I am in love with him – or her." His eyes blinked slowly with a drunken heaviness. "Don't you see their alters sometimes? Actually *see* them?"

Jack crossed his arms in front of his chest like he was contemplating life, but he understood exactly what Buck was saying. Jack's own thoughts were swirling and circular, much like his body that swayed and rolled with the lingering effects of the whiskey. He slumped hard into the back of the bench and shook his head. "Buddy, this shit is crazy. I am having a difficult time wrapping my brain around this, to be honest. Lemme...Let me get this clear. You are a gay man, fucking a man who thinks he is a woman? And not in a...a transgender person kind of way, but in a split personality psychosis kind of way. Are you in love with her?" He trailed off into thoughts of Belinda, who was in love with Samuel, the alternate personality of Mr. Jenkins and scratched his head.

Buck bobbed his head up and down in the comforts of the re-set hood and looked down to the broken pieces of glass near his feet. His hands and toes were cold, but he was so nervous that he was sweating. The entire underside of the shirt near his armpits was soaked now, which only made his body colder.

"I don't want ya'll to fire me. I'm trying to deal with this the best I can, but it's getting to the point where it's hindering my work and my focus – not to mention, I'm falling in love with a mental patient."

"So...when you guys are intimate...I mean, how does that work?" Jack was genuinely confused, and there was nothing perverse in the question, so far as he meant it.

"Mr. Reed. Come on. I don't want to lose my job! I love it here. Ya'll treat me like family." He pressed his index finger and middle finger into his forehead, causing an unnatural bend. He noticed his lips were dry and licked them with whiskey-flavored saliva.

"We think of you as family, too...Buck." Jack stared at his face, then sniffed back a tickle that began to make his nose itch and his eyes water. Before the wave of emotions took over, he shook his head to refocus. "Well, shit, buddy, you gotta stop fucking the patients!" Jack slapped his knee and laughed, but he knew for a fact that Buck was a true professional and had never ever indulged in any irresponsible activity – not until now. He had seen him break up fights, confiscate and destroy illegal drugs, report the things he was supposed to report, and go out of his way to make sure Northern Lights was a safe place for its patients. He had security tapes to prove Buck Lynn's history, without compromising his morale fiber. He also knew that this was a one-time thing... especially when Buck didn't giggle at the joke. "Sorry. Sorry. This is serious. My apologies, buddy, but you can't blame me for being curious and picking on you about it. This is a doozey of a situation you got here." His jacket shuffled as he shifted to get more comfortable on the bench again. The night air was increasingly becoming colder by the minute, but he couldn't break himself away from his spot. Not wanting to push the issue past the point of no return, Jack tried to say one last thing about it before making Buck so uncomfortable that he would never confide in him again.

"Listen, I won't pry anymore about that stuff, but you have got to end this before it takes a turn for the worse. You can't get involved like this. Just appreciate their alter personalities from afar and call it a day. In the end, these people will never be able to give back completely. They can't return the love you feel for them because they don't exist..." He paused to clear his throat as he turned away from Buck to get his shit together before emotions overwhelmed him again. He certainly did not want to be a skinny old man, blubbering on a bench in a vineyard. His dry cotton mouth, a precursor to tears, almost choked him, but he took a deep breath to curb the welling. "And Ignacio is fading. *She* is taking over; that's why they are here, buddy. They need help, but they also need a place to grow old happily, or the best they can anyway, with their alters. Or in Ignacio's case, as his alter. You want to be happy here... You want them to be happy here, right? Then leave this alone, because you cannot comprehend the pain of the fade."

Tears brimmed at the edge of Jack's lower lids, but he tried to laugh, shaking out the unmanly feelings with nervous and poorly timed bursts of sounds. "This place is like a no-kill shelter for animals if you want to be politically incorrect. It's fucked up to say that, but it's the truth. Jill and I...and the staff here, have difficult jobs taking care of these people." He looked at Buck, who was intently listening to his every word. "It's not easy, Buck, and I get why you feel pressure to share yourself with someone here. But you shouldn't, and you know that." Jack shook his head and let his eyes wander off into the distance. "But you shouldn't. That's why we pay well and have the unconventional environment that we do."

Buck's chin slightly pushed back into his neck in disagreement over this last comment about pay. Jack sat up, then forward, resting his elbows on the edge of his knees. "Eh, don't give me no shit about your pay, buddy." He laughed to shake off the seriousness of the conversation. Not even his favorite employee needed to see his sensitive side. "If you want my advice, end this relationship and we won't tell Jill. If it doesn't go well, we will move Ignacio back into the clinical corner of the mansion."

Buck was surprised that the concern Jack Reed showed with such conviction and passion seemed to be reserved for the facility as a whole, and not the individuals within it. So Buck, never one to back down when it came to patients' rights, had to remind his boss, "Now, ya'll know that is like solitary confinement with perks. I've told you the patients are not happy when they are there. I know I wouldn't want to be trapped in a place like that, no matter how much exercise and alternative therapies my schedule was filled with. I'd come out of there bat shit crazy, I think. That's probably why he was released into general population thinking he was his own damn mom! I mean, ya'll had him in there for years!" In frustration, Buck pulled out his little jar of Carmex from his pants pocket. As he applied the warmed jelly to his cold lips, his heart broke for what he knew he had to do regarding Ignacio. His sighs were deep and heavy, just as it was with the weight of the burden on his chest. He mumbled as he finally owned up to what was really going on by saying it aloud. "I'm in love. Shit."

The depth of Mr. Reed's understanding was indescribable. He missed his son.

Jack finally submitted to his emotional state and showed the intense compassion he felt for Buck. "In our defense, they were volatile when they arrived. Buddy, that boy built a world around him that didn't exist; a whole college, for Christ's sake. A fucking make-believe world where he thinks he admitted himself into an institution! It'd almost be laughable if it wasn't the fucking truth. Do the right thing and end this." A wave of dizziness washed over his body. "I need to go in now before I fall asleep on this bench," he said quietly. "Good night." Jack patted Buck's back again and then rested his hand on his broad shoulder, squeezing it in a sincere, fatherly, and yet distant and respectable, manner even though he wanted to linger. "He can't love you back because he is fading away, and once he is gone, he will be no more." Jack paused and tried to speak again, but it came across quietly, his words hidden beneath drunken mumbles and emotional distress. "The pain of the fade is a nightmare."

Jack couldn't stay any longer. He couldn't. Abruptly, he began to walk toward the mansion before the urge to turn and run back for a hug confused them both. What he needed to do now was have a private moment alone. He turned to walk backward as he shouted, "I'm glad we talked! I'm an open door if you need to talk again, okay, buddy?" His effort to make it seem as if the conversation hadn't disturbed him only proved the opposite.

From the bench, Buck assured him that he would confide in him again if he needed to, and that he would do the right thing by ending the insane relationship he had gotten himself into.

As Jack strolled closer to the back door of the mansion, though, he didn't worry about Buck's decision. He knew that his exemplary employee would always be on the upside of the morale swing. He and Jill had made sure to teach their son, Jason, all that they could about right and wrong before he'd split into his alternate psyche – Buck Lynn. Jack knew first-hand that alternate personalities could not love you in the way you wanted them to because they did not exist... even if they had been around for eleven years. The pain of the fade lasts a lifetime if you let it. He genuinely understood the desperate state Buck was in, to reconnect with someone like himself. Normalcy in life, to build such connections, was all any human desired to be truly happy. But he and Jill could only imagine its depth. Their experience of trying to reconnect with their son had officially begun twelve years earlier, when Jason had faded and left his body, but filled it with a personality they didn't know. Jack Reed walked away, proud of his son, no matter his sexual orientation or the color of his imaginary skin. *Dissociative Identity Disorder*, he thought, *is a mother fucker.*

DIRTY CHANGE

After unsuccessfully trying to have a conversation with Ute and Hilda Schmidt about the state of affairs at Northern Lights, Maggie Koontz was frustrated. They couldn't share her anxieties or console her with concern and understanding. They only offered giggles at her simpleton explanations and laughter when she asked them what 'obstruction of justice' meant. As she passed the receptionist desk, proceeding to the first hall towards her room, the twins, seated in the bay window of the lobby, once again called her 'Kaput Cuntz' amidst unsuccessful attempts to stifle the volume in their voices. In return, Maggie began to understand that she truly had no friends at Northern Lights, and desperately missed her husband – not to mention that she now suffered from the knowledge that her free six-month treatment wasn't curing her guilty eating habits.

Maggie slid her hand discretely into the pocket of her thrift store corduroy pants and pulled out a fifty-cent piece coin that she'd found on the floor near the vending machines. She shifted her eyes to the right and left to ensure that no one in the lobby or the hallway in front of her was looking before she put her hand to her mouth, just as if she were stifling a cough. She slid the coin from between her fingers, placing it flatly onto her tongue as if to take Holy Communion.

A warm, tender hand on her shoulder startled her into swallowing it before she was ready, ruining the moment she'd been about to savor. The round metal wasn't lubricated enough to slide down her esophagus the way it should have, making it feel slow-moving and high up in her throat. Her face scrunched in pain as she tried to swallow hard to push it down.

In her peripheral view, Samuel's dark skin appeared first as he bent around her and then placed himself in her way. He smiled awkwardly, exposing his ill-fitting partials that had unfortunately been bent out of shape during a fight he'd recently been involved in. He tried to strike up conversation pleasantly enough, about biblical verses, and ask when the next Bible study would be, but Maggie knew better.

"I don't know why you think you can trick me."

"I did it once."

"I let that happen. What do you want? I have Thursday group in fifteen minutes and I can't be late again." She

crossed her tiny arms in front of her chest in a defensive posture and looked behind her at the clerk who was in-processing a new client. Exaggerated movements at the bay window
caught her attention then, and she twisted her torso to see Ute
standing behind a bent-over Hilda, pumping her stumpy legs
and hips into her sister's backside. When they were confident
that Maggie was watching, they shifted into another mock
sexual position. Hilda now stood with her hands behind her
head as if she was being arrested. Her huge, sagging breasts
looked surprisingly uplifted from the pose of her arms as her
sister knelt before her and bobbed her head up and down near
Hilda's crotch. Not to be outshined by her more dominant
twin, she made the motion of giving oral by jacking her hand
left and right near her face and pushing her tongue outward
on the inside of her cheek. Maggie was appalled.

When she turned to look at Samuel again, he was smiling
from ear to ear as his eyes traveled up and down her curves in
such a lustful way that you would have thought he was looking at her naked flesh. "Ooo wee, little Magpie, you got some
good Christian titties on you." He leaned into her space, getting as uncomfortably close to her ear as she allowed. "You
ever want to know what a black man tastes like, I may be able
to help you out. Get you a taste of my African seed."

A knot bubbled in her throat with disgust. "You need Jesus."

"Jesus ain't got nothin' to do with this, little mamma." He grabbed his crotch and pulled at a bulge that was stiffening under his hold. He leaned into her space again to look intently into her bright blue eyes. "If you don't want my anaconda to think about sliding between your tight pussy lips, you can tell me where the fuck my girlfriend is." Thinking of her, he closed his eyes and inhaled the smell of strawberry shampoo, and then he backed away to watch the woman before him shift her arms into a tighter, more insecure pose.

His breath smelled like a wet ashtray. The rancid odor made Maggie's eyes scrunch closed as she shook her head to shake it from her nose. Unexplainably, her mouth began to water, but this at least made swallowing the lump in her throat a little easier. "I'm not her babysitter, Samuel. Go ask the twins. They think they know everything. Excuse me." Maggie motioned for him to move so she could pass and go about her business. The corduroy between her legs rubbed together with her first step, though. Samuel quickly sidestepped into her path and slid his hand over the buttons on her shirt, and then filled his palm with her right breast. He gave it a sexually charged squeeze, tugging it lightly enough to pull her petite body forward. She gasped as her eyes broadened, exposing the details of their crystal blue pattern. He glared over her pale face, noticing her flawless skin and then scanning specifically over the natural red hue of her lips, which seemed to mesmerize him more so than the intoxicating fear in her eyes.

A burning sensation immediately pulsed at Maggie's ears as they turned red. Discovering his erection pressed against the side of her hip, she produced enough saliva to feel it tickling down the inside of her cheeks, and she swallowed twice. A vivid image of secret piercings through the tip of his penis and other metallic adornments on his genitals flashed before her, as if she knew for a fact that they were there. The spit uncomfortably pooled under her tongue again as they stood staring at each other for what seemed like a lifetime. Her breast, having never been handled in such a forceful way, was oddly stimulated. Maggie was the first to break eye contact, with a sick feeling in her stomach, and she pulled away from his manhandling grip. "Don't ever touch me like that again!" She placed the back of her hand up to her lips. "I'm going to vomit."

She pushed past him and briskly walked down the hallway to the closest bathroom.

Maggie felt his eyes watching her scurry the entire length of the hallway. The twins laughed while jiggling their boobs up and down and making other obscene gestures.

Within the safety of the bathroom, she experienced a full-blown panic attack while hovering over a toilet to let the drool fall out of her mouth. She cried while dry heaving and prayed for it to end. Eventually, she succumbed to the first stages of exhaustion, which felt like the almighty Lord was truly listening. When she plopped her corduroy-covered butt on the cold tiles and leaned herself onto the seat of a bowl, she was able to catch her breath – intermixed with dealing with the stench from the rim. Habitually, she reached for her necklace, which by now was surely at the bottom of sludge water in some sewer treatment plant and covered in feces. Her ears burned profusely. She moved her hand from her empty neck to her heart as she relaxed her head against the stall partition. Finally, Maggie closed her eyes for a peaceful, private moment.

Trying to achieve sanctuary after being violated, Maggie heard Belinda's loud singing.

Fish don't fry in the kitchen; beans don't burn on the grill.

Took a whole lot of tryin' just to get up that hill...

Fuck, fuck, fuck, well, we're movin' on up, to the east side.

To a dee-luxe apartment in the sky.

Maggie tried to ask her to leave, but Belinda's voice was so loud. More vomit pushed its way up and out onto the floor. At least Belinda wasn't singing anymore. Maggie practically fell asleep over the sink.

Maggie was always eating weird things, and was probably sick from it again. Belinda paid no attention to it and began to brush her teeth. A gold chain from her neck hung wildly as she brushed. Eventually, she spat a wad of foam in the sink as the chain dangled at the edge of the porcelain. "Was Samuel looking for me? We are supposed to rendezvous before group." She hastily tucked the necklace back into her shirt and winked at Maggie in the mirror. "I mean, I know you are like, all Bible all the time and shit, but you are a woman. You know love. You know lust." She winked at Maggie again as if she should know exactly what she was talking about. "That man makes my pussy wet – what can I say?"

The vulgarity of the comment nauseated her.

There was a long moment of silence while Belinda chose her next words. Then she rinsed her toothbrush under water.

"He grabbed your boob, didn't he? Did you like it? I know it made your clit tickle." She laughed at herself. "Oh, for Christ's sake, Magpie! You need to get you some good dick before you go back home to your missionary-vanilla husband. He won't know. I'm certainly not going to tell him." She bent over the sink to rinse out her mouth with water. When she lifted her head, she wiped away moisture from the corners of her lips. "Ugh, I can't get this goddamn taste out of my mouth."

Maggie thought of all the sexual juices that could possibly be rotting between her teeth.

"Don't give me that judgmental look. It's like a metallic, dirty taste. Like nasty-ass change from the bottom of a sweaty, homeless guy's shoe. I don't know how you eat shit like that. I'd rather eat a dick any day." She pulled a red lipstick tube from her pocket and applied it as she leaned in closer to the mirror. When she pulled away from the mirror to rub her lips together, she paused for a moment to think and gently shake her head in approval. Reminiscing, she said, "Or pussy. I'd much rather eat pussy. Anyway. You gonna be alright? As much as you hate me, and believe me it's mutual, I sort of feel bad when you are upset. Don't worry about Samuel. I'm going to take care of him real good right now." She quickly flicked her hair up and over her head as she suddenly bent over to jostle her hands through it for volume. The smell reinvigorated the scent of strawberries. There was something rather beautiful about Belinda's preparation as she stood fluffing her hair. When she was finished, she stood straight again, flipping her blonde locks up into the air and letting them fall to her back. Her beautiful breasts jiggled within the bra which flung the necklace out over the center of her silk shirt. At the end of the gold chain was a cross that was very familiar to Maggie; only this one had spots of encrusted brown residue in and around the crevices.

Belinda inhaled deeply as she threw her head back to look at the ceiling and shake her hair one last time. As her body shimmied, the cross necklace pulled itself back into her cleavage again before Belinda returned to a proper stance and then spun around to check her appearance.

Maggie hinted that she didn't need to expose herself like that to be noticed and desperately wanted to clean the questionable filth from the necklace.

"I knew you would say that, to ruin a good moment between us by reciting scriptural philosophy. Listen, I don't want to miss group again, so I need to go get my orgasm on, so I can focus. I'd ask you to be adventurous and come with me, but I know you won't." She giggled and then mumbled her next thought out loud. "Cum with me."

Belinda saw the necklace in the mirror that was distracting Maggie. She looked down and grabbed the pendant while she explained that she'd gotten it from her uncle when her parents had died, and she was sorry that it looked the same as Maggie's. "I had it in my locker and didn't want to wear it because I knew it would upset you since you said you ate yours." She looked down at it and tried to dig away a dark flake that was stuck around the jewels.

Maggie didn't say a word.

"Which reminds me...there is that fucking taste again." She snorted hard with her nose, bringing phlegm up and out of her mouth so that she could spit it into the sink. "Dirty change." She popped her lips together in the mirror one last time and then pranced out of the bathroom with a renewed, straightened posture. Her shoulders were pushed back in perfect form, too, creating a curvier, uplifted silhouette. Just before she pushed the door open to walk out, she said, "Don't be afraid of sexuality, Maggie. I heard him. You are beautiful with your good Christian titties. You can be spiritual and enjoy the taste of African seed. There is nothing to feel guilty about, Jiminy Cricket – you know what I mean?"

Belinda winked into the empty bathroom and then pushed the door open with the butt of her ribbed, corduroy pants.

KNOWLEDGE IGNITES

Ignacio paced back and forth in the empty craft room while he bit at the hangnail on his right middle finger. As he tried to clip the jagged edge with his teeth, the dimples in his face appeared and disappeared with each muscle movement. Alone, he walked around tables that were filled with scraps of brightly colored paper, themselves adorned with intricate dried noodle designs. As he circled one of the tables for the fifth time, thoughts of therapy as infantile as crafting with pasta really began to piss him off. How the hell was a hot glued pasta rendition of a landscape supposed to help him figure out his sexuality? Northern Lights had started all this shit anyway.

Ignacio took a breath before his blood pressure escalated beyond a level that could be retracted so easily. Maybe years of pretending to be mentally unstable had simply caught up with him. He exhaled and tried to run his fingers through his hair, but a dizzy spell took his balance. His body pushed into a locked cage where they kept the hot glue guns, scissors, and any other crafty items that could potentially be used as weapons against the staff. He stared at the items between the metal woven mesh that separated him from them. The space included beautiful jars of sparkling color...spectrums of tangible rainbow flecks – glitter. He pushed himself off the cage to pace again. He didn't want thoughts of Buck to make him smile.

He looked at the clock above the doorway to the hall. The next pasta craft session would be occupying the room in fifteen minutes. Where the hell was Buck? He knocked over a cup of unsharpened pencils with his finger, just to be defiant. He almost needed to hear the clinking of the pencils, just to break up the awful sound of silence.

It seemed to take forever, but finally Buck opened the door while Ignacio scooped and dumped various dried noodles onto the floor.

Startled, he immediately began his verbal attacks. "Where the fuck have you been?" He flicked a single stuck noodle from his sweaty palm to the floor.

Buck, walking tall and proud into the room with that commanding presence he had, smiled through his pain. "Nice to see you, too. I had to restrain one of the weekenders. She flung poop onto the back of Charlotte's head. Roger in maintenance said he thought he saw her holding onto it for at least twenty minutes…"

Ignacio interrupted him. "I can't keep doing this, Buck. I'm not gay."

Buck gently cupped the back of Ignacio's head when he was close enough, and kissed each of his dimples, temporarily silencing the frazzled Mexican who stubbornly accepted the affection – although he acted as if the action was appalling.

Buck looked into his dark brown eyes while gingerly holding his partner's head. "You are right."

"Pendejo! That's it? No fight? You're not going to ask me why or – or be sad?" He shook his head from the warmth of Buck's hands to free himself from the closeness that either comforted him or smothered him, depending on the moment. The shock over Buck's non-reaction was as stunning as a family member's death notification. Unwavering truth pierced straight to the center of his heart. Recognizing that Buck was giving up on the fight to love him was agonizing, as he saw it.

Buck knew he had to explain himself, yet again, to his lover. "You say it's over every time we are together, so, you know, I just think you are right this time. This can't go on – for many reasons."

Buck's perfectly contained emotions and hidden expressions began to erupt from within. His hands began to tremble as he choked back the incredible urge to cry. In an effort to show Ignacio that it wasn't an easy decision to let go, Buck tried to return his hands to the back of his head.

Ignacio was less than comforted. "Get your fucking hands off me, you faggot!" he screamed as he pulled Buck's hands away and stepped backward to position himself into a defensive stance. "You can't end us. I fucking end us. We are done!" He straightened his arms to the ground and balled his fists at the end while his anger seethed from within, swelling the veins in his neck beyond their extended capacity. His ears began to burn as waves of heat seared upward into them.

Heartbroken, but desperately trying not to show it, Buck chose his words carefully. "I'm begging you, please. I can't date a patient. I've been telling you that." Buck placed his hand over his chest and took a step back. It was a genuine display of his sincerity and his growing uncomfortable disposition.

As Ignacio's mixed messages continued to spew from his mouth, he continued. "I'm getting out soon. When the docs sign my paperwork, I'll be done with this place, and we could have moved on...but you got me all twisted up and

I'm telling you that I'm not a fucking queer!" He pointed his fingers into Buck's face as his body lunged forward, warning him to back up. "I like pussy." He popped the letter P in Buck's face, saying it again and spraying a little spit and hot breath onto his mouth and chin.

"Stop it, Ignacio." Buck took a step backward, turning his face from side to side as he pulled his chin inward to retract every portion of his body from Ignacio's forward insistence. The power dynamic shifted with every inch he lost. The Mexican was gaining precious real estate on his torso, and pushing his face into the natural biological heat cushion that surrounded a person when they got upset. This invasion created the sensation that Buck could vomit at any moment. After swallowing hard, Buck managed, "I thought you loved me."

"I cannot love another man. I am not gay!" Ignacio yelled as he pushed Buck in a macho, alpha male display – although his knees felt weak.

Buck tried to correct him without sounding condescending, but after the conversation he'd had with Mr. Reed, he knew he had to set his feelings aside and do the right thing. "You are gay, actually. I hate to do this, but you can't push me around and..."

"Fuck you." Ignacio pushed at his chest again, this time with more force and with crazy-focused eyes that seemed to be coated with the color of...anger.

Buck's voice boomed louder and more prominently baritone after he spread his legs to stabilize his stance. "I'm telling you to stop. Just stop!"

"Or what, Buck? You gonna rape me again – take advantage of my sensitive mental state here at Northern Lights? I don't love you! You made me lose my focus, you prick, and I'm putting myself back on track as of today, so I can find my fucking mother." Ignacio pushed Buck's chest as hard as he could, but when his stance held firm, there was nothing he could do but unleash his anger on his face, neck, and chest. His slaps and punches were wild and erratic as he lost control of the separation between his reality and Juana's. In a full burst of raging, uncontrollable emotions, he kept slapping at him even after a trickle of blood oozed out of Buck's nostril.

Buck stood his ground as Juana pushed her way into the physical world of Ignacio's body. As she clawed and beat at Buck's chest, he began to cry from his broken heart; from the truth of who he was in love with and the pity he'd begun to feel for a person who was completely insane. When her breathing finally returned to a normal rhythm, her hair was left wild and unkempt with the tips tickling at the moons on her cheeks. That's when Buck gently escorted her to a chair at the nearest craft table. His skin stung in a heated pain that he had never felt before. The inside of his nose burned and itched with dripping blood which was warm until it hit the top of his lip, where it cooled in an uncomfortably thick wetness. Yet, he pulled the chair out for her.

She sat willingly, but stared at the floor for a long moment before looking up at him, noticing for the first time that he had sparkling green eyes. Her face scrunched together as she blinked profusely in confusion and shook her head to refocus. When she looked again, they were the familiar chocolate brown color she loved.

From beyond the craft room, Ute peered through the small window in the door with her beady, aged eyes that were bloodshot from smoking medical marijuana and her most recent dose of a new prescription. Her giant sagging chest smashed against the door while she pushed herself closer to witness Buck kneeling before "Juana" and looking deeply into her eyes while he lovingly tucked her, curly locks behind her ear. Ute rubbed at her dry eyes wondering if what she witnessed was a result of the blue pill she had never taken before. She could see Buck's emergency cell phone light blinking from inside the pocket of his nurses' uniform now, although he must have had it on silent because he never answered it. The pair began to talk as tears streamed down their faces. It was a silent film much like Ute remembered from her childhood – only, this time, it was in color and the people in it were...colorful. She mumbled 'baunkerhaus' under her breath, but continued to watch through the glass as her head swirled.

Juana cried as Buck tried to calm her with his deep, soothing voice and southern, sweet tone. "You are confused, aren't you?"

Defeated, she nodded her head yes. "I'm so fucking confused that my brain feels like it's on fire. Oh my God, your nose is bleeding, my love."

Buck's voice, tender and true, calmly asked, "Do you trust me?"

"I guess." Juana sniffed back the snot that was pooling in the back of her nose and wiped the tears away. "Go on. Explica, pendejo. I'm listening."

As gently as he possibly could, Buck explained she was the alternate personality of a man with Dissociative Identity Disorder. "You know, like Mr. Jenkins and Samuel," he said.

Juana smiled as if she was waiting for the punchline. "So, I don't got tits and a pussy? So, if I masturbate, am I fucking myself?" She laughed, pushing her dimples to the surface of her make-believe face, and sat back in the chair again, disbelieving every word that was being said.

Buck didn't move or crack a smile. The blood under his nostril glistened in the terrible lighting.

Juana played into what she thought was a terrible joke. "Do you love me or this man?" She smiled.

Buck shook his head. He pushed a curl away from the eyes that he loved. He answered honestly. "You."

THE DISSAPEARANCE OF JASON

Within the perfectly organized office of Jill Reed, surrounded by beautifully oiled wood architecture of the mansion's glory days, Jack stood on the opposite side of the desk. He leaned over Jill's monogrammed pen set to share a moment with his wife, who was slouching uncomfortably in her leather chair. Her composure and effort to maintain any semblance of professionalism was gone now that she was in her husband's presence. The antique clock behind her desk chimed as the automatic air freshener misted its lavender scent into the air just as she had set it to do. Both noises made her jump a little as she finished explaining the scandalous situation she – they – were in.

Jack's boney fingers spread out over a disheveled file with Maggie's name on it. His face was as worried as it was angry.

Referring to Maggie's breaking and entering, he asked the undying question. "How did she get into your office, Jill?" His tone held a bit of accusation. "And a gun? Why the hell didn't you tell me five days ago when it happened? This isn't good, not one bit." He shook his head in disbelief. Jill pulled her hands up to her face to cover it for an extended moment before sliding her fingers through her white bangs. She'd honestly thought she could handle everything on her own.

She exhaled, which relieved some of the frustration, but it left her open to other, more complex feelings – namely, what actions to take next with her husband. It was the first time in years that she'd truly lost control over anything related to the facility. Jack saw that she was biting her lip on the inside to prevent it from quivering, but it wasn't working. He knew that her emotional investment in the facility didn't come without cause.

Jill looked desperately into her husband's eyes and held her stare as her face took on a look of anguish. Only Jack understood the gravity of their desperate state of twelve years earlier when Jason had come home from medical school as a different person. The day Jason's body had walked through the door as he'd introduced himself as Buck Lynn had solidified the bed and breakfast idea. When it hadn't been pulling in enough money to sustain itself, let alone their son's medical bills, they'd taken the opportunity from Germany with one condition. Other than the twins, it would become long-term health care for DID patients. Researchers from around the world had caught wind of the endeavor; the Reeds had never worried about finances again. However, no success came without a price.

Their price was lying to personalities that did not exist. Mainly, their son, their youngest ginger-haired child, who believed he was his own lover.

Jason had never officially come out of the closet, but they'd known. Somewhere in the mansion, there was a box of photographs of their son with his "best friend" – they'd been enough to prove their suspicions.

Unfortunately, they'd never had the pleasure of meeting the real Buck Lynn. In their son's fourth year of medical school, they'd learned that Buck's father had been killed while serving overseas in Iraq. Additionally, he was dealing with the newly discovered information of a half-sibling he'd known nothing about. Jason confessed that this tragedy had pushed Buck into depression, and that he himself was developing anxiety over the stability of his so-called friend's mental state. Jason cared about people in general, but Buck Lynn pulled at his heartstrings more so than any person in his life. He even wished he could take his place so that Buck didn't have to go through this suffering.

The unforeseen truth behind those remembered words made Jill shudder as she pulled out of her thoughts to stand up. She continued to stare at her husband in something of a trance while back-stepping toward the clock. It was a gift from Jason. Jack subtly shook his head no as his forehead wrinkled and his eyes closed gently over the pain his wife was about to bring upon herself. But he said nothing, as she wouldn't listen; she never did.

She gingerly pushed the bottom of the clock to the left, revealing a small hidden panel that opened to an even smaller nook in the wall. The nook housed one item.

As she pulled a bulky flip cellphone from behind the antique clock, Jack watched and calmed himself without speaking. He knew what her familiar actions meant, but a part of him wanted to hear the voicemail, too. Even though he'd heard it often enough to recite every word and every inflection in his son's last message.

Jill carefully brought the phone over to the desk and sat it next to Maggie's disheveled file. She pressed the button that powered the device on and, as it ran through its start-up process, she sat delicately in her chair, scooting it as close to the desk as it would go. Jack walked around the desk to stand at his wife's side as she gently folded her arms and rested her head on them. Jack stroked her beautiful hair and moved it away from her face while she welcomed his fingers to her aging skin. She closed her sad eyes then, pushing fresh tears out of them as she sniffed every few seconds.

There was nothing Jack could do to comfort her, so over the past few years he'd trained himself to simply be quiet and let her have her moment of remembrance to honor the son they'd lost. He quietly reached out to grab the cell phone, and pressed a few buttons which clicked loudly before setting it to speaker. He placed the phone back on the desk again, this time in front of Jill's face. She sighed deeply and then opened one eye enough to see the phone, and to press the correct button. A man's voice that was similar to their favorite employee's, but without an accent, began to speak.

"Mom, Dad, um, hi. It's Jason. I was just calling to talk to you about something important, but I don't want to do it on the phone, so I don't even know why I'm calling to begin with. Jesus, I'm going insane. *(nervous laugh)* Listen, don't worry, it's nothing bad; I just, well, my friend Buck and I are planning to come home for spring break next week, so maybe it can wait until then. *(grumbling)* Maybe it will cheer him up. I need him to feel better. Yeah. Oh, that's him calling on the other line now! I have to go, but I love you both. Dad, get your moonshine ready! Mom, mark that on your calendar or you'll forget. Jason comes home in a week! Mark it! Love you!"

Jill clicked the button to play it again, but only let the recording run long enough to hear him say his name. She continued pressing the button in such a way that it repeated *Mom, Dad, um, hi. It's Jason* over and over again as her tears spilled onto the desk.

Two days after Jason had recorded the message, Buck had committed suicide. The mental break of their son had occurred soon thereafter. He'd gone missing for two months before police escorted him out of North Carolina. He'd been caught attempting to break into Mrs. Lynn's home, with Buck's identification and credit cards in his wallet.

A neighbor who'd reported the incident had told police that he seemed as if he "…knew where he was going, like he lived there his whole life." The report went on to detail how Jason had tried to enter through the front and back door of the home before walking around to press at the windows, checking for one that may have been unlocked. All of this had occurred while Jason repeatedly screamed, "Mamma, let me in! I forgot my keys!"

Luckily, Mrs. Lynn had been out that weekend and hadn't had to experience that additional madness after the death of her son. Jill remembered trying to apologize over the phone, but Mrs. Lynn had been hysterical and hung up after calling Jason 'crazy' several times. Jill had never found out if the other woman had known the nature of the boys' relationship, but she guessed that it didn't really matter.

When Jason had been able to return home, it had been after jail time and a call from the state. The woman on the phone had been professional, but nothing prepared a parent for: *'He's suffering from a deep psychosis and needs to be evaluated.'*

Buck Lynn had to have been someone really special for her son to quit his own life, just so Buck could live through him.

Jill understood that there was nothing she could have done at that time to prevent any of it. But there was a guilty part of her that felt, had they been wealthier, had they just paid for the right kind of treatment immediately following his breakdown, maybe Jason wouldn't have faded away.

As she trailed off into deeper thoughts, Jack gently closed the flip phone after pulling it away from Jill's fingers as they hovered over the replay button. "Jilly, that's enough for today. Time to deal with the child we gained rather than mourn the one we lost. He's in the west wing doing his security checks and he will be in here soon to secure your office. It's time to close out for the day."

Jill sat up and wiped her streaming tears away, then ran her finger across her nose like a child. She sniffed a few times while looking at the cellular phone in her husband's hand before pulling tissues out to blow her nose. She put the phone back into its hiding place, made sure her hair was in perfect order, and then sat in her chair with a false confidence.

"We need to deal with this gun issue," Jill managed.

Jack let go of the breath he'd been holding. "God, I almost forgot. Police involvement would shut us down. Shit. Is it loaded?" he asked as he walked around the desk to sit in the chair opposite his wife. He knew that this wasn't the main concern, but to him, it was a valid point. Jill was at a loss for words.

He asked, "What papers did she take?"

"The twins' entire folder, Jackie. I already told you that."

"Fuck."

"Yeah."

Jack swirled his palm over the top of his thinning hair

and then placed his index and middle finger on his forehead, pressing them there in frustration and creating an unnatural backward bend. "Well, you need to make nice with her or steal them back or something," he said.

"She says she sent them to her husband, but they could be anywhere. Who is the husband of a woman that doesn't exist?" Jill leaned back in her chair.

In disbelief, Jack thought of an infinite number of people 'Maggie' could have mailed documents to. Did she mail them to the uncle – the dead uncle of Belinda? Was he the make-believe husband of Maggie? He scratched his head hard and rubbed at his temples. "You are not kidding – they could be anywhere. Um, if we find the gun, we could shoot her?" Jack shrugged.

"Soooo not funny." She shook her head in dismay while the corner of her mouth upturned in a guilty smile. The two of them looked beyond each other – thinking, brainstorming. After a very long and intense moment of contemplation, Jill spoke first, but it wasn't about the gun. "Everything we have done has been for Jason. We just want them to feel like they live normal lives, right, Jackie? Our intentions are good. Things were going so well until Ignacio arrived. Then Jason wouldn't stop talking about letting him into general population. Normal population. What's normal about that Mexican? We should put him back into clinical."

Uncomfortable, Jack suddenly knew that he had to tell his wife the truth. "Jilly, babe, we can't do that." He leaned forward to put his face in his hands and sighed.

Jill sat up and leaned over the desk, placing her elbows on a pool of her own tears. She was listening. Intently. "What are you not telling me, Jack Reed? I can feel ya got something up your sleeve."

He was extremely hesitant, but Jill was patient. Finally, through a sigh that was bigger than the first, he said it out loud, so it would stop screaming through his head. "Buck is in love with Ignacio." He spoke into his hands with his eyes closed, afraid to see her reaction as he mumbled, *There – I said it*, several times thereafter.

Her mouth fixed open, locked uncomfortably in that position. She found that she was unable to move. Unable to do anything. When she finally did, it was forced and stiff as she tucked hair behind her ear and then tilted her head to aim it in his direction as if she hadn't quite heard what he'd just said. There was no need to repeat it, though; she'd heard every word. Her eyes searched the spaces between Jack's fingers for his eyes, which peered out from the dark. He shook his head up and down without moving his sprawled hands from his face to confirm that what she had heard was correct. His tongue nervously licked his bottom lip under his sweaty palm.

When Jill spoke, she had to stop to clear her throat before beginning again. "Ig – Ignacio? The one who thinks he is his homicidal mother? What happens when her personality comes out? Does he love Juana?"

"I don't know. He said he sees Juana, though. Like we see Buck."

Jill hit her palm to her chest so hard that it thumped as she screamed. "I don't see...Buck! I see my son acting like another person and I – I fucking play along!" Spit had flown out of her mouth as she'd yelled, she was so upset.

"Jesus, you don't have to scream at me! I know what you mean. But, Jilly, all these years later, don't you see his alter when you look at him? Not once or even just a little?"

Jill crossed her arms over her heaving chest. She didn't want to agree, but she had to. There were times when she replaced images of Buck's face from the photos over her son's. But they were always the two-dimensional, frozen smiles of a black man she'd never known.

For a second, she trailed off to consider the innocent

days when she and her husband had had big dreams in college, and then she came back to the terrible nightmare she was currently living. "This is too much. I can't fucking deal with this, Jackie! I'm about to lose my shit. I just need to work...I'll make some phone calls to deal with the gun. Can you give me a moment, darling? Please. I don't want to call, not in the state I'm in." She fluttered her manicured nails at the sides of her face to unnecessarily point out the fact that she was frustrated, which was already obvious.

"Fine, Jill. Better do it soon, before Buck comes in."

A booming voice with a southern accent shook the room then, as well as Jack and Jill Reed. "Buck's already in. My apologies, ya'll – I was just locking up. I could give you a few more minutes if you need me to."

The awkward silence lingered as three sets of eyes from the former Reed family darted around the room and in between each other.

Buck stood with his thumb up like a hitchhiker as he used it to point to the beautiful door behind him. "I think I'll come back. I have to check the lobby and the smoking room anyway." He back-stepped, but Jill shot up from her chair and shouted for him to wait. Jack just smacked his forehead and begged his wife to please sit down and let him do his job.

Jill snapped at her husband, then walked over to Buck while she fussed with her business attire to make sure she was presentable. She stopped when she approached his personal space and noticed that he'd jerked his head back to express his discomfort with how close she'd come. "Look at my face. Really look. What do you see?"

Buck leaned left, noticing Mr. Reed in the patient chair rolling his eyes and shrugging before he shook his head and then tucked his mouth under his gently curved fingers to prevent himself from saying something stupid.

"Come on. Look hard," Jill insisted.

Buck, who had played this game before, snapped the 'D' ring of keys onto his belt loop and tucked the dangling portion into his pants pocket. He tugged his uniform shirt downward before respectfully crossing his hands over his waist to lean forward. He gave Mrs. Reed a focused and sincere look. His eyes scanned her hair; whiter than anything. Her nose was petite at the bridge, drawing down perfectly into a little ball at the tip that was reminiscent of a more attractive Mrs. Santa Claus. Her face was symmetrical with gently curved laugh lines surrounding her mouth like parenthesis. Her eyes, a beautiful bright green, were the only things that seemed different – other than the natural progression of aging. Their beautiful color was and always would be as vibrant as the day she'd been born. However, the whites of her eyes were dimmed with a hue of pink from the tears she'd shed over the son who didn't recognize her face. Buck noticed the black mascara she used to cover red eyelashes. It had smeared a little from moisture and settled on her bottom lid like smudged and smoky paint.

"Mom," Jason said.

Jill's face lifted and released the tension in her lips and forehead. Her heart literally skipped a beat as she struggled to inhale. She turned to look at Jack, who was still seated with his fingers over his mouth and returning her look with sad, worried eyes. He didn't have to rain on her parade. Jill smiled with a renewed sense of hope before looking back at her son.

"Ma'am," Buck repeated. "You are as lovely as the day I started working here. A classic beauty."

Her face melted as every feature drooped downward in utter heartbreak. "No," she begged the first time she said it. "Nooo," she stretched out the vowel the second time.

Buck sighed painfully, as it hurt him to give the wrong answer, which he knew he was doing – no matter what compliment he ever came up with. He called out to Mr. Reed for help as Mrs. Reed begged him to look again. Jack couldn't help, though, and Buck knew it, but he stood up to retrieve his wife just the same. Suddenly, Buck held his hand up as if he was stopping time to speak. From across the room, he apologized to Mr. Reed for what he was about to do. "I'm sorry. I have to say something."

Jack shook his head no with wide eyes.

"Yes. I cannot let this go on, ya'll, this ain't right." Buck watched Mr. Reed signal with a mocked slicing motion to his neck, which clearly enough meant that he should cut it out. His dark eyebrows scrunched together in a scolding gesture as the 'no' headshake became faster and more jerky.

Jill turned to look at her husband to counteract the cues of a non-verbal conversation, but he suddenly stopped moving and returned to a neutral facial expression.

"I have to," Buck said to Mr. Reed. "Ma'am, I think you are a beautiful woman, no matter how many times you ask me. But I've worked here too long, and I know the rumors about how ya'll lost your son, and how I remind you of him – especially you, Mrs. Reed. If I can be bold here, ma'am, it makes it uncomfortable for me to work here when you do this, and I can't keep that a secret anymore."

His voice was much deeper than her son's on the recording, and Jill wondered if it was part maturity or self-training from over the years. He had settled into the baritone quite nicely, although she remembered his struggle with it after he'd first introduced himself as Buck.

She looked hard into the details of his face as her eyes began to mist. His beautiful crystal-clear eyes complimented his flawless skin that, as a child, had been blessed with freckles across the bridge of his nose. As an adult, the color had been muted just like the intensity of the red in his hair had, but he was and always would be recognized as a ginger. As she wondered how he did not see his own face in the mirror, she also reflected upon why she could not see the face of his heart.

A wet glassy pool of tears began to coat her eyes as she tried to see the man he presented to the world. His details began to melt together and blur in a watery blend of color. While she attempted to wipe the tears away, he spoke frankly about how devastating it must be to lose a son. But this unkinked the hose to her waterworks and she cried so much that she could no longer see. "Please, ma'am, I'm only trying to be honest here. Cuz ya'll know you are like my family, but it's too much to see you this upset every few months, over all these years. Do you understand? Every few months for over a decade. It breaks my heart."

Jill wiped the hot tears from her cheeks and tried to breathe normally as she refocused on the figure in front of her. He was right; it had been over a decade of torture. Her makeup at this point was a sloppy, smeared mess that had bled into the gentle creases of her aged skin. She knew that touching it up wasn't going to cut it; she would have to wash it off and start over. Thank God it was the end of her day, where she could just retire for the evening with her extremely supportive husband who loved every pruning inch of her.

Obsessively wiping the last of her tears away, she threw her head back to inhale and then exhale through her nose. When she pulled her head forward into the neutral position again, her eyes automatically closed as she steadied her breathing while fidgeting with her wedding band. When the dizziness faded, she could feel two sets of eyes upon her. The men were silent as they watched her rotate her head a few times, relieving stressful sounding pops from the back of her neck, but they didn't speak or move. When she finished, her eyelids were relaxed and closed. Then she placed her hands together as if she were going to say the Lord 's Prayer, and brought them to her face. Her two index fingers rested gently on her lips as her thumbs tucked under her chin. She mumbled at first, but cleared her throat to speak a moment later.

"You are right. You're right. Jason has been gone for years...at some point, I need to accept it and stop grieving." Her closing words of mourning behind the bazaar tragedy of her son's disappearance couldn't go on forever. She felt an agonizing sort of comfort in the way Buck was bold enough to express himself, though, and it seemed as if his very words gave her permission to let go.

She shook her body, letting her arms drop and her neck sway. Her posture sank into itself as she sighed while the weight of the situation spilled out of her pores. A warm sensation calmed her clammy skin and, rather than attempt to stifle it like she normally would have, she let it tickle past the hairs on her arms. It relieved an internal ache that had lain dormant, but ever present. Her face, drooping in heavy sadness, began to retract into a lighter and more pleasant expression. Not smiling, yet happier just the same, she finally felt ready to face the truth.

She let her eyes blink open for a split second, then a full second, and then another as the blurring began to formulate details of Buck's chocolate skin and naturally curled eyelashes. His smile was warm and contagious. He was very tall, and towered over her tiny frame – which strangely made it seem as if he was a protector of the evil world she lived in. His muscles pushed at the inside of the nurse's uniform he wore, though it remained professional looking with his pens neatly hung inside of his breast pocket under the embroidered Northern Lights logo. His perfectly shaped lips held just the right hue of pink to make him look healthy and strong. He was a stunning looking man, really. No wonder her son had fallen in love with him.

With her hands relaxed at her sides, she said, "He's gone...but there are other things to be thankful for. Thanks, Buck. Maybe I just needed you to be honest with me for me to see it. I see it now." She turned to her husband. "I see it now."

He smiled while keeping his thin lips together in one of the most sincere, heartfelt moments he had ever shared with his wife, even including the birth of their youngest son, Jason.

Buck, completely unaware of the emotional trauma he had just put Mr. and Mrs. Reed through, rested his hand against Jill's upper arm. "I really hate upsetting you like this, ma'am. It tugs at my heartstrings."

Mr. Reed, realizing that everyone needed a break from the thickness in the air, pressed his hands to his knees to help himself stand up. "Let's go have a puff on the bench, Buck. Mrs. Reed can lock up here and you can clock out early to-night, okay, buddy?" Jack walked over to the two of them and rubbed his wife's back before kissing her forehead.

Buck nodded to Jack, and then turned and walked to the door of the office to give them a private moment.

Jill was so excited to tell her husband the truth of the situation that she couldn't wait for the door to completely close behind Buck before she leaned into Jack's ear. "I see it. I honestly do."

Jack pressed his face into the beautiful hair that covered her ear to correct her. "You see him."

PAINTING WITH FIRE

The newly replaced florescent lights in the craft room were exceptionally bright as some of the patients of Northern Lights struggled to create their masterpieces. The glare in the wet paint agitated each and every one of the twelve people in the room, too. Their assignment for the two-hour block of time was to create an image of a happy moment in their lives, each of which they would later discuss in group. Ignacio was miserable with this particular task, as he was unaccustomed to sharing in a creative, artistic way. He struggled to dip the brush into the paint without smashing the bristles to the bottom. The pressure he used to load the bristles with color was too intense, always resulting in unintentional blobs on his paper. Despite this, he was not defeated – rather, he was still determined to make his doctors happy, and so he carefully lifted his heavy hand for a better stroke.

Belinda was seated at the same group table, across from Ignacio and his fantastic dimples. Although they were hidden when he was not smiling, she knew exactly where they were. She looked at him after each of her own brush strokes was made, hoping to make him smile so that she could see his natural indentations, but his face was inches from the tip of the handle as he concentrated on his work. As he lifted his head enough to reload his brush, which he absolutely didn't need to do, she giggled at the sight of him poking his tongue out from the corner of his mouth. A glob of paint fell onto his happy moment, pulling him right out of his concentration.

"Mother FUCKer!" his voice boomed through the hushed atmosphere, making one patient jump enough that he knocked over a cup of colored pencils. Displeased with the sharp break in the room, everyone scowled or rolled their eyes at Ignacio as the pencils awkwardly hit the floor in a muffled clatter; except for Belinda, who smiled.

"You've been around Samuel too long. Just dip half of the brush, like this." She dipped the hairs of her brush into the cheap paint and pulled it out to demonstrate a stroke on her own paper. "Then you can gently pull it or push it to get different types of lines. You see?" She finished her stroke, then watched Ignacio struggle with every step. She returned her eyes to her own paper and swirled the paint. She rather enjoyed watching it blend together to create one final image. The harmony of it soothed her. "Have you seen Maggie?" Ignacio asked, shaking Belinda out of her brushstrokes.

"What do you want with her?" She looked stunned, and then turned her head away to roll her eyes.

He hunched forward to make sure he was quiet. "I saw her eating change in the lobby. Long term residents don't usually have change – only the open admittance people. She might have something for me, that's all. We have an arrange-ment." He sat back into his chair and then cleared his throat. Then he tried to push and pull the brush like she'd demon-strated – with a concentration that unintentionally pushed his tongue out of his mouth again.

She leaned onto the table to answer him with a gentle smugness. "I know what's going on. Maggie and I are cool now. You can't blackmail her anymore, and she owes you nothing because the ring is probably still in your pocket." She smiled with confidence. When she pulled away to sit back into her chair, she realized that she had placed her ample breasts in a portion of her painting. Now a line of smeared red color spread itself across the mid-line of her breasts. She tried to wipe off the paint, but only made it worse.

Ignacio shook his head and smiled at her mistake. His dimples finally made their grand appearance, and for a mo-ment, Belinda was seduced by them.

Quietly, he explained, "She said she would do it for the

innocent souls I have tortured. That's her backwards way to be nice. Unlike you, she's a good person and doesn't mind-fuck people with her vagina." Without skipping a beat, he cleaned his brush in a jar of water and loaded a new color on the bristles. "Maybe if you were more like her and a little less whore…"

He'd known from day one that distractions like sex would throw his mission off course. They only got him a longer stay in a renovated mansion, painting happy la la moments to impress doctors. When he thought about it, he began to swell with anger at Belinda because, honestly, she was the one who had started it all. A little piece of him pushed the blame onto her lap for creating chaos in his life.

Belinda cocked her head while she flipped him the middle finger. The tempo of her breathing increased then, as did the intense pink flood to her cheeks. Her mouth was slightly open when she licked the inside of her teeth with her tongue. "You are so damn dumb. I feel bad for you."

Ignacio never looked up from his painting. "Ah, shut up, Belinda, and just paint your happy picture."

Her profound disrespect made him livid. She was lucky his grandmother had drilled it into his head not to hit women – otherwise, he would have given her a much-deserved smack across the face that would be hard enough to leave a handprint on her cheek.

Belinda didn't care about her shirt this time, and leaned over her painting again to make sure Ignacio heard every word she was about to say. "Where is Juana? Tell your mom she tasted like dirty change."

Ignacio immediately stood up, knocking his chair backward. The therapist stopped writing notes and the others in the room froze. "What the fuck did you say?"

Then Ignacio realized he was not in control of the movement in his arm. It had reached over to her side of the table, knocked the brush out of her hand, and then smashed his palm into her painting. After his hand was wet, it pressed and swirled red paint all over Belinda's shirt. He viewed this action as if it was through a keyhole and he was unable to stop any of the motions. When he spoke again, it wasn't his own voice he heard – it was the soprano again, the female voice of his mother.

Belinda laughed as she stood to her feet and touched the red color for no apparent reason. "You crazy bitch. Who did that?" She smiled as she leaned in further, as if she was inspecting Ignacio's face. "It doesn't matter, really. I can't believe Maria had two chances to raise good people and fucked it up twice."

The therapist running the crafting event pushed a hidden silent emergency button under a picture on the wall, but no one noticed, and no one moved.

Belinda flailed her arms in the air. "Let's go, bitch! I know it was you! What are you trying to do, protect your son from being a fag?" she shouted as the wet paint on her shirt clung desperately to her skin.

Juana, standing with the back of her knees touching the chair, was completely thrown. However, she was not going to let this skinny white girl push her back into a body she was barely getting used to. Juana balled her fists and rubbed the back of her hand against the moons on her face. She was the Firestarter.

A rage burned within her that was so intense she could almost see floating embers dancing across her vision. She tried to lunge forward then, but suddenly her body felt heavy. There was a rumbling in her mind and then chaos erupted as if many people were arguing in the closed space of a car. Together, they agreed to pull Juana from the driver's seat while her foot was on the gas. She thrashed and screamed as they maneuvered systematically to shut her down. Eventually, she was subdued.

Back in control of his body, Ignacio struggled to breathe

as panic and paranoia washed over him. He had to put his hands on the table to stabilize his body. Sweat seeped from his pores as his cheeks filled with heat. The new fluorescent lights were obtrusive and somewhat painful. He flinched while trying to regain focus. Belinda was standing across the craft table from him, with open arms and one leg forward in a very aggressive pose. The blonde's posture reminded Ignacio of the gang members in his mother's birthday video. He hadn't known white girls had that kind of attitude. It was impressive for some reason, and strangely, suggested an element of respect for him.

Ignacio shook his head and managed to utter, "What the hell?" while he rubbed his eyes and blinked as if it was painful. He scanned the room to see the therapist standing in the back of the room in fear. "What the fuck kind of pills are you giving me, man? I'm going batshit in here!"

The door to the craft room slammed open, making everyone in the room jump and jerk. Paper on a shelf behind the door slid off and fluttered to the floor. Every patient, plus the therapist, turned their heads to witness the culprit of the noise entering with his dominating presence. His voice alone required attention, pushing for everyone in the room to put their hands on the tops of their heads. Somehow, the elongated 'S' that accompanied some of his words disappeared in the seriousness of the situation, but the melodic southern twang carried through even over his angry demands. Three other men followed behind him with green uniforms that no one had ever seen before, each holding electroshock Tasers. One of them with a severely crooked nose, as if it had been broken many times, seemed to be the higher-ranking sergeant with additional embellishments on his shirt.

Having felt a great sense of relief when Buck walked into the room, Ignacio tried to speak first. "Something is wrong. My body – my fucking body is moving without me. I would never hit a girl!"

Buck told Mr. Cheyez to stop talking, and instead looked to Maggie, who was standing with slumped shoulders. She gripped the crucifix around the neck of the body she shared. She squeezed at it so hard that her knuckles were white. "Ms. Koontz, are you bleeding?" Maggie was crying. Her tears glistened under the horrible lighting as they pooled at the bottoms of her lids and then finally fell down her cheeks. She shook her head no and then mumbled that it was paint.

Ignacio scanned the room again to watch the reactions of the therapist and all the other patients, but no one was re-acting the way he'd expected. As his frustration mounted, he began to run his fingers through his hair and grab a little of it to tug. He shook his head like a dog several times, as if to shake off the craziness before looking to Buck for help while lifting his hands as if he was going to be arrested. "I didn't touch her. My hand did, but I didn't."

Without a response, Buck waved his thick fingers in the air, initiating the guys in green to go forward into the room to control the situation. The guy with a crooked nose waited for a visual cue from the therapist, who pointed a peace sign horizontally at Ignacio and Maggie. With his rank and authority, he directed the other two while he walked around to stand behind Maggie – who was still crying. He demanded she put her hands behind her back while he held one outstretched arm up to the group, warning them not to move. Maggie sobbed as she looked down to the craft room tiles, mumbling, "What did I do?"

The two men in green stood on the right and left of Ignacio, who'd initially jerked his arms away from theirs as they'd tried to bind them with rubber cuffs. Buck was the one who shouted for him to stop, which he did. Eventually, everyone watched as the two were escorted out of the craft room with ample distance between them.

Before leaving the room, Buck grabbed the painting Ignacio had been working on.

After looking at the image, he ripped it in half, and then in quarters, and he continued ripping it until the pieces were small enough to flutter like large confetti into the trashcan. He rubbed his hands together to dry the wet paint from his fingers and turned to walk out into the hallway. He had to inhale and hold his breath there to hide the overwhelming disappointment he felt, because he couldn't understand why the happiest time of his life had been painted in fire.

RAINBOWS AND WRECKAGE

By the time the Mexican had come to their area of Northern Lights, Hilda and Ute had been a part of Northern Lights for almost nine years. And after their rare disorder had financed the switch from bed and breakfast to an institution, it had been an odd request by Mr. and Mrs. Reed – that the facility be primarily dedicated to housing Dissociative Identity Disorder patients – but the request had been granted. Their request had enabled Northern Lights to serve as a controlled social experiment from which researchers could compile data and blow the medical communities away. As far as the government and researchers were concerned, it was a perfect set-up for a two-for-one expose. Additionally, the constant switching between personalities had kept the twins entertained. Then an unexpected symbiosis had happened, over time. The strange paring of disorders had led to a mutually beneficial relationship between people. The sisters' behaviors that were negatively judged outside of social norms were acceptable within the mansion. Their antics neutralized the confusion of other patients' personalities and their physical bodies. Researchers had theorized that the duality of the sisters' minds and bodies working in a highly cohesive manner actually grounded the DID patients.

The bonkerhaus, as the twins called it, was constantly on thin ice with everything the patients did while under microscopic scrutiny from eyes around the world. Jack and Jill were responsible for detailed daily reports and financial logs. They had books for taxes, and the real books for researchers hidden somewhere in the mansion. It was very dirty under the carpet of truth, which was helping people with DID live 'normal' lives. The Reeds knew this project was going to provide medical breakthroughs across the globe – even if part of it was unauthorized, illegal, and definitely under the table. It could cause an international rift, should something go wrong. One researcher had written: 'Northern Lights is a sad attempt to create a false sense of normalcy among its trapped human Guinea pigs' – before she pulled her sponsorship. It only took a few months before she'd returned. Despite her moral compass, the project was just too big to ignore.

Hypermania was far less interesting than the dynamic of the human connections among people who disassociated from themselves. And the impact of what the facility was trying to do was further promoted by the tragic and yet progressive story of Jason Reed – otherwise known as Buck.

Buck was an advocate and pioneer of his own disorder even though he didn't know he suffered from it. When his parents had stopped traditional counseling, and moved him to the mansion, the butterfly effect thereafter had been nothing but positivity. He'd finally been happy.

This was what Jack and Jill wanted for all DID patients, even though the practices they pursued were unconventional. Patients were left to believe they were in fact their alter personalities. The idea was to simply let them live. Period. The different alters were accepted and nurtured as if they were in fact two different people. That was it. Simple, really; live and let live.

Getting patients there without disrupting what they believed was normal was another story altogether. The mental health facility, although partially real, was something patients could believe in and it was the thing that kept them from leaving on their own.

It had worked for eleven years. Files were held on each patient, as well as their alternate personalities. This proved to be very helpful with doctors, as some of the patients had created extensive backstories. Relationships were allowed to form even though the façade was that they were forbidden.

And counseling was offered for their additional disorders and activities, but to keep them busy; anything to make it real and comfortable.

Everything had been going well until the Mexican arrived in the summer of 2013 via a transfer of the state. At that time, Ignacio had been a first semester college student who was considered hostile. He'd been placed in the farthest corner of the mansion, which was equipped with more security, a full-time medical staff, and scheduled activities. The patients in the clinical side had no idea that the other side existed at all.

"Juana" was a special case. She was an alternate personality of Ignacio Cheyez.

She was also his estranged real-life mother who'd been charged with multiple counts of premeditated attempted murder, arson, and even other charges entirely after turning fifteen. The real Juana had been institutionalized until she was 18 and then sent to a maximum -security prison in New York. Despite attempts at rehabilitation, Juana Cheyez had immediately thrown herself into the prison gangs. She'd been hanged by rival inmates by the time her son, Ignacio, was three and a half years old.

Ignacio had never known Juana, but a maternal obsession had begun when he was seven. It had continued and progressed throughout his childhood. Then, in his first semester of college, Ignacio had begun to show signs of an alter which quickly turned into the dominant personality. All parties involved in his life had agreed with the state to send him to Northern Lights. His loss of reality, along with his hallucinations, had put him in the clinical wing for nearly two and a half years.

The hostile nature of the alternate personality had required therapies of suppression, though. This was against the philosophy of Northern Lights, but it had been necessary. When the alternate personality had finally been repressed, Ignacio had been considered for release into the general population of other DID patients. It had been on a probationary period, of course, but all of it had also been at the suggestion and pressure of Buck. He'd felt a deep connection to this particular patient as he'd observed him from afar.

It had been an elaborate logistical nightmare to organize a false sense of liberty in a human being. Ignacio Cheyez had had to believe he was self-admitting.

Ignacio's caseworker, Lydia, had spent a lot of time with him to implant certain details of believability. She'd coordinated the whole event. It had been important that his brain stay on track with his perceived reality, or the plan would have blown up on everyone. Buck's file had to be part of the lie. Lydia had assured the Reeds that, since both Ignacio and Buck were stable, everything would work out. It took a genius to manipulate minds, and yet there had been rumors among staff that she'd used sex as a tool. Maybe she had, too, but everything had gone as planned until she'd left.

Buck – who was protective of his heart for reasons he couldn't remember – had let go. Ignacio – who hid his sexuality under his maternal obsession – had let go. The intense connection between the two of them had pushed Ignacio's instability to the forefront. For Buck, it had been too late. His heart was committed.

Being in love with a DID patient took things to a whole new level, but what he felt was true and wonderful; it filled his mind, body, and soul with indescribable warmth and comfort. It healed every wound in his heart with hope and laughter. When they were alone, it was as if they were handmade by God himself to be together. They understood each other without speaking and enjoyed silence. They didn't need to fill it with entertainment or meaningless conversation. Their alone time was invaluable, as was their connection and ability to understand each other.

Great relationships were built on communication. Not just the verbal, but other non-verbal cues like winks and nods that could mean so much more than the quick action itself. And emotional connections, with this nonverbal communication between Buck and Ignacio, had blanketed their love with confirmation that they were in fact soul mates.

Researchers had convinced the Reeds to let their love work itself out. Everyone had been curious to determine who loved who. Was it Buck who loved or was it Jason? Was it Juana or Ignacio? Although these questions were interesting, the Reeds had deeper concerns. Jack and Jill just wanted their son to be happy.

The records on the tumultuous relationship between Samuel and Belinda were shattering theories, though. There seemed to be an element of symbiosis when love entered the equation. Belinda and Samuel were quite the odd couple, but they loved hard. The love had transferred itself into Mr. Jenkins and Maggie's devoted friendship. This balance created improvements in their destructive behaviors. And knowing all of this made it all the harder for the Reeds to decide what to do about their son.

The Reeds conflicted with what part of Northern Lights was actually helping. So many elements played a role in a patient's stability that it proved to be nearly impossible to categorize. Then, though, the question became, did it really matter?

It did, apparently, when love got messy.

The harder Ignacio fell in love, the more he tried to run from it and the more Juana appeared to protect his fragile heart. But Buck loved her, too. He wanted nothing more than to show her a way to love without destruction.

Inevitably, the heartache it had taken for him to push Ignacio away had been altogether too much to handle. What he'd thought would be best for them both had resulted in a backfire of torment and anguish. He knew what he had to do was to surrender himself to love. No one ever said that doing it would be easy.

Over the past week, Buck had prepared to express himself and his love to everyone. He was ready to take the next leap of faith and fully commit himself to a relationship that, although unconventional, was perfect. He struggled with his decision to leave Northern Lights, but concluded that he was tired of living this way, under the watchful and strange eye of his employers. It was time for him to step out of the comfort zone that had been his reality for many years, to experience what could be a long future with Ignacio, if he would have him. He was certain that they should be together – somehow.

Buck was tired of maintaining the lies at Northern Lights. The original intentions, to let DID patients live as normally as they could, was turning into the biggest grand manipulation he had ever known. He'd fallen in love with a patient now, and he simply wanted a fresh new beginning with the truth. He'd concluded that he needed to leave his beloved Northern Lights job.

It was Thursday, Ignacio's craft day, when he was compelled to quit analyzing the complexities of their relationship and quit repairing what wasn't broken. The plan was to tell Ignacio later that night in his room, that he was giving everything up to be with him. When a man made a plan that was as concrete as the wall he'd been banging his head against, things changed. He welcomed and bathed in the calm that washed over him.

He was happy all day. Smiling all day. He actually enjoyed laughing with the twins and listening to them chuckle through stories that he had heard a million times before. His vision seemed vivid and clear; the floors looked shiny, almost new, and the white on the walls brightened as he walked by them. Happy people saw the world differently, and Buck was no different.

When he got the call that there was a problem in the craft room, he didn't really think too much of it. He was sort of on autopilot. Securing tense situations with Samuel had prepared him for pretty much anything anyway. Except this. When the second alarm was triggered, alerting security to the requirement for additional guards on Juana Cheyez, his heart sank.

When he walked into the craft room with extra guards, his heart pounded irregularly with blended emotions as he made eye contact with Ignacio. He wondered if anyone noticed his cheeks beginning to blush under his dark skin. He felt an odd sense of pride for a moment because he was looking at his man, and relief that it was just a spat between him and Belinda. Ignacio looked good that day for some reason, in his stupid *are you a Mexi-can* shirt. But Buck had to be professional. He had to give the signals to move in and forward to control the situation.

Two security guards stood on each side of Ignacio as they struggled to rubber cuff him. Buck felt the embarrassment Ignacio was going through as eyes around the room watched him jerk his arms away. He shouted at Ignacio to stop, and hoped he would understand that he only wanted a peaceful ending to the situation. His lover seemed to pick up something hidden in his tone, but nonetheless he let the officers cuff him as part of their protocol. All eyes in the room were bouncing back and forth between the fighters, disrupters of the craft room chi. Eventually, Ignacio and Belinda were escorted out with ample distance between them.

Before leaving the room, Buck grabbed his lover's painting, curious to see what he'd painted as the happiest moment in his life. After discovering a fire burning people out of a building, though, he was sickened, and ripped the image in half, and then quarters until the pieces were small enough to flutter like confetti into the trash. Now, he wondered, was their love crumbling into ashes of insanity?

BOLD MOVE

After their immature fight in the craft room, Ignacio and Belinda were escorted through the halls. They were taken to opposite sides of the main lobby until the situation could be verified and controlled. The cuffs held the arms of the hosts, but Juana and Maggie were in control of the bodies.

Buck stood with crossed arms in the middle of the lobby with his firm butt cheeks touching the front of the receptionist's desk. He was genuinely pissed. The patients who were already there could hear him snorting like a bull through his nose while his eyes swatted back and forth between the two of them. With a head nod, he gave permission to the guards to remove the rubber cuffs. "I'm gonna take these cuffs off ya'll, but I don't want to hear a peep until I ask some questions. You hear me?" They both nodded their heads yes, Maggie more timidly than Juana, whose head nod was a little more defiant. "What happened in there? Mrs. Koontz, you go first."

Juana rolled her eyes as she rubbed at raw skin around one wrist, where the rubber had ripped a band of hairs out from the skin. Maggie soothed the tender underside of her own tiny wrist in a downward stroke on the front of her shirt, which was still wet with blended color and an angry red handprint smear. Her annoying voice mumbled and whined at the same time. "Ignacio blackmailed me into stealing, and I won't do it." With perfect timing, Buck held his hand up to stop Juana from interrupting without taking his eyes off Mrs. Koontz, as if he knew an interruption was going to happen. Maggie's eyes batted between his lifted arm and Juana, who was staring angrily from across the room, and then she continued. "I'm tired of being the small fish in a big pond, so Belinda stood up for me and he went bonkers!"

Buck held his other hand up to signal a pause from her. She immediately stopped talking and positioned her body to stand in a demure, child-like position. In a strange pose of an open-armed crucifixion, Buck looked at Juana. "Is this true, Ms. Cheyez?" he asked. His voice was deep and firm with a twist of hidden emotion that only his lover and Juana picked up on, while the rest of the people in the room focused on his elongated, feminine 'S' consonants.

Juana's face sunk and jerked backward with the bitter sound of the formal name. It hurt more than anything to hear it that way, but the outward reaction was anger. She pushed her index finger into her chest with shock before she pronounced each syllable with interwoven hate. "Oh, is it my turn to speak now? Okay, fuck you, Magpie!" She lunged forward with her teeth pinching the bottom of her lip.

Buck shouted for her to stop, and Juana did, and Maggie jumped in place, then spoke out of turn. "I'm going to keep praying for you, Buck, because other than your...homosexuality...you are a really good person." The patients who were in the lobby didn't know if they should stay or leave. Out of curiosity, the remaining patients began to filter toward the chaos.

Juana lunged again. The security guard tensed with his hand around the Taser on his belt before Buck neutralized him with a taught straight arm that forced his fingers to spread so wide that the bottom of his hand looked white. "Stop!" his base roared through the lobby, bouncing endlessly off of every wall. He only had two arms, two hands, and a room full of jumpy people. His eyes bounced around the room, but it was too much chaos – and he knew he didn't want to be the one in control anymore. With a low, sincere grumble, he said, "I'm done. I quit."

***

Buck had a good life working in a job that he loved, even

if it was chaotic at times. His employers were welcoming and so good to him that it felt like they were family. With an indescribable force, he wanted to do the right things for their acceptance, but he was losing himself in his work. The fact was that, for a decade, he'd been very lonely, and internally sad for some unknown reason. Working here was the only thing that distracted him from his thoughts, which were sometimes too big for his head to wrap around. Where else in the world could he find employment with bosses who cared as much as they did? This had definitely been a factor in his longevity at Northern Lights.

His job was good, and he appreciated the work, but what he desired and felt he deserved was overall joy and love. That's all people really wanted, despite jokes about money, power, or making it rich. Watching a worldwide documentary about happiness, Buck had discovered that the happiest people on earth didn't have much in terms of wealth and monetary goods. Nor did they have luxuries; in some cases, that meant they didn't even have running water. Buck was that kind of a guy, though. Not the 'I'll-be-a-minimalist-and-find-joy' guy, but the lonely one who on a Saturday night watched documentaries about happiness.

Parental love or friendships aside, the human need for a

partner had been completely absent in his life until the Mexican had arrived. Juana, the complex personality in clinical, had intrigued him. She'd fascinated him in a way that no other DID patient had before. He'd begun observing her from afar and made efforts to be around for checks or conveniently chatting with other staff members when she was nearby. This had been especially true after Ignacio had worked with counselors to suppress Juana and become the dominant personality again.

Two and a half years had transformed into a fondness and familiarity he felt that was unmatched when it came to the other patients around him, both in and out of the clinical wing. Rather than indulging in self-desires, Buck was altruistic. He wanted Ignacio to be genuinely happy. He had many conversations with the staff and the Reeds about releasing Ignacio to general population, eventually becoming the major catalyst for making it happen.

And after Ignacio had 'admitted himself', Buck had gotten the opportunity to get to know him on a personal level. He'd begun to understand who Ignacio was, and helped him break down emotional walls. Whether or not they were Juana's demons was unknown, but sometimes people just needed to talk and feel like someone was listening for them to let it out. Buck and Ignacio had needed the friendship of each other; the love had come unexpectedly. It had never been definable.

It perplexed the German psychologists monitoring Northern Lights activities and intrigued them at the same time. Where in the books could you look up: *gay man becomes dead gay boyfriend and falls in love with two personalities of a DID patient*? You couldn't search that on the internet.

Buck, thinking he was your average man making a living, was completely unaware that he was part of the epic novella at Northern Lights. He believed he was a person who just wanted happiness, like the happy toothless people smiling in Saturday night documentaries. After working with DID patients at Northern Lights for nearly a decade, Buck had been ready to meet someone who understood his job and understood him. The observation stage on the clinical side had opened him up to a possibility of love from the inside – that was the connection.

It had hit so fast and so hard that every day had been like a punch in his chest that took his breath away. Their faces lit up when they saw each other. Their eyes lifted upward, their ears pulled back when they smiled, and a rush of blood pushed through the surface veins of their skin – making each of them glow when the other walked into the room. People could fight it all day long, but feelings of love did things to the heart and mind on a scientific, biological level. They could be measured by blood pressure elevations, hormonal secretions, and pupil dilations. There were things you could visually see when two people were in love. The researches had known it was happening before Buck and Ignacio had even admitted it.

Buck knew it was worth it, insane ashes be damned, and it was time to take the next step. He'd had a good run working for Mr. and Mrs. Reed, but it was time in his life to move on. People were going to judge him no matter who his partner in life was, and being lonely for another ten years due to fear of judgment was not a happy option. In the lobby, once again breaking up fights, was not where he wanted to be.

He addressed the patients, the staff, the guards and everyone in earshot. "I'm done. I quit. Ya'll hear me?"

INSANITY

Buck continued to rub his forehead as he took a minute to relax behind his closed eyes. The other patients in the lobby dodged their eyes around, searching the small gathering for anyone who might have something to say in the seconds after Buck had announced he was quitting. The perplexed faces in the room watched him stand against the reception desk. Even the guards looked at the lead guard with the crooked nose for guidance, but he shrugged his shoulders and gently shook his head while still trying to follow the orders Buck had given moments earlier. But Buck had had enough, and it was over; his eleven-year stint was done. He'd let it all go the moment he said it, and now he began to hum a deep inaudible melody while everyone wondered if he was going to rub a hole in his forehead.

Maggie leaned in to whisper to the guard on her left, asking him if, in fact, he was humming. Perplexed, the guard hesitantly nodded his head to confirm that he was – possibly. Maggie pulled back to her neutral position and polished the cross on her necklace, still dumbfounded as to how it was there. She pushed the pendant into her mouth and flicked her tongue on the bottom of the cross where Jesus' feet would hang. The metal tasted divine.

At first Buck's humming seemed to sooth him as he rocked and drowned himself in the notes he had been listening to over the past few weeks. He continued to rub at his forehead as everyone waited with bated breath for what, they did not know. While the hushed room watched the rhythmic sway of his body, Buck lost himself in the darkness beneath his eyelids to wander in the music he had been rehearsing. A quiet, melodic harmony of guitars began to strum and get louder as the mariachi of three began to fill his head. He envisioned the trio playing in time on their instruments with beautiful large-brimmed hats that were traditional in style and elegance. When the melody slowed to a calming and yet perfectly timed chorus of guitar strums and the accompanying violins held the elongated note of introduction, Buck began to sing.

His deep voice, smoother in song than it was in speech, and with an overall gently unexpected vibrato, waved through his first few notes, pleasantly surprising everyone in the room. The Spanish pronunciation of the lyrics seemed effortless, but the hours he'd spent practicing were how this had come to be. His intent had been to serenade Ignacio when the right time presented itself, but he felt compelled in this moment, and the presentation of his sincerity was evident. As he sang the first line, he slowly stepped to Juana as if no one else was watching, or judging.

The translation was this: *What beautiful eyes you have. Beneath those two eyebrows. What beautiful eyes you have. They want to look at me, but you won't let them; not even to blink. Graceful Malaguenan.*

Everyone listened to each heartfelt note, shocked that this strange outburst was happening right before their eyes. Although no one in the room knew exactly what he was saying, the head guard standing next to Maggie pointed to his puckered lips and made a kissing sound as if he knew the song was a love ballad. Then he quietly mouthed – "I think he said *kiss*; he's singing about kissing." He was smug, but really had no clue. Maggie's mouth dropped as she tilted her ear in the direction of his voice to let each beautiful sound enter her head. Something about it resonated within her, and she rubbed at her stomach, which felt warm and in knots.

Buck's face was soft and relaxed as he sang the first verse of serenading love. In the second verse, he sang with a little more conviction, making his eyebrows scrunch together and creating a deep yet sincere crevice between them.

Kiss your lips; I wish I could, graceful Malaguenan. And to tell you, beautiful little girl, that you are stunning and bewitching like a rose.

Juana was fidgeting uncomfortably as she scanned the lobby for disapproving eyes. No one was looking at her, as they were all fixed on the southern gay man singing a traditional mariachi song in Spanish. When he completed his walk to Juana, standing right in front of her, Buck placed his balled-up hand over his heart and sang another verse as he shook his head, emphasizing the words that he felt with every fiber of his body.

If by being poor, you think less of me, I'll give you a reason. I don't offer you riches; I offer you my heart – in exchange for the things I lack.

His voice began to waiver with emotion as Juana finally returned eye contact. Buck's eyes slowly pooled with a swell of tears as he continued to sing a lyric in the song that demanded a fervent delivery. The passionate, loud notes required a deep breath, an open mouth, and a slight bend in the small of his back to push his words to the high ceilings of the Northern Lights lobby.

For how much I would sing for her. Oh, for how much I would sing for her – for nothing!

As he sang and moved closer, the guard next to Juana stepped away to allow the drama to unfold, as he, too, was mesmerized. Droplets of moisture popped out of Buck's mouth as he clearly sang the consonants of each individual word. Then he paused to begin again with a softer, deeper, and more raw sincerity before finding his crescendo into a dramatic and elaborate finish.

I told her that with just a kiss, one single kiss and a tender glance, my beautiful woman. That you are stunning and bewitching. Like a rose.

He held out the note as he reached in to gently touch Juana's cheek. His mind saw the moon-shaped scars Ignacio spoke of so many times as his fingertips brushed over dimples and facial stubble. The lobby was so quiet that the silence felt heavy in the room. Buck leaned in to Juana to make sure that what he was about to say would be private.

"I'm in love, and I will help you both discover sanity."

Their moment was preserved, as the people around them couldn't hear his baritone whisper.

In the distance, a heavy footstep seemed to get louder

and quicker. As the two men stood frozen, embracing in each other's minds, an average, bowlegged black man stomped from a hallway into the lobby with his hand wrapped around the grip of a tiny, curvaceous ladies pistol.

The Mexican's disrespect over the past few months had been suppressed by a Christian man and his moral convictions, but Samuel didn't follow these biblical rules. In fact, this suppression of anger by his host had only escalated his anger. The ornate, embossed etched gun entered the lobby before Samuel – who trailed behind it, a tight grip with one finger delicately hovering on the trigger. He took aim at his intended target when Maggie and the guards turned their heads to witness his actions. She opened her mouth to scream as the guard with the crooked nose reached for his Taser, but he was too slow, and Samuel put a bullet through the guard's ribcage and accidently into Maggie's shoulder. The horrific gurgling sounds the guard made in the seconds before he died were drowned by the screams of onlookers and by Maggie, who was holding her bloody shoulder and shrieking hysterically while pinned under the weight of the guard.

Buck immediately spun around and held his hands out to tell Samuel to stop, but Samuel was after blood. "You Mexican bitch! Did you think I would let you get away with hitting me? I smelled her fucking strawberry shampoo!" He stepped harder and closer as he aimed the gun in Juana's general direction. Buck thought quickly, using his long reach to grab the gun and jam his oversized finger between the trigger and sudden death. Samuel tried to pull back to shoot, but nothing happened. The remaining guards began to move in to subdue him, but they were fearful of being shot. Rather than get too close while Buck was still grappling with Samuel, they watched the scuffle ensue while they pretended like they were trying to step in. As Buck and Samuel wrestled in a circle, trying to punch and gain control of the pistol that latched them together, it somehow dislodged and spun off into a potted plant that was right next to Juana who immediately picked it up. In Juana's persona, she was confident without second thoughts, because the Firestarter didn't doubt. She was the rebellious gang member the newspapers wrote articles about. Although Buck had softened her, the woman she knew herself to be was unafraid of a pistol and definitely not afraid to put a bullet in a man who was attacking her love. Without hesitation she aimed the barrel and shot a bullet into the intertwining body parts of the two men. A spray of blood spewed outward from the center, dropping them both to the floor.

Now in her own body, Belinda mustered enough energy to pick herself up from underneath the deceased crooked-nosed guard to run to Samuel, screaming for him to please not be dead. The bullet in her shoulder caused a burning sensation which made her howl in pain as she knelt by his face to repeat that they were going to have a baby, pleading in his ear. Her tears fell to the aged black skin around his eyes, which made him seem as if he too was crying, but Samuel was near death, and Mr. Jenkins refused to acknowledge her, instead calling out to his daughter in mumbled last breaths.

The onlookers scurried and ran from the lobby, through hallways, outside the main door, and some even hid inside the smoking room for cover. The security guard who was about to retire shuffled his way into the reception desk area and pressed the emergency button as he watched Juana slump to the floor with the beautiful pistol in her hand. Her torso hit hard next to the body of Buck, who had a hole in his stomach that was oozing with dark blood. The guard aimed his Taser from behind the desk, but did not pull the trigger as the room hushed to an eerie calm, other than Belinda's sobs between painful groans. He, too, was conflicted with the emotional explosion that was happening before him.

Frantic screams of a woman – faded at first, but growing

louder – overtook the calm as Mrs. Reed ran toward the lobby with medical personnel from the clinical wing running behind her. The footsteps were panicked and heavy, like those of frightened wild horses, as the group cut through the lobby to treat the causalities. Mrs. Reed's white hair, which was usually perfectly in place, was whipping backward as she ran. Her business attire and heels neither helped nor hindered the pace at which she rushed straight over to Buck. Two of the medics helped Belinda to her feet, but she resisted and screamed that she was not leaving Samuel's side as a third checked for a pulse on him with a stethoscope and shook his head.

"Jason! Jason!" Mrs. Reed yelled, and threw herself to her knees next to her unresponsive son, bending low enough to surround his face with her dangling white hair. She tapped his cheek as a medic was trying to dress the wound in his abdominal area. "Buck. Buck, are you in there? Don't you let my baby die!"

"Ma'am, I need you to move. Ma'am, move out of the way so I can help him!" the medic shouted to her while she tried to look for signs of life. Her face was so close to his that the tips of their ball-shaped noses were almost touching while she scanned his face, seeing the son she remembered from eleven years ago – before his lover's suicide had changed their lives. She sobbed as she scooted away from him. Her complete loss of control over a dismal future that she'd been forced to watch had made a grieving mother snap. She violently shook her head back and forth, making her hair seem as if the tips were reaching for an escape away from the woman to which they belonged. She jumped to her feet, wobbling on her pumps with heavy black mascara running down the tops of her cheeks.

Juana lay motionless on her back with the gun loosely dangling between her fingers and onto the floor. She was staring blankly at Buck with a distant, lost gaze in her eyes.

Mrs. Reed crawled to her, bent down, and grabbed the gun from her loose hands in one effortless swoop, and then she pointed the barrel inches from Juana's long black curls. "He dies, I shoot. Do you understand me?" Her voice wavered through her tears. The pistol shook violently, as she had never held a weapon before in her life and the fear of what she was about to do was washing over her. Tears pushed the dark, smeared makeup further down her cheeks and then left a clean line as the path it traveled cleared away the foundation she was wearing.

Emotionless, Juana stared at the man on the floor. "He

loved me. He saw me and loved me." She mumbled with a Spanish accent while tears began to push at the edges of her bottom lids, waiting for their moment to stream down her brown skin. "Is he dead?"

Mrs. Reed shook her head violently as she screamed, scrambling her wild head of hair again which had become damp at the roots. "Don't say that! Don't you ever fucking say that!" Words shot spit out of her mouth as her emotional pain spilled into each heavy syllable.

Juana looked up to her with huge, childlike eyes. "Is he?" Jill winced as if the question had slapped her in the face.

The old guard interjected from behind the reception desk. "Mrs. Reed!" He aimed the Taser at her back, but he knew it was useless in this situation. "Right now, you are the one with the gun in her hands! You have the power to walk away, Mrs. Reed," he said, hoping she would stop the madness on her own with a little push of clarity from the facts of the situation.

"You shut the hell up, Arthur. She shot my son!" She trembled harder as hot tears oozed from her eyes, through her smeared makeup and down the clean path off her chin to the floor. She had trouble holding the small firearm in position, as the torque in her arms made it seem as if she was holding a fifteen-pound weight – especially under the stiff stitching that was pulling from the sleeves of her business jacket.

Arthur was firm this time. "Mrs. Reed, your son died eleven years ago. I know you don't want to hear that, but God damnit, it's the truth, so walk away, Jill!" She reset her finger over the trigger in preparation for a final squeeze that would end the cause of her present pain. Buck moaned from the floor, distracting her eyes long enough for Juana to throw herself on top of him. Jill screamed at her to get off her son, but she didn't move; in fact, she held on tighter.

The medics, trying to attend to Buck, pried and pushed the Mexican away as best they could with their blood-soaked gloves. Buck writhed in pain as the commotion around him escalated. The medics began to panic while trying to save his life. They, too, began to shout at Juana to let go, and yelled at the guards who were repositioning themselves in their first real attempt to help pull her off.

Belinda begged and pleaded for everyone to stop as she tried to break herself free from the restraints the medics had placed around her so that they could dress her gunshot wound. Arthur tried to repeatedly shout over everyone, demanding that Mrs. Reed walk away.

The screaming and yelling over the bloody, twisted chaos clogged the ears of everyone in the lobby, until the twins' laughter grew louder from the same hallway that Samuel had taken his last angry steps along. It pierced through the commotion in an awkward, uncomfortable manner that seemed unnaturally sinister. The medics continued to render aid to Buck and Belinda as everyone tuned their ears to the sounds of the cackling of the elderly twins. There was something eerie about the silencing effect it had throughout the lobby. For a moment that lasted far too long, everyone's eyes were fixed to the frumpy figures waddling toward them in utter joy with their mouths wide open and their heads thrown back as if the funniest joke in the world had just been told. Arthur, who just wanted to retire in peace, quietly held his left hand up and waved his open palm and sprayed out fingers in a motion that was supposed to tell them to stop as his eyes returned to the gun in Jill's hand.

From the twins' point of view, he was ducking down behind the reception desk while holding his Taser in his right hand and saying hello with the other. Ute Schmidt grabbed her sister's fat fingers, and tugged her to encourage their skipping into the lobby as they giggled like devil children.

Once they skipped down the remaining length of the hall and were about two steps into the lobby, they stopped to take in the epic scene that shocked them both into the first silent pause anyone had ever witnessed them experience. The twins viewed the blood and the tears of everyone in the lobby, and then analyzed the situation in a ten second visual scan.

A strange wave of lingering burnt gases from the firearm gently billowed past the twins' noses and then faded as if it had never been there, the smell soon replaced with the biological scent of blood and exposed body fluids. "Und vee are the crazy ones?" Ute looked to her sister, who mirrored her rolling eyes.

Hilda, still holding Ute's hand, shouted to Jill. "Frau Reed, drop it so doctors can save his life if he's not already dead."

Jill looked down to the human on top of her son and tossed the gun to the floor near a young guard who frantically secured it. Arthur shook his head in relief but wondered why she'd chosen to succumb to their demand and not his. Juana released her hold on Buck when she heard the weapon hit the floor, and then she scooted away so that medical personnel could prepare him for emergency transport.

Ute sniffed and lifted her nose in the air like a dog. "Love is in the air." The twins smiled at each other as they began to playfully dance.

Their actions mesmerized everyone, and no one who was watching could take their eyes off the twins while they laughed and swirled around, this time in a circle with their hands latched together as the pivotal point. It was only a few seconds later when Hilda broke free from the playful dance to skip her old frumpy body to the center of the lobby, where she stopped in front of Belinda and rubbed her fat belly in a teasing display of insanity.

"Love made that pretty frauline!" Belinda was shocked, and immediately grabbed at her stomach with her available hand. Hilda laughed hysterically and pointed to the bandage around her shoulder that was seeping, and then to the dead man on the floor. She turned and bent over Mr. Jenkins, who finally seemed at peace as he rested in a pool of bright red arterial blood. "Love sent you to das bonkerhaus. Love sent you home." She faked a creepy, overly exaggerated sad face as she held her hips while hovering over the body which had once housed two men. Then, assuming Mr. Jenkins was going to heaven, she pointed to the sky. Ute, who was giggling uncontrollably, kept shaking her head up and down while she let her less dominant sister dance around the tragedy of the room in a sick display of insane truth.

Hilda shimmied around the medics as they counted to

three in unison and then hoisted Buck onto the stretcher. She pushed her hand and arm between the medics as they lifted Buck, to push the pad of her fat finger onto the center of his forehead. He didn't respond in any way to her intrusive touch. "Die Liebe hat dich zerschmettert," she whispered.

Ute giggled at first and then laughed out loud before mocking her words in English. "Love has shattered you! Love broke you! Kaput!"

Mrs. Reed mumbled to herself for them to please stop, but her plea was dismissed as Ute retracted her hand and spun her body in a delightful and yet wobbly twist, stopping in front of Mrs. Reed. She gently placed her curled index finger under Jill's quivering chin. With a raise of her arm, she lifted Mrs. Reed's face and stood on the balls of her feet within her orthopedic shoes. Ute's beady eyes, surrounded with aged and spotted skin, offered no solace in contrast to the gentle tone, with which she spoke as if she genuinely cared. "Dance in the eye of the hurricane."

There was a pause of deep reflection before Hilda moved her hand to let Jill's face fall to her chest again in profound sadness.

As they began to wheel the stretcher away, Hilda swayed her body as if she was dancing to a lovely orchestral melody with one arm crossed over her torso and the other stretched out, holding hands with an imaginary partner. Ute laughed euphorically as she frantically clapped her hands and side-stepped left then right to her sister's rhythm.

Juana, sitting with a fixed catatonic stare on the floor, did not look up to see Hilda dancing; nor did she observe the change in her fluid arm movements that now signaled a more jagged and posed jerking to a new song. As Ute mocked traditional American Indian tribal dances, she howled and cackled in laughter. She then began to bounce in place and grunted as her sister pretended to inhale smoke from a fire – one that originated within Juana. While the twins continued their imaginary drumming beat , Jill tried to follow the medics, but was unable to look away from the Schmidt twins.

"Your fire is not purifying! Your. Love. Burns." Ute's German accent was thick, but it didn't get in the way of her clearly saying each necessary word while her sister continued to grunt and howl.

Distracted by the twins, Jill stumbled into the stretcher which the medics had stopped at the archway to the hall. One was checking for a pulse deep in Buck's neck while another tried to listen for breathing and watch for the rise and fall of his chest. By the look on their faces and the way they slowly moved their hands away from his skin, Jill knew his physical life had finally come to an end. Like Mr. Jenkins, he was finally free.

Immediately, there was a wrenching in her gut that made her feel like she would vomit at any moment. The sadness propelled her forward into a slow walk to her son. She had to see that he was gone before she would believe it. Jill placed her right hand gently onto his chest and pressed down while closing her eyes. The dance of the Schmidt twins faded into background noise as she searched for the strong beat of her son's heart. Her logical side knew it wouldn't be tapping at her palm, but the reality of it somehow numbed her. When she looked up, the green color in her eyes was muted like dying grass when the summer's too hot for its delicate blades. She was distant, with an emotionless face. As the twins laughed and shouted in mocking ceremonial chants and loud irregular screams, Jill turned and walked to the young guard who was mesmerized by the twin's theatrics. She slid the gun from his grip as easily as if he'd been giving it to her and turned to aim the gun at Juana's forehead.

There was a scream that didn't come from the Schmidt twins then, and suddenly everyone stopped moving. Juana didn't flinch as she lunged at Jill grabbing the gun out of Jill's hands and turned it on Jill. "Is your fire worth the fade?"

Jack, who'd entered the lobby during the commotion but had slipped out undetected, returned with his own pistol in hand. "Hey! Was yours?" And as he yelled, he pulled the trigger. The single bullet in the chamber had been meant for his own broken heart. Instead, the bullet entered the body of Ignacio, killing him and the alternate personality who'd animated it.

In the wave of silence that hushed the room, a whimpering woman began to sob. Jill repeatedly asked, "Why did you do that?" as she looked to the floor with tears falling upon tears. "I would have..." She trailed off. The guards, with no training on this kind of emergency were too shocked to move. Jack carefully lowered the smoking barrel of the pistol to the floor and looked around the lobby with guilty eyes that begged for understanding from the those who remained in the lobby and the judgemental walls between them. Jill was shaking uncontrollably as she stood by his side now, unable to control the tears or the string of mucus falling from her nose.

A few patients who'd initially scurried away during the beginning of the drama began to carefully return to the lobby as a suddenly quiet calm bounced between the walls. They were curious to see who'd pulled the trigger and began to whisper when they saw Jack holding a gun.

Jack stared at the cross on his son's motionless chest for a moment, and then briefly at the deceased head guard. His eyes, already filled with tears, looked to Mr. Jenkins who had once saved a little girl from a blazing fire, and to Belinda, with a bullet hole in her shoulder. Ignacio's body was slumped, lifeless on its side, only a few feet from Jack's hysterical wife. He was ashamed to think that he and Jill had failed to provide Buck and their patients with normal, safe lives.

But he was wrong.

EPILOGUE

It was the middle of the day and a television in the lobby of the mansion was airing channel 8 news. The volume was low but audible and the seating around it was inviting. Yet, no one was watching it. A woman and her son walked passed it to set comfortably on the newly installed patio. The sweet smell of the vineyard was in the air and much more alluring than the broadcasted story.

A year ago, two patients, one staff member, and a guard were fatality wounded and one patient was seriously wounded at Northern Lights, a mental health facility in Jefferson County. The community was stunned and left with a lot of questions and theories. You sent these questions to us here at WKTN Channel 8 News and on social media. We wrote about the losses of the families in this tragic event and, on the one-year anniversary, we wanted to share some perspective on what lead to the carnage and what has happened since.

If you have never heard of Northern Lights or its extraordinary residents, you can most likely research it and find words like groundbreaking, innovative, or pioneering. That is because the facility, run by Jack and Jill Reed, implemented nontraditional methods of treatment. The facility, funded predominately by private research groups, treated many patients with serious conditions as well as those less severe, non-permanent residents. However, the focus was on patients that suffered from the same condition; Dissociative Identity Disorder, otherwise known as DID or multiple personalities.

In the investigation that followed the incident, the assessments of researchers found, oddly, that the treatments the patients received, that lead to the tragedy, actually accomplished the mission of the facility. Patients benefited because they did not live on a steady plateau of previously charted ground. They were allowed to feel, fail, succeed, grow, and live without margins. This freedom and flexibility, within treatments, was deemed commendable yet risky. Some would argue that although ground-breaking, it was the lack of stricter, more structured methodologies that led to four untimely deaths and the ultimate shut down of Northern Lights.

Aside from their unprecedented treatments that the medical community at first dubbed as self-guided, and their unique clientele, the building itself has a history. Mr. and Mrs. Reed renovated a vineyard mansion for their permanent residents.

Some of the upgrades included a state of the art monitoring system, specialty treatment rooms, and an overhaul in electrical systems. A section of the mansion was also secured for specific patients harboring hostile intent. Unfortunately, the shooting last year could not have been prevented no matter how much effort the Reeds put into the upgrade of safety systems or in the treatment of their staff and patients.

One of the six residents, that became a part of this devastating event, was Jason Reed, Jack and Jill's son, who began showing signs of DID twelve years ago. He was the reason the couple established Northern Lights. In a press conference last week Mrs. Reed spoke to the people of Jefferson County to thank them for their support on the anniversary of her son's death.

"Our son Jason and his alter "Buck" wanted a different kind of care for mental health patients. We did our best to accommodate that for him, for them, and for us. Thank you for your support."

The Reeds were able to make the conversion back to a bed and breakfast with the help of volunteers in the community who heard their story. The conversion took eight months to accomplish and it will open next week, under a new name that will be unveiled at the opening ceremony

Among the other deceased patients from the tragedy, are a security guard, whose family has asked us not to name; Sam Jenkins, a sugar mill worker of Ohio who is survived by his daughter Gloria Semer and grandson Aaron and Ignacio Cheyez of New York whose mother made national news as the gang leader of the Quinceñera Fifteen Fire Starters. When asked about the fatal outcome of Northern Lights, Mrs. Reed had this to say.

"Each of them had tragic events in their lives. But they loved no matter what. Isn't that the point? Mr. Cheyez, Mr. Jenkins, and our son, loved beyond boundaries. This is what Buck tried to tell us all along; happiness lies within and beyond the sadness we overcome. To allow the good and the bad and all of the craziness in between is – a normal life. For the residents of Northern Lights, finding the balance between tragedy and triumph was how they discovered sanity."

Today, the Reeds run the bed and breakfast with the help of three previous clients and one addition, a baby named Jason "Bucky" Beckler. Jefferson County welcomes a new beginning from this tragic history. From everyone at WKTN Channel 8 News – goodnight.

Acknowledgements Note

One night, while giddy from a lack of sleep and pregnant with twins, I found myself speaking of a range of comical characters that developed out of jokes. Excitement grew as the ideas inspired me to draft "Vineyard Nuts," my first light-hearted comedy. However, that book never quite manifested in full. What it turned into instead was a multifaceted tale of discovery surrounding institutionalized patients.

And I've learned not to question the writing process, but would like readers to note that, although the disorders in this book are based off of true symptoms and disorders, they have been tailored for the purposes of this fictional story.

Now, I owe thanks to so many folks. Thank you for being subject matter experts in a myriad of odd genres, for giving me quirky advice or simply being fantastic muses. Collectively, you made this crazy book happen. In no specific order, thank yous go to: Eddie Dennis, Geonoah and Cassie, Felipe Casillas Jr., Jonathan Perez, Cheryl Martin, Juan Angel, Kailyn and Harmony, Jessica Alvarez, Jo F., Adolfo Serna,

Jaylene Hohman, Tyler Hashimoto, Joshua Douglas, Kory Rohrdanz, Angelo Broyles, Emely Espinal, Joshua Tagliaboschi, Chelsea Garay, Charles Blanding, Anthony Waller Jr., Candace Barney, Autumn Abramczyk, Bruce Tolley, Dustin Page, Jon Stiffler, Leigha Chhay, Leigh Farina, Andrew Bobbe, Mandi Marek, Michael O'Connor, Denise Caddy, and Sonja Everard.

Specific thanks also go to: Nancy Jimenez, Francisco Bernardino, Elmi Sanchez and Amanda Gallegos for translating "Malaguena Salarosa" into English. There are so many beautiful versions of this song, but our collaborative efforts helped me take the appropriate creative liberties with the lyrics for adaptation into the story. Also, I owe thanks to Melchior Mueller-Spude for letting me get away with painfully crude German accents for a bit of comedic relief.

ABOUT THE AUTHOR

 Emma Janson was born in Ohio but left to join the Army when she turned 17. She served for six years at Fort Hua-chu-ca, Arizona and Hanau, Germany.

After leaving the Army, she moved briefly to Ohio and then on to Las Vegas to enroll in the National Guard while also attending UNLV. To pay for college, Emma became a dancer and a mud-wrestler while she waited for the National Guard to finally recognized her request to release her, in order for her to rejoin active duty. But, be-fore Emma could rejoin the service, she had to go back "into the closet" after having announced her status as gay the prior year.

Emma served honorably as a member of the Airborne and was deployed to Iraq and Afghanistan. She was medical-ly retired in 2015 and now lives back in Ohio with her twin daughters where, time permitting, she pursues her love for writing. *Discovering Sanity* marks Emma's third book.

CREDITS

This book is a work of art produced by
Incorgnito Publishing Press.

Jennifer Collins - Editor

Matthew Bucemi - Proofing Editor

Star Foos - Artist/Designer

Daria Lacy - Graphic Production

Janice Bini - Chief Reader

Michael Conant - Publisher

December 2017

Incorgnito Publishing Press

Direct inquiries to mconant@incorgnitobooks.com

CPSIA information can be obtained
at www.ICGtesting.com
Printed in the USA
LVHW04s0712170618
580548LV00002B/2/P